NORTH
POLE

elf village

SANT
WORKSHOP

REINDEER
STABLE

JENNIFER CHIPMAN

For everyone who's ever believed in the magic of Christmas... or wanted their Hallmark movies to be a little spicier.
This one's for you.

playlist

- Christmas Must Be Something More - Taylor Swift
- Santa Tell Me - Ariana Grande
- A Place in this World - Taylor Swift
- My Only Wish (This Year) - Britney Spears
- Lost - Michael Bublé
- 'tis the damn season - Taylor Swift
- All I Want for Christmas - Mariah Carey
- Christmas Tree Farm - Taylor Swift
- Cold December Night - Michael Bublé
- I'll Be Home - Meghan Traitor
- fOoL fOr YoU - ZAYN
- Poison Ivy - Jonas Brothers
- Christmas (Baby Please Come Home) - Michael Bublé
- Mistletoe - Justin Bieber

- Glittery - Kacey Musgraves
- I Choose You - Sara Bareilles
- Until I Found You - Stephen Sanchez
- Underneath the Tree - Kelly Clarkson
- Like It's Christmas - Jonas Brothers

contents

1. Ivy   1
2. Teddy   8
3. Ivy   14
4. Teddy   22
5. Ivy   32
6. Teddy   40
7. Ivy   50
8. Teddy   59
9. Ivy   66
10. Teddy   75
11. Ivy   83
12. Teddy   99
13. Ivy   108
14. Teddy   117
15. Ivy   125
16. Teddy   132
17. Ivy   140
18. Teddy   149
19. Ivy   160
20. Teddy   168
21. Ivy   175
22. Teddy   190
23. Ivy   201
24. Teddy   210
25. Ivy   223
    Epilogue   234
    Extended Epilogue   246

    Acknowledgments   257
    Also by Jennifer Chipman   259
    About the Author   261

1
ivy

31 days until christmas

I drew a red x through today's date on the calendar —another day closer to Christmas. Only one month to go. The thought brought a smile to my lips as I swiped another coat of red lipstick on my lips and adjusted my green velvet dress.

This was my favorite time of year. And not just because of the holiday cheer, the peppermint hot chocolates, or the gingerbread cookies. No, it was because this time of year, everything felt truly *magical*. There was something about the season that I absolutely loved and always had. Ever since I was a little girl, I remember getting excited when *Rudolph* came on and how holiday music blasted in the car as soon as the calendar flipped to November. I'd dreamed of a snowy white Christmas, for cold crisp air that paired perfectly with a peppermint hot chocolate, as long as I could remember.

Though every day was Christmas here at *Santa's Christmasland*.

As one of Central Florida's premier theme park destinations, millions of people visit the park each year, coming through our front gates to experience a holiday overload. Each park area was themed, from Santa's Workshop to the North Pole Village. You could ride Reindeer Flight—a roller coaster, the Holly Jolly Train that went around the entire park, or a sleigh ride through Santa's Village. Plus, there was a skating rink and an entire room filled with artificial snow so guests could have snowball fights and build snowmen. We even had a bakery that looked like a giant gingerbread house where they pumped scents into the air to encourage them to purchase treats.

And, of course, *the star on the top of the tree*, as they said, was a meet and greet with Santa Claus himself. Not the real Santa, of course, but that didn't stop parents from purchasing photos with him and kids from whispering their wishes into his ear.

This place was all Christmas, all the time. And it wasn't just the kids who loved it—it was the adults, too. Maybe that was why they kept coming back, year after year.

I loved walking through the empty park each morning, enjoying the calm before we opened. An instrumental version of *All I Want For Christmas is You* was currently playing in the background. After guests arrived, it would be non-stop busy until close, so I tried to savor these moments. The entire place was decked out in garlands and red bows, and the thousands of lights that decorated the area were already lit up. The fans on top of the buildings that would blow soap to simulate snow weren't running yet, giving me a temporary reprieve from that, at least.

Even if none of it was real, it felt like magic to me. It wasn't the fake snow that was pumped into the air, the decorations that hung on every corner, or the smell of sugar cookies baking across the way. All of it was ridiculously over the top, and I loved every single bit of it.

This was my happy place. After all, I'd never seen actual snow, but I'd always believed in Christmas *magic*.

Though, if someone had told me when I was younger that one day, I was going to be working at a North Pole themed amusement park, I would have laughed. But that was me. Ivy Winters. Head Elf at Santa's Christmasland.

I'd started here at eighteen while getting my degree, and now, seven years later, I'd worked my way up to being a manager, overseeing the operation and being in charge of the other employees. It was amazing what it took to keep a place like this running every day.

Though sometimes, it felt like it was hard for people to take me seriously, given that I was a whopping five foot two inches and wore a green velvet dress every day.

Never mind that I was twenty-five and had a management degree from the University of Central Florida. Just because I worked at an amusement park didn't mean I wasn't a professional. An elf costume didn't mean I didn't deserve to be treated with respect. I blew out a breath as I adjusted my name tag, feeling grateful that at least I no longer had to wear the candy cane striped tights every day. Honestly, I could have opted out of the dress, too, but my employees had to wear it, so I wore it too.

"Ivy!" I turned, seeing my dark-haired friend rushing towards me as I headed towards the employee only area behind the park where my office was located.

Sarah and I had met during property orientation all those years ago, and she was the closest thing I had to a best friend here at work. She held her costume in her hands, which made sense, considering it was a sweltering eighty degrees outside today, even though it was almost December. That was just how it was here, though. I'd long since grown used to it.

This place was as close to the North Pole as you could get in a state where the temperatures barely ever dropped below sixty degrees. When it hit fifty, the locals put on their down jackets.

"Hey, Sarah." I gave her a warm smile, tugging on the sleeve of my dress.

"Morning." She beamed back at me. "I thought I was going to be late. The bus took forever."

Joys of theme park work: having to park in a giant, sprawling parking lot before being bussed to the actual location. It was also why I was chronically early. Sarah, on the other hand, was chronically late.

"Hey, at least you made it." I looked at the clock. Her shift didn't start for another fifteen minutes. Everyone would hustle to their spots after they punched in, and then we'd be ready to open at ten on the dot.

She blew a piece of dark hair off her forehead. "Yeah, thankfully. I can't afford another point on my record card."

"Ready for another fantastic day in Santa's Workshop?" I asked her, leaning against a locker. She was one of our photographers for our Santa meet and greet.

A snort escaped her lips. "Oh yeah. Absolutely riveting."

I jabbed at her with my elbow before Sarah shoved her bag into its spot, grabbing her striped and fur-lined getup so she could change herself.

While she changed into her costume, I went into my office, busying myself with the next round of schedules that needed to go out—thankfully, I wasn't in charge of the entire park.

I lost myself in my work, too focused on the spreadsheet in front of me, not hearing Sarah until she leaned her hip against my desk, the bells of her shoes jangling.

"Did you hear about the new executive that will arrive tomorrow?" She was fully dressed and had clearly grabbed

4

her equipment from the camera storage room since her camera was now hanging around her neck.

"Oh, God, that's *tomorrow*?" I groaned. It had been on my calendar for weeks, and for the life of me, I couldn't fathom why the company that owned the park would send someone just a few weeks before Christmas, but then again, this was a company that profited off of the holiday.

"I've heard he's young and really attractive."

"Sarah!"

"What?" She fluttered her eyelashes. "I'm just saying it would be nice to have some eye candy around here." My friend held up her camera. "I'm stuck staring at Santa all day."

"Something you never let me forget." I playfully rolled my eyes. "I thought you said there were plenty of single dads to ogle?"

Sarah shrugged. "It's not as fun as it used to be. Besides, the chances of me running into *Mr. Right* while working as an amusement park photographer? Please. *As if.*"

I'd watched enough Hallmark movies to never say never, but she was probably right. The chances of meeting anyone here seemed low. Most of our employees were college students, and I definitely wasn't into twenty-year-old immature guys who just wanted to party every night.

"How do you even know this new guy is single?" I asked, saving and exiting the document. I'd finish it later.

"Don't you listen to the rumors?"

I quirked an eyebrow. "No. I'm too busy doing my actual job."

"Sorry, I forgot you have actual *responsibilities* these days."

"Something I *tried* to remedy." I'd offered her an assistant manager role over a year ago, though she declined.

"I like my job." She sighed. "Besides, it's not forever. Once

...sh my master's degree, I'm out of here." The company was paying for it, which was an excellent incentive to stick around.

"Still." I sighed, then looked up at the clock. "You should probably get out there. Park opens soon."

"Any plans for tonight?" Sarah asked me as she headed towards the door.

I laughed. "You know me. Going to go home and curl up with a good book." Back to my lonely apartment. I didn't even have a pet to keep me company, even though I'd always wanted to get a dog. Maybe one day.

She rolled her eyes. "One of these times, I'm going to get you to come out with us. The piano bar is so fun, I promise."

"Eh." I shrugged, giving her a small smile. "I'm alright. But thank you for thinking of me."

I was okay being alone. After all, I had been alone for as long as I could remember.

"Alright, suit yourself. I'll see you out there?" She asked, knowing I'd come by several times during my rounds. I liked to check in on my staff, making sure they had everything they needed so the operation ran smoothly.

I nodded, waving her off, trying not to look too deeply into the empty spot in my chest.

It was almost Christmas—my favorite time of year—so why was I suddenly feeling so achingly lonely? It had been too long since I'd been on a date. That much was true.

Maybe I needed to remedy that. Maybe one of these nights, I'd actually take her up on her offer and go out for drinks after work. Meet a handsome stranger, let him take me home...

Biting my lip, I realized I'd been staring off into space. I couldn't afford to be distracted. Not when I had so much to get done. Besides, I couldn't afford to dream.

In the end, I'd just get my heart broken again.
And that was something I wouldn't let happen.
Never again.

2
teddy

30 days until christmas

*a*nd that's the end of our tour." Jeremy, the head of operations for Santa's Christmasland, gave me a firm nod. We were standing in the middle of the North Pole area, each side lined with small shops and food locations, the entire place decked out in decorations.

The Christmas themed amusement park was a part of my family's business holdings. Claus Family Enterprises was all I'd ever known, since my father had groomed me to take over my whole life. I'd gone to business school, getting a degree in Finance while learning all I could about corporate management. Now, here I was, attempting to understand each facet of the company. I'd started with the toy manufacturing branch, and now I was moving on to the theme park division.

We both looked out of place in the middle of the park, surrounded by all things Christmas, while wearing business suits, but luckily, it hadn't opened yet for the day.

It was still quiet. They'd turned the lights on but left the

8

music loop off, a glorious break from the endless Christmas music. I was pretty sure if I never heard *I Saw Mommy Kissing Santa Claus* again, it would still be too soon. I resisted making a face, given that Jeremy was still standing in front of me. He wouldn't understand my aversion to the song.

"Thanks, man." I stuck out my hand for a handshake. "I appreciate it."

"Of course. If there's anything I can get you while you're here, just let me know."

I nodded. "Will do."

They'd set up a temporary office for me for the few weeks I was here to study the business operations and evaluate the budget. I had some ideas about expansions and improvements—ways we could grow the park into a bigger tourist destination to keep people coming back year after year—but there was only so much a spreadsheet could tell me. And now that I was the Chief Operating Officer for the company, it was all in my purview.

Though I enjoyed being on the road, I also didn't mind being here, cooped up in an office. At least I was useful here. Back home, well… I wasn't the same as my jolly old man. I couldn't be the figurehead the way he could.

Especially when my dad was a big picture kinda guy. He preferred to focus on the smiling looks on kids' faces versus how we could cut costs or increase efficiency. But that didn't put food on the table, either. At least I could put my degree to use, keeping the business going. Our family might have been running a successful toy enterprise for the last few hundred years, which had turned into countless other investments. However, that was even more of a reason that it needed meticulous organization.

Wandering through the park on my own after bidding Jeremy goodbye, I grabbed a cup of coffee from the giant gingerbread house shaped bakery and a gingerbread muffin that melted in my mouth. A flash of reddish-blonde hair caught my attention, but the woman was gone in a flurry of green before I could take proper notice of her.

Maybe this place wouldn't be so bad. It was kitschy and cliché, but there was a charm in it as well. Plus, the park was highly profitable, and I planned to keep it that way.

My phone rang as I headed back into the office, and I waited until the office door closed before I hit the answer button. "Hey, Mom."

"Teddy." I could practically hear her smile, even though I couldn't see her face. "How's Florida?"

I looked around me. "It's fine. Hot, but expected." Even if this place looked like Christmas threw up all over it, it still didn't feel the same as it did this time of year back home. I missed the cold and the snow. "Dad's got nothing to worry about. I'm going to make sure everything here is running perfectly before I leave."

"That's good." She made a non-committal sound with her throat before adding, "You always do such a wonderful job, honey."

"Mom," I said, feeling like there was something she wasn't saying. "What is it?"

"Are you going to make it home for Christmas?"

I pinched between my brows. The big day was still a month away, but could I finish here in time to head back? "I don't know. You know how crazy it is this time of year. And I have a lot of work to do here—"

"Still." She cut me off. "I know your father would love to have you up here before he leaves for his rounds. It's not the same without you."

With a sigh, I spun my office chair around to look at the singular framed photo I'd placed in my new office. "I know. I've never spent Christmas anywhere else."

It was strange to think about spending it somewhere other

than with my parents. Especially when the hotel room I was sleeping in for the next few weeks was cold and empty. No Christmas decorations, no endless stream of my mom's delicious sugar cookies and hot chocolate.

Maybe I was a little homesick. That was what months of being on the road would do to you. But that's what it had always been like, ever since I was little.

One downside of Christmas being the family business. Not that anyone around me would understand that.

"Listen, Mom, I should go. I'm still settling in here and want to make a good impression on the employees." Plus, I had a lot to do to get my proposals ready to show the board. "I'll let you know about Christmas, alright?"

"Okay, Teddy. We'll talk soon?"

"Of course. Love you, Mom."

"Love you too."

We finished saying our goodbyes, and then I leaned back in my chair, running my hands through my hair.

Was this really all my life was going to be? Jet-setting across the world, checking in on our families' businesses, but never really *living*? I sighed. Twenty-seven years old and I still hadn't figured it out.

Maybe it was time to open myself up to the possibilities.

SITTING on a bench surrounded by giant candy canes, I couldn't stop thinking about my mother's call. For the last hour, I'd been wandering the park on my own. The Candy Cane Forest where I currently sat was a newer addition: a walk-through area filled with sweets, peppermint hot chocolate, and candy cane stands. It led you to Santa's Workshop if you kept walking along the path. Not the real one, of course.

No actual toys were made in the park, despite a dark ride that went through a toy factory, but it all made me strangely homesick.

Of course, I hadn't exactly had a normal childhood, though my parents had always made sure I knew how loved I was. Still, I sometimes wondered what it would be like to grow up here. To spend Christmas together, gathered around our tree, opening presents on Christmas morning.

Sighing, I heaved myself off the bench. It had been a few hours since I'd had that muffin and coffee, and I wouldn't get anything else done by sitting here and staring off into space.

A loud noise drew my attention to the area outside Santa's Workshop, and I noticed a crowd had formed. What was going on? It sounded like an angry guest yelling at one of our employees.

This was one reason I hated it down here. People were so entitled. They thought they could complain about every little thing just because they'd paid to be here. Parades getting postponed because of rain. Lightning closing the outdoor rides. You name it, and it *ruined their day*. Of course, they wanted a full refund. But it never stopped there.

We were in the business of making people happy, and creating magical Christmas memories for our attendees, but that didn't mean I would tolerate someone treating any of our staff poorly. We had great employee retention at the park because we took care of our workers and made them feel valuable. It was one cornerstone of my family's business.

Thankfully, because of the weather, I'd left my suit coat in the office when I'd left for my walk earlier, though I was still wearing my forest green tie. There was no chance of blending in around here.

An angry parent was practically red in the face, yelling at a young woman dressed in green velvet. Though I hadn't met her during my tour, she must have been an elf who worked in this area.

I definitely would have remembered if we'd met before, though. Her long, strawberry blonde hair was enough to capture my attention, not to mention her delicate facial features and slight frame. Not that it was important right now when she was getting berated. *Dammit.*

"Well, that woman's definitely getting coal this year," I muttered out loud. A child's eyes grew wide, looking over at me. *Oops.* It hadn't occurred to me that anyone would be listening.

"Don't worry, Peter," I promised the kid with a wink. "Santa told me you definitely made it on the Nice List." He gaped at me, tugging on his parents' sleeve as they walked away, further from the confrontation that was still happening.

I needed to put a stop to this. There were too many people around, and cellphones pointed at the situation. Still, the employee looked completely unfazed—a smile on her face, a pretty pink blush on her cheeks.

"I'm sorry, Ma'am," she said. "I understand that you're unsatisfied, but that's the policy here in Santa's Workshop."

This girl. Damn. She was fearless. The way she stood tall, even though she had to be close to five feet when she took off her heels, the tilt of her jaw that said she wouldn't back down...

I glanced at her nametag. *Ivy.* I definitely wouldn't be forgetting that name.

"Excuse me," I said, coming to stand next to the employee, who just gaped at me. "What seems to be the problem here?"

3
ivy

*M*y day had been going great until one of my elves had come over the radio to let me know we had an *unhappy* customer outside of Santa's Workshop. Rude customers were a common occurrence in any customer service job, but I couldn't stand it when they went off on my employees who were just doing their jobs the way they'd been trained to. Plus, they were on vacation. What could really be so wrong that you feel the need to tell off someone who was selling reindeer plush for a living?

I knew if they could handle it themselves, they would, but some visitors just would not let it go, and that was when I came in.

"I want to speak with whoever's in charge here," came the snotty voice as I walked outside. Holding myself back from rolling my eyes, I pasted a fake smile on my face even as I groaned internally. It was easy to find her, considering she was the only red-faced person here, standing much too close to my elves.

Clearing my throat, I looked at the woman—a mother, I

assumed—whose energy screamed *I'm going to get what I want*. "Hi. That would be me."

She looked me up and down as if appraising my green velvet dress that hung on my slender frame and the green velvet bow in my hair. Sure, I'd swapped the shoes that jingled for a pair of red heels, but I was still small, and I knew it. I couldn't believe how many Christmases I'd spent asking Santa to let me grow a few more inches. Of course, it never happened, just like all the other things I'd wished for, but that didn't stop me from trying every year.

"*You're* in charge?" she asked, sounding skeptical. "Are you sure there's not anyone else I can talk to, honey?"

I hated when people belittled me and how often this happened. Instead of saying anything, I gave her my best customer service smile, hoping that, at the very least, she'd change her tone with me. "Yes, I'm the manager here, so I'm the one who can help you, ma'am. What seems to be the problem?"

"That *elf* out front was completely inappropriate in front of me and my child. She made her cry. And right before our photo with Santa, too."

"Oh, I'm so sorry," I said, that fake smile still plastered on my face. "What was her name so that I can talk to her?" I really hated when people tried to walk all over me. Besides, over the last few years, I'd hired all the other elves here. I knew there was no way any of them would have been rude to the woman. Even when it was warranted, that smile stayed plastered on our faces. And we'd all been there.

"Uh, it was—" She looked like she was trying to rack her brain to come up with it. "Something like Sugar... or Cookie... maybe Candy? Our entire experience was ruined."

I nodded, knowing I'd have to check with Tory out front to hear what happened. "Sorry to hear that. I will certainly talk with my staff to make sure they are following our procedures."

"Okay, well, I want a refund for how I've been treated."

"Was there something wrong with your picture?" I cocked my head to the side, enjoying the way my earrings jingled as I did. I liked to think they were one reason I'd been having an extra good day. Throughout November and December, I rotated through my collection of Christmas earrings, and today's pair was a bunch of dangling colored bells.

"Well, no—"

"Then I don't see what the problem is." I gave her my sweetest smile. "If your photos are satisfactory, then I'm afraid I can't refund them." And I certainly didn't have permission to refund park admission. That was a little over my head.

"You're being very rude to me, and I don't appreciate it," she quipped, her arms crossed over her chest as she angrily tapped her foot on the ground.

"I'm sorry, Ma'am," I said. "I understand that you're unsatisfied, but that's the policy here in Santa's Workshop."

"Excuse me," a man's voice spoke up behind us. I was surprised by the timbre of the voice, deep and soothing. "What seems to be the problem here?"

"Can't you see we're a little busy here, *Buddy*?" Angry mom whirled around, and when my eyes moved to see who'd interrupted us, I took him in.

Dark brown hair. Deep green eyes. A frown spread over his face. Wearing a tie the color of Christmas trees.

"I think your husband was looking for you, miss." My Christmas savior in disguise, apparently, told the woman. "Something about the photo being done and your daughter wanting a candy apple…?"

She turned bright red, spun on her heel, and stormed off.

I planted my hands on my hips, lips quirking up in

amusement as I watched her go. Turning to the stranger, I furrowed my brow. "I had that handled, you know."

"Sure you did." He hummed, clearly entertained by the whole situation, looking me over as if appraising me.

I narrowed my eyes at him. "I am perfectly capable of doing my job."

A little smirk curled up on his face. "Never said you weren't."

Resisting the urge to roll my eyes, I tried not to analyze why this man was getting under my skin so easily. "Right." I cleared my throat. "Anyway, I've gotta get back to work, so…"

"Sure. I'll walk with you. I'm heading that way, too."

"What?" I stopped, and he spun on his heel to face me. He raised an eyebrow, and I felt all the blood drain from my face. "You're the new executive." I should have guessed from his attire, but the thought hadn't even crossed my mind. At least he hadn't contradicted me in front of the guest.

He nodded. "I am. Theodore Clau—Clausen." He cleared his throat, sticking out his hand like he wanted me to shake it. "Nice to meet you…"

"Ivy Winters." Placing my hand in his, I felt a little jolt run up my spine at the contact. "Sorry. You caught me a little off guard back there. I'm a manager here."

"You are?" His eyes flickered to my ears and then back to my eyes.

I crossed my arms over my chest. "Why wouldn't I be?"

"It's just… You're so…" He seemed lost for words.

"Watch it, buddy," I said, narrowing my eyes at him.

He glanced at my ears again, and I pushed my hair over them, suddenly feeling oddly self-conscious. "Teddy."

"What?"

"My name. Not Buddy."

I laughed. "You're not from around here, are you?" He

looked confused, and I shook my head. "I really need to get back to work."

"Sure, sure." He gave me a wave and then stopped and turned. "See you later, Ivy."

I scowled. "Not if I see you first!"

Stupid, stupid. What was I even thinking?

A WARM, steaming mug of peppermint hot chocolate was just what I needed to get my day back on track. Sitting at my desk, I'd kicked my heels on the floor and tucked my legs underneath me. I'd always been more comfortable sitting like this, even if everyone made fun of me for it.

Putting on my Christmas playlist, I got back to work. I'd skipped lunch—no surprise there—but I'd just grab a bite to eat on my way home like I always did. There was always too much to do, schedules to sort out, personnel issues to solve, and that didn't even include walking around the park to check in on everyone. I tried to be as active of a manager as possible. That was one reason I'd stuck around here so long— employees were treated well. Maybe we dressed up as Santa's Elves, but we had a damn good union behind us.

"Knock, knock." The voice at the door startled me.

I looked up, surprised to find my eyes meeting Theodore Clausen's—Teddy, I reminded myself—for the second time today. "Hello. What can I do for you?"

He took his time inspecting my office. It wasn't overly decorated, mostly because I hadn't even had time to put out the tiny tree that normally sat on my desk this year. A few photo frames were on my desk, one of me graduating from UCF, diploma in hand. One with Sarah, the second summer we'd both worked here, during one of the Christmas in July summer-themed events. We both had big smiles plastered on our faces like the magic was all still new and everything was fun. There was one with me and one of my foster sisters from the Christmas I lived with her family. One of the best ones I'd ever had.

If only it had lasted.

I wondered what it looked like through someone else's eyes.

His perusal of my space gave me ample time to study him. That long, brown hair that touched the top of his ears. It looked soft like you'd want to run your fingers through it. He was clean-shaven, though I imagined he'd look equally attractive with stubble and that strong jaw. Pink, full lips. And those cheekbones? Ugh. To die for. And yet, none of that compared to his physique. He wore black suit pants and a white button-up shirt with a forest green tie, but he'd rolled up the sleeves, revealing delicious forearms. With those broad shoulders, I could just imagine—

"Ivy?"

"Huh?" My cheeks warmed. Oh, god. He totally caught me ogling him. This was embarrassing. No, strike that, mortifying. He already seemed to think I couldn't do my job. I couldn't have him firing me for checking him out.

"It's nice. A little small, though."

"Oh." If it was possible, I was pretty sure my blush deepened. "Thank you. They used to joke that it was a broom closet, but then when it became my office…" That it was me sized. Because I was so small. Ugh. It wasn't funny then or now.

He frowned, straightening. "I'm sorry if we got off on the wrong foot earlier."

"I *did* have it handled," I insisted.

"I know." He held up his hands. "But people were filming, and I couldn't stand the way she was talking to you."

"Oh." My temper diffused a little, and I brushed a piece of hair behind my ear. "Well, I guess you're not a *total* scrooge."

He chuckled. "Definitely not. Christmas is my favorite time of year."

"Then why are you spending it working at an amusement park instead of being home with your family?" I glanced at his left hand but didn't see a ring. Not married, then. Still, he could have a girlfriend back home. It didn't matter either way though, because technically he was my boss. And I was *not* interested.

Teddy raised an eyebrow at me as if to ask, *why are you?* "I'm trying to wrap up a few projects before the holidays. Seemed the best time to see how this place operated and get the lay of the land."

I snorted. "Yeah, the busy season is definitely the *most fun* around here."

"It's crazy, but I think I love it." He picked up a tiny wooden reindeer off my desk, running his thumb over the carvings. It was small in his massive hands. God, what was wrong with me? I didn't usually notice stuff like that.

"Yeah?" I bit my lip. "Honestly, it doesn't feel like there's anywhere else like it in the world. I started here right after I graduated high school, and I just... never left." Some might call it complacency, but I was content, and wasn't that enough? Maybe it was too much to ask for a perfect fairytale life—I'd certainly never had that to begin with—but this was enough for me. "And now I'm Head Elf at Santa's Workshop, and how many people can say that?"

He placed the reindeer back down on my desk, a hint of amusement dancing over his lips. "And you like it?"

I raised an eyebrow. "Is this a standard question you're asking all employees or just me?"

"Just you."

A shiver ran down my spine. "Oh." I met his green-eyed

gaze and nodded. "Then I guess, yeah. I like it. Why? Does that make a difference for you?"

Teddy smiled. "Maybe it does."

He stood up, heading out of my office, then looked over his shoulder at the last moment. "See you tomorrow, Ivy Winters." The matter-of-factness in his tone, the way his stare was full of determination... all of it was hot.

He was just plain attractive. I hated it because I didn't want to like him.

"See you tomorrow," I mumbled back.

4
teddy

25 days until christmas

My phone buzzed as I tapped my ID badge against the sensor to enter the employees-only area of the park. I'd been here almost a week, and it felt like I finally had my footing here. Pulling it out, I looked at the caller ID and then sighed. *Dad.* I'd call him back later. I wasn't quite ready to talk yet. It wasn't like we'd fought, but the last time we'd spoken had been... different.

I knew exactly what he wanted from me: to find a wife, bring her back home, and settle down. Have two point five perfect children. And eventually take over his legacy. It wasn't just the family business—though honestly, they ran almost perfectly, even without our participation—it was all of it: no pressure or anything.

Never mind that it had ended terribly when I'd dated in college. Try explaining to a woman that you wanted to take home for the holidays that she needed to pack for subzero temperatures. Oh, and home?

22

The North Pole. Yeah, I wouldn't have come with me either. After that, I'd stopped dating entirely. It was easier to tell the girls that I was from Alaska and laugh it off when they found out my last name was Claus.

Nobody here knew my last name or that I was one of *those* Claus. It felt almost wrong not to tell Ivy my actual last name, though. Plus, I just had this feeling any time I looked at her. Something I couldn't quite identify, but it was there, lingering under the surface…

Dropping my stuff at my desk, I surveyed the room. It was a big corner office with windows that looked out over the park. Nothing like the tiny one they'd given her. She'd joked about everyone calling it a broom closet, but that was practically what it was.

How could I fix that? She deserved better than to be shoved into a tiny space.

While I was down here, I'd made it my mission to experience everything the park offered at least once. It was the only way I could get a truly informed overview of all the aspects of the park operations: attractions, food services, merchandise —every role played a vital part in the park running smoothly. Even our custodial team, overseeing sweeping and trash, kept this place looking pristine.

Looking over today's to-do list, I took a drink of the coffee I'd grabbed from the hotel on my way here.

"God, that's gross," I muttered, grabbing the cup and dumping it in the sink. My mug from the Gingerbread Bakery had been incredible. Maybe I'd just sneak over and grab another one before starting my work.

I'd ditched the formal suit today and instead wore a pair of slacks and a red button up, rolling my sleeves up to combat the Florida humidity, forgoing a tie entirely.

Luckily, the line was short, and I stepped up to the counter. The entire place looked like Christmas threw up all over it, and that was saying something, considering where I was from. The menu was all Holiday-themed drinks and cookies, from sugar cookies to peppermint and even eggnog drinks.

"Hey. Can I get a large gingerbread latte?"

The barista adjusted her gingerbread cookie patterned apron before writing my order down. "And what's the name for that?"

"Teddy." I gave her a small smile as she input my order into the system.

"Whipped cream?"

I opened my mouth to say no but then said, "Sure, why not?" I was in the mood, and what was the harm? What was the point of life if you didn't indulge yourself every once in a while?

"And can I get one of those gingerbread muffins?" I asked, pointing at the display case. It was the last one. My mouth watered just thinking about how delicious it had been yesterday. The North Pole was filled with amazing treats, but I absolutely needed the recipe for these.

"Of course." She nodded.

"Thank you, Hollie."

"No problem." The girl blushed as I handed over my card.

"Oh, you're—!" She exclaimed, and I placed a finger over my lips.

"Shhh. Wouldn't want everyone in the park to know, right?"

She nodded. "Of course, sir. Sorry."

This was why I didn't want people to know who I was. But it was hard to ignore the Claus Family Enterprises company card with my name printed on it. Still, they didn't know who I *really* was. That was a secret I couldn't share with anyone—no matter how much I wanted to.

After paying, I took my plated muffin and sat at one of the

small tables by the window. Even the stool was themed to match like this entire place really was made of real gingerbread. I waited for my latte to come out as I took a bite of my muffin, trying not to inhale every last bite.

"Sorry, he took the last one."

"Who?"

I looked over at the counter, catching the barista pointing at me—and an irritated looking Ivy, who looked like she could have shot daggers out of her eyes. Scary. She looked like an angry kitten.

"You."

I gave her a sheepish grin. "Sorry. They're delicious."

"I know." She crossed her arms over her chest. "That's why I've been getting one every morning for years."

Raising an eyebrow, I licked my thumb, like a trace of icing might remain. "I didn't see your name on it, sweetheart."

"Ugh." She rolled her eyes, muttering under her breath, "You're so annoying." I'm sure she didn't mean for me to hear it, but I had uncannily sharp senses.

She turned back to the barista, ordering something else, and surprised me by coming down to sit in front of me.

I'd only caught glimpses of her over the last few days, as it seemed like anytime she saw me, she ran away before I could approach her. Now she wanted to talk?

Ivy took a sip of her drink—an iced, extra-sweet sugar cookie blended coffee—and I raised an eyebrow.

Even annoyed at me, she was a vision in green velvet. Stunning, with that strawberry blonde hair—that shined golden and red in the sun—curled down her back and her bright blue eyes that sparkled like snowflakes falling from the sky. Today, she was wearing a fresh pair of earrings than she had the last time I'd seen her—a set of sparkly Christmas trees—and she'd done her hair differently.

Yet there was something else in her bright blue eyes I couldn't quite identify. *Loneliness?* Or was that just my imagination? She had said she liked it here, but there was a hesitation I couldn't help but hear in her voice. But maybe I was just projecting my own feelings onto her.

"So..."

She did her best to look properly annoyed while eating her cinnamon scone. "I can't believe you took my muffin." She scowled, though the expression was more cute than it was intimidating.

"You know what they say. You snooze, you lose." I smirked, licking my lips. "What's on the docket for the day, Poison Ivy?"

"Seems like I should be the one asking *you* that. Do you even work?" She gestured to the table, which held our cups of coffee and empty plates.

"Of course I work," I scoffed. "Part of my visit is experiencing everything the park offers. I'm making a list of potential upgrades to the park."

Ivy looked skeptical. "You are?"

I took a drink of coffee, studying her closely. What was it about her? "Yes. That's my job. What did you think I do, anyway?"

"I don't know." She lowered her voice, leaning in conspiratorially. "I wasn't sure the stuffy executives actually did anything."

A laugh burst free from my lips. "I promise you, that's the farthest from the truth."

The strawberry blonde in front of me just hummed. "Maybe."

"You're teasing me, aren't you?"

She rolled her straw between her teeth, giving me a cheeky grin. "Potentially."

"What about you?" I asked, wanting to get to know her better.

"What about me?" Ivy repeated, looking confused.

"How'd you end up working here? Why Christmasland?"

She picked up her necklace chain—one that had been tucked underneath the neckline of her dress—and fidgeted with the snowflake pendant. "It's a long story."

I glanced down at my watch and shrugged. "I've got time." I leaned back in my chair as I sipped my coffee and watched her.

"I've always loved Christmas. When I moved here for college, I got a job here working as an entertainment handler, and I never left."

"And you like it?"

"What's not to love? Being surrounded by the magic of Christmas every day?"

"Oh, you can only imagine." I had more experience with that than she'd ever know.

"Hm?"

I chuckled. "Nothing. And what about your family? Where are they?"

Her face fell. "Oh. I... It's just me."

"I'm sorry, Ivy. I didn't mean to pry."

"No, it's okay." She stared down at her drink. "It's always been just me, though, so I'm used to it. I lost my dad when I was small. When my mom passed away, I ended up in foster care." She looked out the garland-covered window, toying with a pendant around her neck of a small silver snowflake. "All I had left of her was this necklace with my name etched into the back. I barely remember them, I was so young. Sure, I have vague memories of my mom, but that's it. And my dad... all I know is that losing him destroyed her." Her blue eyes looked so sad, and I briefly thought of comforting her.

Of laying my hand over hers on the table, so she knew she wasn't alone.

But I didn't think she'd appreciate that, so I pulled my hand back into my lap.

Her little brows furrowed. "I don't know why I just told you that." She mumbled something under her breath.

But I did. It was the same reason little kids liked to tell me what they wanted for Christmas.

"Where are you from, anyway?" Ivy asked, changing the subject. "You didn't say."

"Up north." I was aware I was being evasive, but she wouldn't believe me if I told her. Not yet.

She scrunched her nose. "Like... Canada?"

A chuckle left my lips. "Something like that."

"Mmm. I bet it's cold there. Probably have a white Christmas every year, huh?"

"Definitely. It's basically always snowing where I'm from."

"I've never seen snow," she admitted. "I've always wanted to, though. It seems so... *magical*." She sighed, a dreamy expression on her face.

It was crazy, the things I'd taken for granted living in the North Pole all my life. But for Ivy, even this theme park was something special. What would it be like to see the North Pole through her eyes? To see her experience snow, a real Christmas, for the first time?

I shook the thought away. I'd only just met her—it wasn't like I was going to invite her home for Christmas. Besides, I didn't even know if I'd have time to go back.

She smiled at me, tucking a strand of hair behind her ear. "I should go. This was... nice, though. Thanks for the company, Teddy."

"Even though I stole your muffin?"

"Yeah." She stood up with a bit of flounce to her skirts. "Even though you stole my muffin."

And then she was gone, in a blur of green velvet and strawberry blonde, making me wonder if I'd ever noticed how beautiful a woman was before Ivy Winters.

I didn't think I ever had.

"DAD?"

"Hey, son. How's it going down there?"

"Good. Park's in good shape." Overall, I was enjoying the job, even if I wished I was back home. "Sorry I missed your call earlier. I was just getting to work."

"No worries. I just wanted to see if you'd given any thought to what I said the other night?" Dad asked, sounding so hopeful.

About meeting someone? Yeah, not likely. I was already here, learning all the family businesses at his request. When did he think I'd also have time to find a wife?

"The world is different now than when you met Mom." I let out a sigh. "Besides, who would choose this life?" Especially since it meant leaving their family and friends—all of their loved ones—behind. Keeping a secret for the rest of their lives. Pinching the spot between my eyebrows, I shook my head. "No one in their right mind."

"You know I'm not getting any younger, Theodore."

Full name. Oh, he was serious. Everyone always called me Teddy, except for my parents when they were upset with me, and then I got the full *Theodore Nicholas Claus*. In college, I'd tried out Theo, but at home, Teddy had stuck.

"I know, Dad." I blew out a breath. "But it's not like I can just snap my fingers and have the perfect woman appear right in front of me." He let out a hum, and I shook my head, even knowing he couldn't see me. "But listen, that's not why I'm calling."

"Oh?"

"There's this girl."

"Oh. So you did think about what I said."

"No. I mean, it's not like that." It wasn't, right? I mean, she was beautiful, and something in her blue eyes captivated me more than I could explain, but it wasn't... I cleared my throat. "I can sense Christmas magic in her. Which is impossible, unless..."

"Unless she was born in the North Pole. Or..." My dad let out a contemplative noise. "Do you remember that story I told you?"

"Which one?" I asked because my dad loved to tell stories. Besides making and delivering toys, it was his favorite pastime.

"About the runaway elf."

"Dad." I huffed out a laugh. "You can't be serious. Wasn't that like, thirty years ago?"

"Are you going to listen to me or not?"

I rolled my eyes, shutting my mouth, even though he couldn't see me. "Alright, alright. Let's hear it."

I could almost picture my father nodding, running his thumb across his chin as if in deep thought. "She had a daughter."

"What?" I blinked. Why was this the first time I was hearing of this? "And you think that..."

Was there a chance Ivy was actually from the North Pole? It felt like I'd been searching my whole life for someone who would understand me—had I really found her here?

But she didn't know. She *couldn't*. She appeared totally human.

"Maybe. If you can sense the magic in her, there's little other explanation."

"But what are the odds?"

He chuckled. "Maybe the magic of the park attracted that part of her. If she doesn't know, that's certainly one explanation."

"She never knew her parents," I offered. "They both passed away when she was young."

"Hmm." If he was here, he'd probably pat me on the shoulder and give me some wise advice. I didn't understand how he did it, but maybe one day I would. "Guess you should get to know her better, huh?"

"Dad," I groaned.

But he was right. The only way to sort this out was to get to know her better.

That wouldn't be a hardship, though. Not when I couldn't get those sparkling blue eyes out of my mind.

5

ivy

24 days until christmas

*A*fter yesterday's café run-in, I hadn't seen Teddy again all afternoon. Wherever he was—in his office working or taking his time experiencing all Christmasland offered—our paths hadn't crossed.

For whatever reason, I found myself almost bummed that we hadn't. He was handsome, and sitting across the table from him had made my heart beat a little faster. If I was being honest, I wanted to get to know him better. He was attractive, yes, but it was something *deeper*. Like something in him called to something inside of my soul. Even if he drove me crazy and had stolen my muffin.

Hadn't he known those were my favorite? I'd seen him there a few days this week, and I'd always had one each morning.

I still found it strange that he hadn't told me exactly where he was from. *Something like that.* I frowned at the memory of his words. The only thing further north than

Canada was the Arctic Ocean, and it's not like people actually lived on the polar ice caps.

He was dangerous. That much I knew to be true. Because after Christmas, he'd be gone. And I'd still be here, just like I'd always been. So it was better not to get attached. Not to let this crush of mine deepen or engage him in playful banter because it would end up the same way either way.

Still, I couldn't help the way my heart soared when someone knocked on the door frame of my office door.

I looked up, expecting to see Teddy there, but it was just Sarah. "Oh. Hi."

"Don't look so disappointed to see your best friend," she muttered, dropping herself onto the chair across from my desk.

Shaking my head, I smiled at her. "You're early today."

"What can I say? Turning over a new leaf." She draped an arm over the chair. "Now, who were you expecting that you were all excited to see?"

"No one. It's nothing." I pushed my hair back behind my ears, brushing my fingers over my candy cane earrings.

Sarah pursed her lips. "Are you sure? Because I heard you and the new executive were getting cozy in the café yesterday."

"How?" I scowled. "Those gossiping—"

"Relax, kitten. Put those claws away."

I let out a breath. "You know I hate when people talk about me behind my back."

"I do. But I also think everyone's just interested in your new beau."

"Theodore Clausen?" I raised an eyebrow, though that name felt wrong on my lips, like it wasn't quite right. "He's not my *beau*. We're not even friends, really. And he totally stole my muffin from me yesterday. I can't stand the guy."

Lie. It was so obvious that I wasn't telling the truth, but I couldn't let myself feel anything else for this man. He'd just be another person who would leave.

So why did I care?

"Am I interrupting?" came a deep, smooth voice. *Teddy.* Butterflies erupted in my chest. Fuck, I needed to end this. Whatever it was.

"No, not at all," Sarah said, a broad, beaming smile on her face. I attempted to kick her under my desk, but no luck.

"Brought you something." He held up a bag from the Gingerbread Bakery. "Got you one before they ran out." He winked. "Since you like them so much."

Oh. My cheeks warmed. "Thank you. You didn't have to." Indulging myself on sweets from the bakery was my one treat each day, and I definitely didn't need one, but they certainly made a long day better.

"It was all I could do to make up for yesterday." He also made a cup of iced coffee appear, setting them both on my desk. My mouth watered.

Coffee and a muffin? I was being spoiled. "Wow. What service."

My dark-haired friend looked back and forth between the two of us. "Aren't you going to introduce us?" Sarah said, a smug look on her face.

"Sarah, this is Theodore. Theodore, this is Sarah. She's one of our Santa photographers."

"Nice to meet you, Sarah." Teddy stuck out his hand for a handshake. "Keep up the good work."

"Of course." She looked entranced, like maybe I wasn't the only one who those handsome looks affected. Glancing down at her watch, she shot off the chair. "Shoot. I should probably get to work. Bye, Ivy." She turned to the man whose presence made my office seem even smaller. "Nice to meet you, Theodore."

He nodded, giving her a small wave.

"You really didn't have to do this," I repeated. "I wasn't that upset yesterday."

His eyes twinkled with amusement. "Sure you weren't, Poison Ivy."

"Don't call me that."

"Why not?"

"Because you make me sound like the Batman villain. And I don't even have red hair." I furrowed my brow.

"It's beautiful." He cleared his throat like he hadn't meant to say that. "And it's a little red in the sun."

"What?"

"Your hair."

"I..." How did someone respond to that, anyway? I gaped at him. "Yeah." I'd always loved the color of my hair for that reason—blonde with red lowlights. When the girls I'd known in high school were dying theirs, I'd been too attached to my hair color to even consider it.

Needing a distraction from the way Teddy was looking at me, I popped a piece of the muffin into my mouth. It was still warm, and the flavors exploded on my tongue. A small moan slipped from my lips. "So good."

He looked pleased, like an alpha male puffing up his chest at having fed his female. Not that I was *his*. He wasn't mine, either, though. "Thought you couldn't stand me, sweetheart." Teddy winked.

"Can't. You owe it all to this to the muffin, Theodore."

"Sure, sure." He propped his hip against my desk, towering over me. My entire space was filled with the smell of him—masculine, like mountains and snow and pine trees —and all I wanted to do was to take a deep inhale.

"Hey, Ivy?"

"Mhm?" I asked, realizing I'd been biting my lip.

"Do you want to get dinner sometime?"

"Oh. I'm…" I looked down at my lap. "I'm not sure that's a good idea."

"Why not?"

"Because you're my boss."

"Not really."

"Okay. You're my bosses' bosses' boss. Semantics, really."

"There's no rule about fraternization between employees unless I'm your direct supervisor or making decisions about your employment."

"Still… We've only known each other a week."

"And a week isn't long enough?" When had he leaned in so close? "Say yes."

"Why?" I whispered the word.

Teddy pushed a piece of hair behind my ear, his finger lingering for a beat longer than was probably acceptable. Was any of this? Probably not. Still, I didn't stop it. "Because I want to get to know you better. Because you intrigue me like no one else ever has."

"Okay." My voice was shaky when I finally responded.

"When's your next day off?"

I blinked. "Tuesday. But—"

"Great. It's a date. I'll pick you up at eight."

He left my office, taking that dizzyingly intoxicating scent of pine with him, and I realized later that he hadn't even asked for my address.

22 days until christmas

When was the last time I'd even been on a date? Years. It wasn't like that many guys were clamoring to ask me out, considering I wore an elf costume for my career.

Looking at myself in the mirror, I inspected the way the tight red dress hugged my curves. I'd left my snowflake necklace on, letting it rest over the top of my collarbone. It always felt like I was missing something without it.

I'd paired the dress with my favorite pair of heels, giving me a few extra inches of height. Teddy was *tall*, and I wanted to even the playing field a little. I looked myself over in the mirror one last time.

I'd redone my hair, pulling a few pieces back and out of my face, plus touching up my makeup by deepening the color on my eyes and swiping a fresh coat of red lipstick on. The effect was instantaneous, more sultry, and a little sexy.

It worked well with my dress, which dipped down to show a hint of cleavage. Was it too much? We hadn't even talked about where we were going for dinner. Maybe I'd just assumed—

The doorbell rang, and there was no more time to panic about my chosen ensemble.

He was here. *Teddy.*

I blew out a breath, going to answer the door.

"Hey."

"Hi, Ivy." He sucked in a breath. "Wow. You look—wow."

He'd combed his dark brown hair back and swapped his shirt out for a new one. This one was a dark, forest green, like the color of pine trees.

"These are for you," Teddy said, offering me a bouquet of poinsettia flowers. "I thought you might like them."

"Wow." A giggle escaped me, and I scolded myself for acting like an excited schoolgirl on her first ever date. *Come on, Ivy, get it together.* "Thank you. I'll just put them in water, and then we can go. Do you want to come in for a second?"

"Sure."

I opened the door all the way, and he brushed by me, entering my apartment. It was bare, and heat rose to my cheeks as I watched him take it all in.

"It's not much," I murmured, "but it's mine." And it was hard to even afford a one-bedroom apartment in this economy, especially in Central Florida. My manager's salary helped some, but only enough that I didn't have to share anymore.

"You don't have a tree," was the first thing he finally said, turning to look at me. Those green eyes shouldn't have held my attention so much.

I swallowed roughly, looking away. "No point in getting one for just me."

He raised an eyebrow but said nothing else. I was grateful if only so I didn't have to talk about the subject further. Because he knew I loved Christmas, but my apartment was anything but. I hadn't had the time or energy to decorate. When I got home from work most nights, all I wanted to do was sit in a bubble bath with a glass of wine or read a book. Occasionally, I sat down in the little craft corner I'd set up, but that was on a good day.

Heading into the kitchen, I found a vase for the flowers he brought me and filled it with water before setting them on the table.

"That's better," he mused.

He drummed his fingers against the table, distracting me from my thoughts. I took the moment to admire his large hands. Teddy cleared his throat, and I averted my eyes, knowing my cheeks would be red from being caught staring. I couldn't help it. They were well-manicured hands but looked strong, like he wasn't afraid to work. Like he could get his hands dirty.

"They're beautiful. Thank you again."

"Of course. Shall we?" He held out his arm, and I nodded. Grabbing my purse, we headed out the door and downstairs. He steered me to a small red truck—the kind that looked like it should have a tree tied to the back.

"This is yours?" I asked, my jaw dropping open. It was adorable.

He nodded, opening the door for me. "It was the only one left when I went to get a rental."

"I love it." I slid inside, and Teddy's scent surrounded me. He closed the door, and I took a deep inhale of the deep, masculine smell. It was insane how much I liked it.

He chuckled, and the sound ran down my spine, and I couldn't believe how it affected me. Teddy seemed so serious, down to his dark green eyes that looked at me with so much... what? Concern? *Interest?* I didn't know, but part of me wanted to hear his laugh. To know what he looked like with a smile on his face.

"Where to, boss?" I asked, crossing my legs and flipping my hair over my shoulder as I turned to face him fully.

"I'm not your boss, Ivy," he said, furrowing his brow. Teddy stared at my bare legs, and his jaw tightened before he looked away. "It's important to me you know that."

I swallowed roughly. "I know," I whispered.

"Good." He nodded.

And then we headed out on our *date.*

6
teddy

*M*y palms were sweating as I gripped the steering wheel, trying to distract myself from the beauty of a woman sitting in the passenger seat. *Wow* was an understatement. She was stunning. An absolute bombshell. She'd done something different with her eyes, and those pouty red lips begged to be kissed. We hadn't really touched, skin to skin, where we were open and vulnerable with each other.

But did I want to? *Yes.*

Fuck, I needed to pace myself. Maybe I was doing too much, trying to impress her. But the way her eyes had lit up when she saw the truck told me it was a good use of magic. Though I only had so much before I had to return to the Pole.

Still, she was here with me, and I knew I hadn't made up this attraction between us. It was almost electric, and I wanted to explore it. Which meant I needed an excuse to spend more time with her. Maybe then I could figure out what ran through her veins and the reason it felt like something in her called to me.

It had to be the magic I detected inside of her. It couldn't be anything else.

I pulled up to the restaurant, and her eyes lit up. "Are you kidding?" Her jaw dropped open. "This place is so nice. And *expensive.*"

"I can afford it," I said with a chuckle. "Part of the perks of being a stuffy executive."

She blushed. "I didn't mean it like that. I'm sorry for assuming—"

"It's fine," I reassured her. "Besides, you're not completely wrong. Lots of people in positions like mine have lost touch with the company. They lose sight of what's important." Turning to face her fully, I locked my gaze on hers. "I won't ever lose sight of what's important, Ivy."

Ivy shifted in her seat, and I got out, going around and opening the door for her.

"Oh."

"I believe the words you're looking for are, *thank you, Teddy,*" I said with a wink, holding out my hand to her to help her out of the truck.

"Thank you, Teddy," Ivy parroted back, mocking me.

I caught her eyes and grinned. "See, that wasn't so hard, was it?"

"I believe the words you're looking for are, *you're welcome, Ivy.*"

Catching her hand, I brought it up to my mouth and kissed it. "You're welcome, Ivy." There wasn't even a hint of teasing in my voice.

Her cheeks were tinged the slightest shade of pink. "Should we go in?"

With a nod, I guided her into the restaurant, the palm of my hand resting on the small of her back possessively. That tight red dress that clung to her curves dipped low in her back, showing a sliver of bare skin, and it made me feel a little crazy.

After telling the hostess my name, we were quickly seated at an intimate two-person table in the corner, and I did my best to take my eyes off of her. It was hard, though, because I finally had an excuse to study her in excruciating detail.

Those gorgeous reddish-blonde waves. Her beautiful blue eyes peeked up at me through long lashes. Full, soft-looking lips painted red.

She slid her snowflake necklace pendant back and forth on the chain as she studied the menu. I'd ordered a bottle of wine when we sat down, not wanting to get interrupted again too quickly.

Because I was telling Ivy the truth when I told her I wanted to get to know her. I wanted to know everything there was about her. Maybe then I could understand why she fascinated me so.

"What are you getting?" Ivy asked, looking up at me. "I have to admit, I'm a little overwhelmed."

"Probably the pot roast with potatoes and carrots," I said, clearing my throat and trying not to make it seem like I'd just been staring at her. "But I heard the steak is good, too."

"Carrots? What are you, a reindeer?"

I laughed. "If only." She really had no idea where I'd grown up.

"Huh?"

"Nothing." I shook my head.

The waitress came over with the wine I'd ordered and a basket of bread, saving me from further questioning, and we both ordered our meals before she scurried away.

Once she was gone, Ivy propped her chin up on her hands, her elbows on the table as she studied me. "Tell me more about yourself."

"What do you want to know?" I asked, running my fingers through my brown hair.

Ivy shrugged. "I don't know. I feel like I've told you lots of things about myself, but what do I know about you?"

Chuckling, I took a sip of my wine. Where would I even start? "I'm from a tiny town, so when I turned eighteen, I went in the exact opposite direction and moved to a big city for college. I had all these plans." That seemed safe.

She nodded, encouraging me. "And?"

"And I *hated* it. The noise, the traffic, how it felt like I was surrounded by a million people, and yet no one really knew me." And wasn't that still the case? Who really knew me? Even my parents only knew the part of me I showed them.

Everything else—everything I kept inside? That was the real me. The one who longed for all the things I knew I couldn't have.

"So what happened?"

"I graduated at twenty-two. Left the city. Went to work at my family's company. I started in the Finance Department and worked my way up to where I am now."

"Wait. Your *family's* company?"

I tilted my head to the side. "Yeah. Didn't you know?"

"No." She frowned. "Was it common knowledge or something?"

"Suppose not. But *Clausen* and Claus Family—"

"Oh." Ivy slapped her forehead, interrupting me. "Duh. That should have been so obvious, huh?"

"If it helps, I didn't want it to be. I could have started at the top, but I like this part. Getting to see how the company actually works. It helps me determine where I can make changes to improve efficiency. I'm always working on developing our ventures and finding new ways to create capital. I couldn't do that if everyone constantly fell over my feet, knowing I was the heir to the family enterprise." Because when people realized I was worth millions—potentially billions—of dollars, they treated me differently. Thankfully, no one back home cared about that.

"Huh."

"What?"

She shook her head. "I just couldn't help but think how different our lives have been. And yet... here we both are."

"Here we are," I agreed. Reaching my hand across the table, I laid my hand over hers and then squeezed slightly. "And I'm grateful you're here, Ivy."

Our food arrived, and I reluctantly drew my hand away as we started eating. It smelled amazing, and I was glad to have a moment of reprieve from the conversation. It led to a discussion I wasn't sure I was ready for.

We shared some small talk as we ate—Ivy's favorite parts of the park and the places she loved to visit in the surrounding area. In return, I shared my favorite places from my travels around the country, visiting the different businesses my family owned. If she thought it was strange that they all had one thing in common, Ivy didn't mention it.

Switching topics, I drew our conversation back to her. "You said you didn't know much about your parents?"

"No." Hurt seeped from her. "Just that they're gone. Both of them."

"But you don't know where they came from?"

She shook her head. "I would assume the government did, but... they never told me. My dad was in the military, so they moved all over, and all I know is there was no other family to take me in. That's how I ended up in foster care."

I rested my hand over hers. "I'm sorry, Ivy."

"That's just life, isn't it?"

"No." I shook my head. "I mean, I'm sorry that no one

was there for you. If, for any moment in your life, you felt unwanted."

"Oh." A blush covered her cheeks. "I—Thank you."

"Of course." I nodded, taking my hand back. "So, I told you about my career path. What about you? Why management?"

Ivy looked relieved at the change in topic, raising an eyebrow. "What do you mean? It makes sense. And I knew I'd have a stable job."

"You don't strike me as the kind of girl to pick a career because it's practical, Ivy."

Not when she was this fiery spitball who loved to argue with me. I could already tell she wouldn't back down from a fight. She might have fit right in at the park, but that didn't mean she was flourishing here. Eventually, it would kill her spirit. Maybe it already had. Maybe there was something more out there for her.

"Well… I originally wanted to major in art. My favorite activities growing up always included making things. And maybe I could have become an art teacher or something eventually if I'd gone with it. But Christmasland… it's been good to me." She poked around her dish with her fork. "So I can't complain."

"But you're not happy."

"What do you mean?" Her brows furrowed. "Of course I'm happy. I just do that stuff as a hobby now. I have a little craft corner in my apartment, and it's great."

I'd noticed that before, when she'd let me inside her space. The space that was devoid of decorations.

"What do you like to make?"

A smile broke out on her face. "This might sound dumb, but…"

"Believe me, sweetheart. Nothing is going to sound dumb from you." Not when I was hanging on her every word.

"Christmas ornaments." Her face lit up when she was talking about this—something she loved. "My friends are always trying to get me to sell them at markets, but I feel like taking something from a hobby to a job can ruin the fun, you know?"

Ornaments. That was adorable.

An idea was already forming in my head. But did I have the will to upend her entire life? If what I believed to be true was correct, everything she knew about herself was about to change.

How I was going to convince her to come with me, though... That was a separate problem.

OUR DESSERT, though delicious, didn't compete with my mom's white chocolate peppermint cheesecake.

Would Ivy like it? If she even agreed to my idea.

"Should we walk?" I asked her, standing outside the restaurant. It was nice outside for an early December day, even in Florida.

She nodded. "Sure. Why not?" The street was lined with trees covered in string lights, giving it a cozy ambiance.

Ivy shivered, and I draped my jacket around her shoulders.

"Oh." Ivy looked up at me, cheeks pink. "Thank you."

"Don't mention it. Besides, I'm not even cold."

"I bet it's way warmer here than where you're from, huh?"

Definitely. That was an understatement. "It's not so bad," I said instead. "I've got a fireplace in my house. It's cozy to sit in front of on the cold winter nights."

Ivy let out a small sigh. "That sounds nice. I have to admit, I'm jealous."

"The perfect Christmas," I agreed.

"Tell me more about it," Ivy asked, her eyes lit up.

I froze, my heart beating a million miles in my chest as I sputtered, "What?"

"What was it like for you growing up? You said you always had a white Christmas, didn't you?"

Oh. Letting out my breath, I nodded. "Yeah. My dad worked a lot during this season—always has—but Christmas Day was always my favorite day of the year. Finding that special present under the tree, playing with it all day, eating cookies, and watching movies by the fire... Those are some of my favorite memories."

Ivy gave me a hesitant smile. "That sounds amazing."

"What about you? What are you doing for Christmas?"

"Honestly, the last few years, I've just worked."

I frowned. "Where's your *Christmas Spirit*?" That and the bare apartment seemed so at odds with the girl I was beginning to know.

She shrugged. "Perks of working for an amusement park that's open three hundred and sixty-five days a year. Barring any major hurricanes, you work on holidays."

"I suppose you're right." I let out a sigh.

"What are *you* doing?" She asked, throwing my question back at me.

I blinked, not expecting that. "Well... I hadn't decided yet. It's always been my dad's busy season, and I guess I've adopted his work ethic."

"But you're not spending it with your family?"

"I might. My mom's working hard to get me to come home for Christmas. I've never spent one anywhere else."

"I'm sure that will be amazing." A small smile formed on

her lips, but it felt sad. Like my words were a reminder of what she didn't have.

I could change that. Stopping on the sidewalk, I turned to face her. "Come home with me."

"What?" She raised an eyebrow. "I'm not going to—"

"For Christmas," I clarified, cutting her off. "Come back with me. You can experience all of it."

"Are you crazy?"

For you.

"No." I let out a small chuckle. "But I want to spend more time with you. And I want you to know what it's like. A real Christmas."

She looked away, that curtain of strawberry blonde hair covering her face so I couldn't see her reaction. "I don't know, Teddy. That's a lot. And even if I wanted to, I have my job, and I can't just leave right before the busiest time of the year."

"Don't worry about it. I'll take care of it. Like you said, I'm the big boss, remember?" I winked.

"You might just be the most stubborn, frustrating man I've ever met. Do you even know how to take no for an answer?"

"Not when I know what I want." And what I wanted was to see her eyes light up as she watched the snow fall on Christmas Eve. Among other things that I knew I shouldn't. "That's why I'm so good at business."

She bit her lip. "Just business?"

"No, Ivy," I said, leaning in closer to her. "Not just business."

Her breath caught in her throat, and I stepped backward, out of her personal space. Even though I desperately wanted to wrap my arm around her waist and pull her tight against my body.

"I don't know why I keep saying yes to you."

I flashed her a grin. "I do. It's because you like me."

"Absolutely not." She wrinkled her nose. "I definitely do *not* like you."

"Admit it, sweetheart."

"No." Ivy crossed her arms over her chest, a small scowl on her face.

I sighed. "Fine. You're going to make me do this the hard way, aren't you?"

"Do what?" she looked genuinely confused.

"Win you over."

And win her heart.

7

ivy

*T*onight had been *perfect*. The best first date in the history of first dates. Not that I was going to admit that to him. I couldn't make this too easy for him. Besides, I had to protect my heart. If my stubbornness was all I had, I'd cling to it.

And that walk... With his jacket draped over my shoulders, surrounding me with his delicious scent, and the pathway lit with lights, I found myself hoping he would reach over and interlace our fingers together.

My keys were in my hand, and I looked between him and the door. His body blocked it, and the way he towered over me had me swallowing in a breath.

It was easy to forget how tall he was at the restaurant while we'd been sitting down. But now, every inch of difference felt more apparent to me. I came up to his shoulder, barely. I knew I was small, but he made me feel *tiny*.

If I invited him inside, would he kiss me? Did I want him to? *Yes*. I did. And that was the problem. If I invited him inside, I'd want him to kiss me. And if he kissed me, well... That couldn't happen. Because I'd get attached. I always did.

And it would be so easy to fall for Teddy. I knew it would. Maybe that was why I'd been trying to avoid him.

Come home with me. Goosebumps rippled over my skin. Did I want to go? *Yes.*

I loved Christmastime, even if I'd never cared much for the day itself, celebrating alone. Sure, I had friends, but it wasn't the same. It was just another reminder that I didn't have a family, and I didn't need that.

But with Teddy...

It was absolutely, completely insane to want to go with this man that I'd known for a week, but I did. When was the last time I'd taken a real vacation? I couldn't afford to go on any extravagant trips, and besides, it was just me. I'd always wanted to see the world, but doing it alone seemed lonely. Maybe with someone by my side...

"Ivy..." He leaned in close.

"Yes?" I wasn't sure I was breathing. In fact, I knew I wasn't. Any second now, I was going to pass out from a lack of oxygen. Definitely.

But he didn't kiss me.

"You don't have to decide tonight," he reassured me. "Just think about it. I haven't even told my mom if I'm coming home yet."

"But you want to go?" I didn't want him to make this decision because of me.

He nodded.

"Okay," I said, my words a soft whisper. It wasn't an answer, not yet.

"Goodnight, Ivy Winters." He leaned in to kiss me, and my brain short-circuited.

Was I ready for this? I turned my head slightly, and his lips grazed my cheek.

"You don't want to come inside?"

A strangled sound left his throat. "More than you know. But we're not there yet."

"Oh." Why did I sound so disappointed? "But I'll see you tomorrow?"

He chuckled, and the sound filled me inexplicably. "Sure, sweetheart."

The nickname made my cheeks warm even more, but I turned away, not wanting to acknowledge why.

"Goodnight, Teddy," I whispered to his disappearing form as he walked away.

21 days until christmas

"Good morning." Teddy leaned against the door frame to my office, two cups of coffee in hand.

Did he know how desperately I needed that after last night? I'd tossed and turned all night thinking of his offer. I should have been floating on air after such a great first date—I'd laughed a lot and even *wanted* him to kiss me. It had been so long, and I'd gotten all dolled up… Even if I chickened out at the end.

Part of me wished he had come inside, but he was right not to. It was better not to get involved with him—not like *that*. Even if he'd invited me home for the holidays, he would still leave eventually.

Where would that leave me? Alone, just like I'd always been.

I was tired, cranky, and slightly irritable, but just the sight of his handsome face and the delicious smell of coffee in his hands made me perk up. "Is one of those for me?"

"Yes." He looked down at the cups in his hands, moving into my office while letting the door shut behind him. "Thought you could use one."

He handed it over, and I took a deep inhale.

Peppermint mocha. Yum. My favorite.

"Like Christmas in a cup," I said, doing my best to hold back the small moan as I took my first sip. Delicious. "Thank you."

"Don't mention it."

But how could I not? No man had ever gone to these lengths with me before. Especially not inviting me to Christmas with his family. It wasn't like we were dating, but the offer made me feel warm and fuzzy. Though I tried not to let that show, putting on an air of professionalism.

"Did you mean what you said last night?"

"About you coming home with me?" He settled into the chair across from me, watching me with an amused look as I took another sip.

"Yes." I nodded. "Because I appreciate the offer, but I couldn't impose on your family."

"Oh, believe me. They won't mind."

"Still. I couldn't possibly—" I shook my head. "I have a job to do. No matter what your position is within the company, there's no way you can replace me that quickly. I'd have to train someone, and—"

"Why don't you let me worry about that?" Mischief was written all over his face.

"When would we leave, anyway?"

"One week."

"What?" I spit out my coffee, doing the mental math. "But that's still two weeks until Christmas. I can't take that many days off work. I have to pay my rent, Teddy. And my car payment. I know this might be a strange concept, but—"

"Don't do that." He frowned. "Don't treat me differently

now that you know who my family is. I'm still the same me I was before I took you out to dinner."

That was fair. He'd explicitly told me he hated how people treated him after finding out how much he was worth. Was I doing the same thing? It wasn't like I was asking him to pay my rent.

"I just..."

"Please." His green eyes bore into me with so much sincerity that the *yes* was on the tip of my tongue. "What do I have to say to convince you?"

"Where are you from again?" All I knew was he grew up in a small town up north, though I had no idea what that meant. Montana? Alaska? Canada? If every Christmas was a white one, it had to be somewhere up there.

"It's a tiny town in... Northern Canada. You won't find it on any map." He chuckled. "No one's ever heard of it."

"Oh." I gnawed on my lower lip. Why did I want to say yes so badly? "And it snows there." It wasn't really a question. I was just trying to find any reason to say no when I so desperately wanted to say yes.

Christmas in a tiny, snow covered town? It sounded like something out of my dreams—or maybe a romantic Christmas movie.

He laughed. "Yes, Ivy. It snows."

"What are the chances said tiny town is obsessed with Christmas and has over-the-top decorations everywhere?"

"High." Teddy gave me a smirk. "Come on, Ivy. Say yes. I know you want to."

I frowned, holding up a hand. "Wait. I don't even have a passport." I'd never left the country. Had never really had a reason to before now.

"Don't worry. I'll take care of everything, sweetheart."

"Okay." I nodded. "Okay. Yes. I'll come home with you for Christmas." Definitely not what I meant to say. I meant to insist I couldn't, *absolutely not*, but then I'd gone and opened my mouth and done it anyway.

"Great." A grin split his face like he was pleased with himself. "And Ivy?"

"Hmm?" I asked, looking up from my paperwork to Teddy, who still stood in the doorway.

"Pack warm. I'll pick you up."

"You don't have to do that," I said, feeling flustered. "I can get a ride to the airport. Or I'll call a ride. You're already doing enough for me."

"Nah." A dimple popped in his left cheek. "I think I'm doing just the right amount."

"WHAT DO YOU MEAN, you're leaving for *two weeks?*" Sarah shrieked on the phone. As soon as Teddy had left my office, I'd called her. It was her day off, so I couldn't go find her in the park.

"Um, well... You know how you're always telling me I should go out more?"

I could practically *feel* her rolling her eyes. "This is definitely not what I meant."

"He invited me home with him for Christmas, Sar. How could I say no?"

"I mean, yeah. Have you seen that man?" She whistled. *Of course I had.* I wasn't blind. "But still. This is so not you."

She was right. This was completely out of character for me. And yet... "It feels like I'll regret it for the rest of my life if I don't do this. If I don't see where this thing is going."

"You really like him, don't you?"

"No." My denial came way too fast, and I knew she'd see right through me. "I just... after our date..."

"It's okay," she sighed. "I know you're going to fall in love and leave me forever."

Fall in love? That seemed like a bit of a leap.

"Why would I leave you?" I scrunched up my nose. "This is just for Christmas. Besides, he's leaving eventually. The park is just a pit stop for him while he learns all the aspects of the business."

Her tone was full of warning. "Ivy…"

"And he's *hot*," I whispered, a confession that maybe I shouldn't have given. Hot was an understatement. He was undeniably handsome. I'd never been this attracted to someone before Teddy.

"So hot," Sarah agreed. "Do you trust him?"

I closed my eyes, staring up at the ceiling. Yes. I did. Maybe that was the problem. "Yes," I finally answered her out loud. "I think I do."

"Then I think you should go. It's just two weeks, right?"

"Right." Two weeks, and then I'd come back.

15 days until christmas

What did I think I was doing? I'd packed two suitcases with every warm article of clothing I owned—which was, unsurprisingly, not a lot, considering the usual climate of this state. Maybe there would be some sort of store wherever he was from where I could get a few other things to wear. I certainly couldn't wear the same pair of jeans every day if I was going to be there for two weeks.

"This is a mistake. Oh, God. What am I even thinking? I can't be gone for two weeks."

With a stranger. And okay, sure, he wasn't *really* a stranger anymore. I'd known him for two weeks and tolerated his presence—okay, mostly liked him—for at least half of that. But I still barely knew him.

Did that matter when my heart sped up any time I was around him? I'd catch him coming into my office at random times during the day like he just wanted to see me.

And maybe I wanted to see him, too.

"But does that mean I'm not crazy?" I asked myself. Maybe I needed to get a dog. At least then it wouldn't seem like I was talking to myself, which I was definitely doing.

My doorbell rang, and I let out a long breath before opening it.

Theodore was standing outside my door, dressed in jeans and a t-shirt, a sweater thrown over his arm.

"Are you ready?" He asked me, looking at the bags I'd piled around the door.

I shrugged. "Honestly? No." A nervous laugh bubbled free from my lips. "I had no idea what I should pack. I've never even been somewhere cold before."

"You're going to love it."

"I hope so."

He stepped inside, and my breath caught in my throat. Teddy was standing so close to me, his vibrant green gaze locked on mine, and it flickered down to my lips before meeting my eyes again.

"I know so," he finally said.

"O-okay." I let out a ragged exhale. "So, how are we getting there?"

"Flying, of course."

I frowned. "Did you forget I don't have a passport?"

"I said I'd take care of it, didn't I?"

He had, but that didn't mean he'd follow through. What kind of guy could take care of something like that in a week?

Teddy reached behind his back, pulling out a folded blue booklet. I blinked.

"How did you even do this?" I flipped it open, looking at the page with my photo.

Somehow, it felt like I had more questions than answers for the strange things that Teddy did. Still, if it meant I could see the world—even a part of it, I guessed I shouldn't complain. "Thank you." I cradled the document against my heart. "This means so much to me. Truly, I don't know how I can make this up to you."

He chuckled. "Survive Christmas with my family, and that will be all the thank you I need."

Survive? I was going to *thrive*. This sounded like the best vacation I'd had in years.

The *only* vacation I'd had in years. I was going to savor every moment. Especially the ones I spent with this man by my side.

I just hoped I could resist him long enough to protect my heart.

8
teddy

With Ivy's belongings safely stowed in the back of the truck, I closed it, a thrum of excitement running through me at the prospect of being home. Sure, I enjoyed my work, but there was something about a Christmas at the North Pole that I couldn't quite deny.

And there was the mystery of the girl sitting in my front seat. I'd find out if my hunch was true or not soon, though. Everything would be revealed as soon as we crossed the border into the North Pole. Though I'd still have questions.

Part of me knew I should tell her the truth. But what would happen? Would she think I was insane? No one believed me when I told them I was from the North Pole. And she had clearly stopped believing in the magic of Christmas— the *real* Christmas. I knew whatever commercialized version was stuck in her brain was nothing like the things she'd dreamed about as a kid. But I wondered what would happen if I told her the whole truth of who I was. All of it.

Maybe she'd demand I turned around and took her home. Or maybe… a small voice in my mind whispered. *Maybe* she would want to stay.

There was only one way to find out.

"I still don't understand how you did all of this in a week." She stared at her lap in disbelief. "Are you sure there isn't something I should know about you? Are you secretly a foreign prince? Or maybe the FBI? Am I being trafficked?"

I chuckled. "You really love to doubt me, don't you?"

Ivy crossed her arms over her chest. "It's not like that."

"Isn't it?" I raised an eyebrow.

"Why are you like this?" She gave an exasperated sigh, muttering under her breath. "I don't know why I agreed to go home with you for Christmas."

"Because you like me." I grinned. It was almost endearing watching her try to deny it.

"Do not," Ivy grumbled something else, but I couldn't wipe the smile off my face.

She looked over at me, her lips caught between her teeth, and I held in a groan. I knew I hadn't imagined the heat between us. It had been a week since our date—a week of dropping by her office to bring her coffee each morning.

A week of resisting the pull I felt between us. Was this insane? Maybe.

Instead of giving in and resting my hand on her thigh like I wanted to, I kept driving. I needed to get out of the city before getting in the air, but I had to ensure Ivy was asleep first.

Luckily, I still had a bit of magic left.

RIDING on the back of a reindeer with an unconscious girl was harder than it looked.

"Sorry, Buddy," I said, patting my reindeer's neck with

my free hand as I held a sleeping Ivy in my arm. "We'll be home soon."

He made a braying noise as his legs moved underneath us, and I tried to ignore the fact that I had a girl cradled against my chest, her head resting against my shoulder. How right it felt.

I'd only used a pinch of magic to make her fall asleep, landing in my arms with that stubborn mouth of hers finally shut. Honestly, when she wasn't arguing with me, she looked almost... peaceful.

Those pouty pink lips of hers looked soft and kissable, and—I shook my head. I shouldn't have those thoughts about Ivy. Didn't need to be thinking that way about her, period. I wanted her—that was impossible to deny—but I wanted her to want me, too. To accept all of me.

But even wanting that, I knew it wouldn't last. After all, she wasn't *mine*.

Ugh. What was wrong with me? Maybe all of my dad's talk about meeting someone had gotten into my head. But I was fine, really. I didn't need to settle down. At twenty-seven, I was in no rush to find a wife. Or something more than that.

And my dad had plenty of years left before he even needed to *think* about retirement.

Shaking off the thoughts, I focused my attention on the horizon, letting Buddy fly us home.

MY DAD WAS SITTING in front of the fireplace, glasses perched low on his nose as he studied the book in front of him. I almost hated to interrupt him because, for once, he wasn't working. Wasn't checking the list, overseeing work in the workshop, or planning out the delivery schedule for the season.

Here, like this, all I could see was the man who raised me. My father. Not whatever mythical figure the world thought him to be.

My knuckles rapped on the door frame, alerting him to my presence. He looked up in surprise, his features forming into a warm smile before a look of confusion overtook his face. "Teddy. You're back early."

I looked at the calendar pinned to the wall, the countdown to Christmas. "I couldn't disappoint Mom by missing Christmas."

"Christmas is still two weeks away, son. You still had plenty of time to finish what you were working on down at the park."

"I know." I was hyper-aware of that fact. "But…"

"It's about the girl, isn't it?"

Nothing ever got past him. I nodded. "She agreed to come home with me for Christmas." I'd called him a few more times since I'd first met Ivy, telling him my suspicions. Though I couldn't know for sure.

My dad's white eyebrows raised on his forehead. "Oh, she did?" A jolly smile lit up his face. "That's my boy."

"Yeah," I agreed, staring into the fireplace as it crackled. All the fireplaces in the North Pole were wood burning, but they never needed tending to. *Magic.* This whole place was imbued with it. "Though she doesn't exactly know *where* she is."

My father blinked. "What do you mean? You didn't tell her?"

"How could I? She's going to think I'm crazy. That this is crazy. She has no idea who she is, Dad. What she is." Plus, we fought as much as we flirted. Which was—constantly. She'd think I was just teasing her for her height. "I left her in my house. Asleep." Because I was only slightly terrified of waking her up. She was feisty, and I was afraid of her drawing blood. Poison Ivy had claws.

"Where does she think she is, exactly?"

I winced. "A small town in Canada?"

"What's going to happen when she realizes she's not?"

I hadn't exactly thought that far ahead yet. "She's never even seen the snow before. I was thinking I could handle one thing at a time."

A hearty bellow came from him. "You're a little in over your head, aren't you, son?" He ran his hand through his beard. "Help her assimilate, Teddy. Make her feel at home. After all, the North Pole *is* her home."

"Right..." I said, drawing out the word. "If she wants to stay."

Her home. Would it ever feel like that? She didn't have a home in Florida but she had family here. She'd love it, right? Shutting my eyes, I dragged my hand over my face, dragging my fingers through my hair and tugging on the ends.

"You knew, didn't you? Exactly who she is. You always have."

"Now, Teddy. Why would I not have told you that?"

"Theodore!" My mom came in, carrying a tray of home-made cookies with two cups of hot chocolate. "I didn't know you'd be home tonight."

"Hey, Mom." She walked over, wrapping me up in a hug. "Wanted to surprise you." I was thankful for her interruption because I wasn't sure I was ready to hear what my dad had to say just yet. The truth seemed like something that would change everything in my life—forever.

As she pulled away, she patted me on the cheek like she didn't see me regularly. But she'd always been like this. "I've missed you."

I chuckled. "Missed you too."

"I just made a fresh batch of cookies, and there's a whole extra tray in the kitchen, Teddy." She wiped her hands on her apron.

"Okay," I said, though I was still half distracted by my thoughts of Ivy.

"You could take her some," my dad chimed in, a mischievous look on his face.

"*Her?*" Mom asked, looking between us. "Nicholas, what are you up to?"

"Nothing, honey."

She shot daggers his way. "You really think that's going to work? After *how* many years of marriage?"

Dad ran his fingers through his beard, trying his best to appear innocent. "Our son brought home a girl for Christmas."

I rolled my eyes. "Way to throw me under the bus." The words were muttered under my breath.

"Really?" Mom looked shocked.

"Yeah. Her name's Ivy Winters," I responded.

"Wow. So it's serious? I didn't even know you were dating someone. Where is she? When do we get to meet her?"

"Mom." I rubbed my forehead. "Slow down. We're not in a relationship. It's not... like that."

We'd gone out on *one* date. But I'd never brought anyone home before, so of course she assumed. I'd figured she'd just be so happy that I was home for Christmas that she wouldn't look too deeply into why I'd brought Ivy with me.

Of course, I was wrong.

"Theodore..." Her voice was stern. "You like this girl?"

"Of course I do." The words slipped out before I could think better of it. "She's... different. Like no one else I've ever met before."

"Then you better treat her right. Don't let her get away." My mom winked.

I blinked. Was that even a question? Of course I would. "I'm just trying to make sure she has the perfect Christmas," I said honestly. "Speaking of that... Do you think you can do me a favor?"

"Of course, honey. What do you need?"

I filled her in on my plan—or what I had of it so far, and she agreed, a smile spreading over her face.

Now if only I could make Ivy smile like that.

9

ivy

14 days until christmas

*W*armth surrounded me from all sides, and it felt like I was on a cloud. The most luxurious bed I'd ever slept in. The scent of pine trees surrounded me, and I let out a dreamy sigh. It smelled delicious, and I buried my face in the pillow, inhaling deeply.

My eyes flew open. "What the *fuck*?" I didn't have sheets this nice.

What had happened? I rubbed my forehead. The last thing I remembered was…

Being in the car on the way to the airport with Teddy.

Teddy. *Shit.* I sat up straight in the bed, taking in my surroundings for the first time. This wasn't my room. The exposed wood on the wall was definitely a dead giveaway of that. It looked like some sort of wood cabin, rustic yet… cozy. There was a fireplace with an actual fire burning, and when I looked out the window, the world was covered in a blanket of white—double shit.

"Toto, we're not in Kansas anymore," I muttered, rubbing at the back of my head. Where was I? Had he kidnapped me and taken me to a cabin in the middle of nowhere? I couldn't have slept through the entire airport and flight, right?

I regretted making that joke before.

"Oh, good. You're awake." Teddy entered the room, carrying a tray with a pot of what smelled like chocolate and...

"*Cookies?*" I raised an eyebrow. "Are you sure you didn't kidnap me? Where are we?"

He did his best to look sheepish. "They're my mom's recipe. And we're at my house."

"Which is *where*, exactly? And how did we get here? I fell asleep, and the next thing I know, I'm waking up here."

Teddy didn't answer my stream of questions, instead looking out the window. "What do you know about the North Pole, Ivy?" he asked, changing the topic completely.

I frowned. "Like... The one in the Arctic Ocean or the fictional one where Santa is supposed to live?"

He raised an eyebrow. "Fictional? Who said anything about fictional?"

"Come on. You can't tell me you still believe in all of that stuff. You're what, twenty...?" I trailed off, realizing I probably should have asked that sooner.

"Twenty-seven."

Which meant he was only two years older than me. "You can't seriously tell me you still believe in Santa?"

I'd learned the hard way that he wasn't real. Running down the stairs on Christmas morning, only to find there wasn't a single gift for me under the tree... I'd tried to convince myself it was because Santa didn't have my new address since I'd just moved into a new foster home, but later I found out the truth.

"I need to tell you something, but I'm not sure you'll believe me."

He'd said something of the sort earlier when I asked him how he knew me. "Okay...?" I gave him a hesitant nod, urging him to tell me.

"We're in the North Pole, Ivy."

I blinked. "No."

"Yes. The North Pole *is* real. And I know because I'm from here. My full name is Theodore Nicholas Claus. Not Clausen."

"No." I stood up, my face dropping. This wasn't funny. "You're crazy."

"I'm serious."

Did he think that was going to make me believe him? I looked around for hidden cameras. "Is this some sort of elaborate punk? Am I on a game show?"

"No one put me up to this," he said with a sigh. "It's the truth. I knew you wouldn't believe me," Teddy cursed under his breath. "But I'm serious, Ivy," he repeated. "And I know I should have told you sooner, but I didn't know how to tell you. Everything I've told you *is* true. I asked you to come home with me for Christmas because I like spending time with you. And I wanted to explore whatever was between us. But coming here confirmed things."

"Like what?"

"Like, that you belong here, in the North Pole. Your mother was an elf, Ivy."

"I'm sorry. *What?*" I blinked at him. This day just kept getting weirder. Maybe this was all a dream, and I'd wake up still in Teddy's truck. "That's not possible. Elves aren't real. My mother was a human. I'm a human."

"Are you?" He raised an eyebrow.

I glared at him. "Yes. Besides, even if you were right..." I ignored the way his eyes glinted, continuing my statement.

"There's no way I can be an elf." I pointed at my ears. "I'm *human.*"

That damn eyebrow stayed perched on his forehead. Like he was seeing something I wasn't. "Sure, you *appeared* human. But haven't you ever wondered why you're so short?"

"Hey!" I glared at him. It was one thing that he was talking nonsense, but now he had to insult my height, too? "I'm a perfectly respectable height, thank you very much." Irritation was rolling off of me in waves.

Man, why did the pretty ones always have to be crazy?

He snorted. "You're practically fun-sized."

"Don't make me sound like the consolation prize kids get on Halloween when they're hoping for a full-sized candy bar." I crossed my arms over my chest, glaring up at him.

"What?"

"No one ever wants the fun-sized candies. It's a well-known fact."

"That's—" Theodore rolled his eyes. "That's not the point. Why won't you believe that I'm telling the truth? Your mom came from the North Pole. She left and met your father, and they fell in love. But she never returned."

Because she'd had me, and then she'd passed away a few years later.

I fidgeted with the necklace pendant around my neck. "Because the North Pole isn't real, Teddy, and neither is Santa Claus," I said, the last part in a hushed tone because it still felt wrong even if I didn't *believe* anymore. "And I'm thinking you're a little delusional. Are you sure you didn't hit your head?"

"I'm not the delusional one, Ivy."

His gaze flicked to my ears. I covered them with my hands and then shrieked. "What. The. Hell."

Huffing, I threw back the sheets. Stomping through the

room, I threw open a door, hoping it would be the bathroom. Instead, I was bombarded by the scent of pine trees and snow. A closet of flannel, plaid, and cable knit sweaters stared back at me.

Oh, God. This was his bedroom. The scent on his sheets that I'd thought was so heavenly was *him*. Heat rushed to my cheeks, and I avoided his gaze.

"Um. Where's your bathroom?" I asked, slamming the closet closed. The thud radiated through the room.

He chuckled behind me. "Next door on your left."

"Great. If you'll excuse me?" I slipped past him, opening the bathroom door, and then closed myself inside quickly.

I turned the faucet on, the cool water running over my fingers before I splashed some over my face. Maybe I just needed to wake up and realize this was all some sort of strange dream, and I—

Looking into the mirror, I let out a scream. I was feeling more and more out of my element, and I didn't know what was going on here, but it was clear who to blame.

Throwing the door back open, I found Teddy standing right outside like he'd been waiting for me.

"What the *fuck* did you do to me?" I demanded, pointing at my ears, which were now longer and slightly... pointed.

"Woah there, Poison Ivy." He leaned against the door frame, an amused expression on his face, with his arms crossed over his chest. "I didn't do anything."

"Then how do you explain these?" I pointed at my ears. The ears that looked a suspicious lot like *elf* ears. I'd seen the Santa Clause movies. A sick feeling spread through my stomach. "They didn't look like this before." My last words were barely a whisper. I didn't want to hear his explanation. I didn't want to accept that any part of him was telling the truth. They weren't silicone or liquid latex and certainly didn't come off when I tugged on them. When my fingers ran over the tips, I could feel it, the sensation making me shudder.

Which meant... *They were real.*

He blinked like he was waiting for me to catch up to something he already knew.

Your mother was an elf, Ivy. The words sank in, and I froze. "This can't be happening."

"I told you, you're half elf."

Crossing my arms, I glared at him. "Still, *how*?" Even if I was half elf, that didn't explain how I hadn't looked like this my whole life. "This isn't *me*. I don't..."

He sighed, moving over and leaning on the bathroom counter beside me. "There's a magic barrier around the North Pole. When we crossed it..." He gestured to my ears, and my rosier-than-usual cheeks. "The human world doesn't understand. It's why Santa Claus has become nothing more than a legend. There's a magic that protects us here from detection, and it's the same magic that made you look human."

"So, if I leave, I'll go back to normal?" I asked, sucking in a breath. I *could* leave, right?

He chuckled, the sound rough. "Yes. But I'm afraid that *this* is your normal, Ivy. This is who you were always meant to be."

Frowning, I touched the point of my ears once again. *Who I was meant to be?* I never knew who that was. Maybe some part of me wanted to find out.

"How'd we get here, anyway? We couldn't have come on a plane..." I trailed off.

"Would you believe me if I said magic?" Teddy looked hopeful. "And a reindeer?" I gave him a glare that I hoped properly expressed that I thought he was full of shit. He held up his hands. "I'll take that as a no."

One glimpse out the window confirmed we were indeed somewhere snowy. I refused to believe it was the North Pole though. Rubbing the back of my head, I refocused on him. "How long was I asleep?"

"A day. Most of that was spent flying, though." Yep, I was going to pretend he meant on an airplane, even though there was absolutely no way he could have gotten me through an airport unconscious. Private jet, maybe?

Santa wasn't real. I wasn't an elf. I didn't have pointy elf ears.

"You need to take me home. Right now."

"I can't do that, Ivy. Besides, what happened to spending Christmas with me?"

"Of course you can. You're the one who brought me here." I furrowed my brows. "Are you dense?"

He shrugged his shoulders. "It's kinda the busy season around here. Can't afford another trip away."

"Fine. I'll find a way home myself." I moved to the empty doorway. "Where are we? Somewhere in Canada? Or maybe Montana? How did you get me on a plane while I was asleep?"

"I told you. We're in the North Pole."

I rolled my eyes. "And like I said, you're *crazy*. I know I work at a Christmas themed amusement park, but this is taking it a little too far." I crossed my arms over my chest.

How was I going to get out of here? It wasn't like I had any weapons on me. I didn't even have my phone on me. What were the odds I could get away and find the police, explain to them what happened, and have them bring me home?

If there was snow outside, we were somewhere in the North. Considering he said I'd only been out a day, we must still be in the United States, right? Or maybe somewhere in Canada, though that didn't seem likely even if he'd put me in a car and driven straight through.

"Come on. Just sit down, have a cookie, and let's talk

things through." As I moved into the living room, the plate was in his hands again.

"Fine." I sat on the edge of the couch, folding my legs underneath me. I tried not to think about *who* his mom was if he was telling the truth. Picking up a cookie, I took a bite.

Dammit, it was delicious. And a distraction I didn't need. His little cabin was cozy—far cozier than I wanted to admit, but something had only just occurred to me. I narrowed my eyes. "Teddy."

"Mhm?"

"Where did you sleep last night?"

He did his best to look sheepish. "On the couch. There's only one bedroom here, you know."

Oh. God. There was only one bed? I groaned. "You've got to be kidding me." What sort of Hallmark movie did I wake up in the middle of?

Teddy shrugged. "It's fine. It's a comfy couch. You can have the bed."

"No way. I can't do that. This is your house. And it's your bed."

A smirk crossed his face. "So, do you want to *share* the bed, then?"

I did everything I could to keep from stomping my foot, knowing my cheeks were redder than ever. "No! I just—" I rubbed at my temples. "I should take the couch. It's your bed."

He frowned. "No. You'll take the bed, and that's final. A gentleman wouldn't let a lady sleep on the couch."

"A gentleman wouldn't have lied to me and brought me here, either." I crossed my arms over my chest.

Chuckling, he reached over me and grabbed another cookie from the plate. "Fair enough."

"Stop doing that," I said, frowning.

"What?" He asked, looking entertained.

"Being all…" I waved my hand around, gesturing to his face. "*Amused*. Like you think this is one big joke. This is my *life*, Theodore."

His face dropped, all traces of levity gone. Like it was my calling him his full name that made him understand I was serious. "I'm sorry, Ivy." He looked genuine when he said, "But can you just give it a chance? Let me show you around here?"

There was no reason I should have said yes to him, but maybe there was something in his eyes. Or just the look of desperation on his face. Like he really wanted me to give this a shot. Give him a shot.

It was hard not to think about the dinner we'd shared. The coffees he'd brought me, the hours he'd spent in my office. Did he have any reason to lie to me?

But maybe the scarier part was… What if he was telling the truth?

"Okay, fine." I swallowed roughly. "Just, uh… Can I take a shower first?"

Teddy blinked as if I had surprised him by agreeing.

I was still trying to figure out how I was going to verify his claims. First things first, I needed to escape.

10
teddy

*I*vy?" I knocked on the door to the bathroom, the shower water still running. She'd been in there a long time, and for whatever reason, I was getting worried. Was she avoiding me?

Fuck. Had I ruined everything between us?

All things considered, there were about a million ways that our conversation could have gone better. I should have known she'd be upset with me. After all, I'd lied to her by not telling her the truth from the beginning. But I hadn't known the truth of what she was until we arrived at the North Pole. Now, it was clear. How could I have ever thought otherwise?

She was supposed to be here.

A little whisper of something more rippled through my mind, but I ignored it. That wasn't what this was. It couldn't be. I'd given up all hope of that a long time ago.

"Dammit." I smoothed a hand over my face, muttering under my breath. No matter what, I wanted her here. Wanted to give her a perfect Christmas memory. Even if she never chose this life, I'd make it special.

When she came out, I'd take her into town for breakfast.

There, she'd see I wasn't making this up. And then she'd fall in love with the North Pole. How could she not?

When she still didn't answer after I knocked again, I frowned. Ivy might have been mad at me, but she was never afraid to use her claws. Poison Ivy wouldn't hide.

Unless... I reached up and grabbed the key on the doorframe, unlocking the door. The steamy bathroom was empty, the shower water running—and the window was open. Her sweats were discarded on the sink, the new pair of clothes she'd taken in with her gone.

"Shit." This wasn't good. Looking up at the sky, I winced. It might not have been snowing yet, but it was freezing out. Did she even have a coat? Her phone was still in her bag on my living room floor. "Ivy?" I called out.

No response. I needed to find her—now. How far could she have gotten?

"Ivy!" I shouted. It wasn't actively snowing, so I could see a trail of footprints in the snow—one that headed out towards the woods.

Throwing the window closed and shutting off the shower, I went to grab my coat from the closet. My mom had left one behind on one of their visits to my house, so I grabbed it too. It might not fit her perfectly, but it would be better than nothing.

Grabbing a blanket, I wrapped a scarf around my neck and pulled on my coat before heading outside. Luckily, I'd left Buddy in the small stable next to my house, so I didn't have to go far.

Opening the front door, I trudged outside into the snow.

"Wanna go for a little adventure, Bud?" I asked him, smoothing my hand over his snout. He made a noise of affirmation, and I swung onto his back, not bothering with a saddle. "We gotta go find Ivy."

She didn't have too much of a head start on me, and luckily, her footprints were easy to track.

"Stubborn girl," I muttered under my breath. Each step was torture, not knowing how far into the woods she'd gotten.

But then, there she was. A bundle of red and strawberry blonde against a backdrop of green and white. She'd leaned up against a tree, luckily shielding herself from the worst of the cold.

Swinging my leg around and dismounting Buddy, I crouched down over Ivy. My hands wrapped around her upper arms as I looked her over.

"Shit, sweetheart. You're freezing." Her teeth were chattering, and I wrapped the blanket I brought around her shoulders, tucking it into her body.

She looked up at me with those big blue eyes. "You came to find me?"

"Of course I did, sweetheart." I brushed some snow out of her hair.

"I d-didn't mean to get l-lost," Ivy said, tugging the soft throw tighter around her. "I-I was just u-upset, and then I-I got all turned a-around. I-I thought maybe if I could find town—"

"Ivy." Cupping her chin with my gloved hand, I forced her eyes to meet mine. "It's okay." I tried to give her a reassuring smile. "Just let me get you warm, okay?"

She just nodded, not saying anything else, her chattering teeth filling the silence. God, how had I thought she'd acclimate quickly to the freezing temperatures here? To a Floridian, 50 degrees was cold. Of course she wasn't used to this.

"Come on," I said, offering her a hand. She took it hesitantly, and I guided her back to where Buddy stood, stomping his hooves into the snow.

Her eyes widened, but she didn't let go of my hand.

"I'll make sure you two get a moment to meet properly later," I promised. "But this is Buddy."

"Do you expect us both to ride him?" She just stared at me.

I blinked back. "Yes. It's the fastest way back."

She eyed me skeptically. "No way am I getting on his back with you."

"You don't have a choice, sweetheart. Besides, you already have, you know." Wrong thing to say. Ivy startled out of my grip. "Please," I said, voice low. "Let's get out of the cold."

She sighed, like she'd finally decided to stop fighting with me.

Placing a hand on her lower back, I had a hard time not thinking about the last time I'd done the same. The night of our date when I'd invited her to come home with me. That gorgeous red dress had left her back exposed. *Well, look how that had turned out.* I shook away the thought.

"Now, come on. I'll help you up."

She grumbled something under her breath but let me guide her onto Buddy's back. Once she was settled, holding onto his mane, I hopped up behind her.

"Take us home, Buddy," I said, giving him gentle pressure from my calves.

"Oh!" Ivy exclaimed as we started moving, her back colliding into my chest.

"Woah there, Poison Ivy." I wrapped my arm around her waist, keeping her pinned against me so she wouldn't fall off.

The tips of her ears were pink.

"Sorry," she whispered. "I just… I've never even ridden a horse before."

"Buddy's a gentle reindeer," I reassured her. "And he's carried you once before, remember?" She looked back at me, and I winked.

"Maybe I liked it better when I thought I'd somehow just slept through the entire flight, *Theodore*."

"Teddy," I corrected. Why it was so important to me she called me by my nickname, I couldn't explain. Maybe it was that Theodore felt like she was putting up walls, and when she called me Teddy, it felt like I was breaking through them.

She sighed, relaxing against me. Thanks to how close together we were, I could smell her hair—like vanilla and sugar cookies—and I did my best not to bury my nose in it and inhale.

"I just can't wrap my head around all of this... That this place could possibly be real."

Even though I'd grown up here, it still seemed impossible for a place like this to exist after visiting the human world. "I can't even imagine how strange all of this is for you."

"You have *no* idea," she muttered.

We got back to the cabin, and I hopped down and helped Ivy off before nodding at her. "You want to go inside and warm up while I get Buddy penned up?"

"His name's actually Buddy?" Ivy asked, hesitantly peering at him.

I nodded, leading my reindeer over to his stall by his reins. To my surprise, Ivy followed along, not heading into the house. She was all bundled up in my mom's old red coat, plus my scarf and the blanket I'd wrapped around her shoulders, and even though the tip of her nose was pink, she seemed to be doing okay with the cold.

"He's mine," I finally responded. Rubbing down his sides and telling him what a good boy he was, I looked up to find Ivy leaning against the wood, watching me. "Do you want to come say hi?"

"Oh." She gnawed on her lower lip. "I don't know."

"He won't bite. I promise."

Ivy gave a slight nod and approached Buddy, her hand

reaching out and brushing over his snout. A giggle slipped free from her lips. "He's fuzzy."

"Buddy's basically just like a horse," I said, ignoring the glare my reindeer gave me as I patted his neck. He might not have been a *talking* reindeer, but he communicated his moods well enough with his grunts and glares. "He just wants attention. And some snacks." I pulled a carrot from the treat box hanging on the wall and held it out to Ivy, who was still running her fingertips over his nose. "Want to feed him?"

She looked surprised. "Are you sure?"

I nodded, and she reached over, her fingers brushing my palm as she grabbed the carrot.

"This is amazing." She looked over at me as Buddy ate out of her hand. "I can't believe I'm feeding a *real* reindeer right now."

"Believe me, sweetheart. You haven't seen anything yet."

"I might have overreacted earlier," she winced, still petting my reindeer. "I really am sorry you had to come searching for me." She gave me a small smile. No matter how much she wanted to argue with me or demand I take her home, I could tell she was enjoying this. It made just a glimmer of hope spark through my chest. Maybe, just maybe, she would come to love it.

As quickly as that thought came, I tried to brush it aside. My dad's words from last night popped into my mind, and I shook my head. Ivy wasn't staying. No matter how much today had given me hope, this wasn't her home.

And there wasn't anything I could do about that.

"How old were you when you named him, anyway?" Ivy asked, distracting me. She was still petting Buddy, who seemed thrilled to have a beautiful woman giving him attention.

"I was seven when I got him. And Buddy is a perfectly fine name for a reindeer," I grumbled.

Ivy giggled. "Sure, sure. Definitely better than Rudolph."

"I'll have you know Rudolph was one of the best reindeer of all time."

A real, genuine laugh broke free from her throat. It was the best sound I'd heard all day. Maybe my entire life. "All time, huh?"

I crossed my arms over my chest, turning to face her. "Yes. Haven't you heard the legends?"

Her jaw dropped open. "Are you telling me that the story of *Rudolph the Red-Nosed Reindeer* is true?"

A grin split my face. She was just so fun to tease. "I'm just fucking with you, Ivy. Though there *was* a reindeer named Rudolph, his nose wasn't red. And it certainly didn't light up."

"Oh." She sounded strangely disappointed.

I turned and suddenly was all too aware of how close our bodies were. I stared down at her, resisting the urge to reach out and brush the strand of hair off her cheek. "You think you can do better?"

Ivy brushed her strawberry-blonde hair back behind her shoulder, giving me a little smirk. Damn, she was cute. "Oh, definitely. I know I could."

"Let me guess… Brownie? No. Cookie."

I knew I'd guessed correctly when her brows furrowed, giving me the cutest little scowl. "No." When she did that, she looked like a little angry kitten, claws and all.

"*Suuure*, sweetheart."

"It would be *way* better than that." Her head dipped in a confident nod.

I hummed in response before asking, "Did you have any pets growing up?"

She shook her head, looking lost in thought. "No. But I always wanted a puppy. You know, like a white and black puppy with those little brown eyebrows, wearing a big red bow under the tree on Christmas morning?" Ivy sighed. "But it wasn't in the cards."

"What about now?"

"Now?" A snort left her. "Living in that tiny apartment? That's no place for a dog." She sighed. "They deserve a big backyard to run around in."

I had to agree with that. But I could hear the longing in her voice, too. How many things had she missed out on because she denied herself, even now?

What would it be like to make all those dreams come true? To show her what it was like?

A picture-perfect Christmas.

"Ivy." I stood back, leaving Buddy to munch on his hay.

"Hm?" She looked up at me, clearly distracted.

"Are you hungry?"

Her stomach rumbled as if in answer, and she gave me a sheepish grin. "Starving."

"Then come on, sweetheart. Let's go eat."

"Alright." She looked down at herself. "Think I can keep the coat?"

"Of course." She could keep anything she wanted for all I cared.

I couldn't stop thinking about what she'd said earlier. *I really am sorry you had to come searching for me.* It was clear no one had ever put her first before. There was no world where I wouldn't come to her rescue if she needed it.

What she didn't know was that I would have searched the entire world for her.

11
ivy

I couldn't stop thinking about when Teddy's reindeer nuzzled the carrot out of my hand. Never mind the way he'd come barreling through the trees on the back of Buddy to find me.

Trying to escape out the window might not have been my smartest plan.

Not that I was going to complain to Teddy because I'd stolen one of his cable-knit sweaters. It smelled faintly of pine trees and spice, though I was trying not to inhale too deeply. I didn't want him to catch me smelling his clothes. No matter if it calmed my senses or not, there was just something about Teddy that drove me crazy.

I hated that he was right. Cookie would be an adorable name for a reindeer.

I'd always loved animals with food names, even if I'd never had a pet of my own. That dream had never quite gone away, even if I'd given up on so many others in my life.

Rudolph had always been my favorite Christmas movie growing up like some part of me had related to him. Because no matter how hard I'd tried to fit in with the other kids and to make friends, I'd never quite felt like I did.

Maybe one day, I'd have that dream. The big house, all warm and cozy inside, with a little puppy curled up in a basket. A home. Someone who loved me and would never leave me. Maybe I was just destined never to find my place. My person.

Sitting in the North Pole Diner, I took a swig of the hot chocolate that had been placed in front of me by our waitress, Scarlett. God, it smelled delicious: rich and sweet, everything I loved in a cup.

She'd given me a warm smile when we sat down in the booth. I'd caught a glimpse of ears just like mine—long and pointed at the ends—when she walked away after taking our orders.

"Wow. That's good," I said, swiping my tongue over my upper lip to catch some of the whipped cream.

"Best hot cocoa in the entire North Pole," he agreed.

I hummed in response. "This place is unreal." And damn, I wanted to hate this place. But how could I?

"Just wait until you see everything else we have here." He flashed me a confident grin. "You're gonna love it."

I already did.

The storefronts were all painted in various bright colors, decked out in holiday trimmings, and the bakery was painted like a giant gingerbread house, just like at Christmasland. Seriously, the whole thing looked edible. I *desperately* wanted to go inside. I also spotted a bookstore, a store that looked like it sold ice skates and skis, and a clothing boutique.

"It looks like we just stepped out onto the set of a Christmas movie," I repeated my earlier thought in a daze.

"It's great, isn't it?" He grinned. "Come on, admit that you like it."

And honestly—it was great. I loved Christmas. This place

was amazing. That didn't mean I wanted to give him the satisfaction of being right.

"Is this where they got the inspiration for Christmasland?" I raised an eyebrow, looking out the window.

"Probably. Though the park was all my grandpa's idea."

"Wow." I was still looking out the window. "And everyone who lives here is... an elf? Genuinely?"

He let out a sigh. "You still don't believe me."

"I don't know what I believe." I rubbed my forehead. "The entire foundation of my life just changed. I'm just processing."

"When will you accept the fact that maybe I'm telling the truth? That I didn't lie to you, sweetheart?"

"But you did," I whispered. "Why didn't you tell me the truth about who you were before?"

"Would you have believed me if I did?" Teddy said, his voice soft. There was a sad tone to it like he'd told someone before, and they hadn't.

So many things made sense now.

Even so, it hurt. Knowing all those days getting to know him, and it wasn't even the real him. I knew him now, though. This man sitting in front of me—Teddy Claus—this was the real him.

"Maybe not," I said, matching his tone. "But now we'll never know, huh?"

Our food came, interrupting our conversation.

"Thanks, Scarlett," Teddy said, nodding to our waitress.

"Sure thing, Teddy." She gave him a bright smile, the pointy tips of her ears sticking out of her hair as she turned to the side. *Just like mine.* "How's everything going at the workshop?"

The workshop? *Oh, you've got to be kidding me.* I dug into my cheeseburger and fries, pretending like I wasn't interested in their conversation.

"Oh, you know. Business as usual this time of year. Dad kept nagging me about taking a break from everything, but he doesn't have much room to talk."

She laughed. "Tell him to come visit sometime soon."

"Sure thing."

Our waitress left, and I shoved another fry in my mouth, studying him.

"Do you want to see the workshop?" he asked, voice softer than I expected, like he was trying not to spook a wild animal. Whatever I'd expected him to say, it wasn't that. "That's where all the magic happens."

Something twisted in my gut. Had I overreacted earlier? I didn't think I had. Part of me was still trying to wrap my head around all of it: how I had supposedly come from here. That the mother I had never known grew up here.

As much as I wanted to keep being difficult to Teddy, especially since he had lied to me, I couldn't because this place was *amazing*.

"That depends. Does that also include meeting your parents?"

He nodded. "Probably."

"Your father," I stated. "Santa Claus."

My eyes connected with Teddy's, and he gave me a small smile. I wondered if he had any idea how handsome he was when he did that. It lit up his entire face, making his eyes almost sparkle like lights on a tree.

Oh. *Wow*. Okay. I could do this, right? I pushed my hair back behind my ears—a reminder that they were, in fact, still pointy on the ends—and squared my shoulders. "I'd love that, Teddy." It wasn't hard to put a smile on my face, considering I'd just pet a reindeer and was about to see Santa's workshop.

Santa's. Freaking. Workshop.

If I was dreaming, I wasn't sure I wanted to wake up.

He cleared his throat. "Shall we then?"

I nodded, burying the bottom half of my face in my borrowed jacket and Teddy's scarf.

No matter how attractive I found him, I needed to stop thinking about him that way. Needed to stop thinking about all the ways my life could be different.

That wasn't what this was. He'd offered for me to come home with him for Christmas so that I could experience it. Not because we were in a relationship. After the holidays were over, I would go back to Florida, and I'd be alone. Same as always.

But would it hurt to have a little fun while I was here? I bit my lip, watching his back as we headed back out into the cold, trudging through the snow.

Earlier, I hadn't taken the time to appreciate it before, but outside was... amazing. As far as I could see, the world was covered in a blanket of white. I spun in a circle, taking it all in.

Breathing out, I watched as a puff of air formed in front of me. "Cool," I murmured to myself. When I looked up, I found Teddy watching me, an amused expression on his face. "I told you I'd never seen snow before," I said, voice quiet. "Not the real kind. We make fake snow for the amusement park, but... it's not the same." I reached down and scooped up a handful of snow. "It's softer than I imagined." The snow was cold on my bare hands, melting from whatever body heat I still had.

Teddy laughed, the sound making my inside feel warm despite the outside temperature.

"What?" I asked, giving him a little scowl. I didn't need him to find my actions fascinating or for him to watch my every move.

He cleared his throat. "Nothing. You ready for this?"

"Uh-huh," I responded, brushing the snow off my hands.

We walked in a comfortable silence towards the workshop, and I wondered if Teddy was as lost in his own thoughts as I was in mine.

Longing unfurled inside of me. It was easier to pretend I didn't feel that pull of desire when I denied the things I wanted, but looking them in the face, seeing other people living a life I could only dream of... It picked at that wounded part of my soul.

Stopping in front of a large, multi-story building was trimmed in bright lights and painted red, my jaw dropped open. "Is that..."

Teddy nodded, stepping up behind me. "The big building is the factory. My dad's workshop is over to the left—" He pointed at the smaller, quaint looking log-cabin building set off to the side.

Teddy turned his body towards mine, staring down at me with that chiseled jawline and sharp cheekbones.

There was something almost magnetic about his presence. Something that kept drawing me to him, even when I knew I should have been running the other way. He was undeniably gorgeous, but there was something about the spark of delight in his deep green eyes that I couldn't look away from.

He offered me a hesitant smile. "Welcome to the North Pole, Ivy."

"THIS IS THE ORIGINAL WORKSHOP. Or so they say."

"Really?" I wondered how many of the movies had gotten the tale of Santa Claus right and how many had just been pure speculation based on tales of sightings or legends of old.

"Yeah." He nodded. "Back when they built this place, it

was the only structure around. We don't make toys in here anymore, but... well, you'll see."

A rush of anticipation went through me. This was my *catnip*. I had seven thousand questions simmering under the surface, waiting to be unleashed. Could he tell that I was endlessly captivated? I hoped not. Because I still needed to remember that I was mad at him, even if the reasons were slipping away from me.

He opened the room, and we stepped inside, the warmth hitting me like a blast. I might have needed the coat outside, but in here, the fire was roaring. I shrugged it off, leaving my winter clothes on the coat rack by the door.

Surveying the space, I took in the enormous fireplace, and how everything was decked out in Christmas decor. Garlands, lights, and tinsel covered almost every inch of this place.

"*Woah.*"

"This is nothing," Teddy murmured. "You should see my parents' house."

"Who does all of this?" I asked, eyes still wide. Looking around, I noticed a hallway that must have led to the other rooms. If this was no longer the workshop and wasn't where his parents lived, what was it?

"The elves," he said, offering no further explanation. "Come on, I want you to meet someone." He held out his hand, guiding me further into the sitting room.

My jaw dropped. Because sitting in front of the fireplace, wearing a knit Christmas sweater and eating a sugar cookie, was an older man with a long white beard.

Holy shit. I blinked a few times. "*Santa?*"

"Hello there, little Ivy."

My throat was tight. I'd always believed in Christmas magic, and maybe some part of me had always hoped he'd been real. But to be here, to be standing in the middle of the

North Pole, standing in front of Santa Claus... I opened my mouth, but no words came out.

Teddy gave me a small smile. "Ivy, I'd like you to meet my dad, Nicholas Claus. Dad, this is Ivy Winters."

"You're real?" I blurted out, not sure if I was asking a question or stating a fact.

He chuckled. "Of course I am. And I've been watching over you all these years."

Teddy looked at his dad in surprise, but if his lack of knowledge of that should have surprised me, I didn't know.

"Sorry. I think I need a minute." I sat on the couch, looking at Teddy and his father. His father, Santa Claus. Which meant all of this was real, wasn't it? Because how could I see all of this, the man sitting in front of me, and not believe it to be true?

Even I wasn't that jaded.

"You really were telling me the truth," I murmured, rubbing my temples.

"Told you that you shouldn't doubt me." He leaned back against the brick of the fireplace. "I have no reason to lie to you, Ivy."

"I can see that now." Rubbing at my forehead, I tried to comprehend everything I knew to be true. Everything had changed in just a matter of hours. "I just... why me? Why bring me here?"

His dad stood up from his chair, moving over to stand in front of the couch I sat on. "May I?" He asked, waving at the cushion next to me. I nodded.

"Ivy, I know life hasn't been easy for you." Teddy's father took my hand in his, squeezing lightly. "I wish I had all the answers for you. That I could turn back the clock and keep you from heartbreak." His lips turn down, and I can see the sadness in his eyes.

My eyes filled with tears. Because as much as I wanted to

put on a brave face and insist that I was fine, it had been hard. "But you can't," I murmured, knowing my words were barely audible. That Teddy was standing here.

"No." He ran his fingers over his beard as if deep in thought. "But you are here now."

"Why?" I asked again, sucking in a ragged breath that I hoped didn't sound like a sob. *Why couldn't you have found me sooner?* It was the question at the forefront of my mind, but somehow, I couldn't bear asking it.

"Why does anything happen the way it does?" He tilted his head as if considering me. "I do not have answers to the way events unfold." Santa shook his head. "I cannot see what will come to pass. That does not mean that the future cannot be different. Perhaps everything had to happen exactly the way it has so that we could end up here now." He looked at his son, something unspoken passing between them.

"But all that *he sees you when you're sleeping, he knows when you're awake, he knows when you've been bad or good...* It's true, isn't it? You've been watching me?"

He nodded. "There is more to it than that, but it is true I watch over the children of the world. As for your background... I am afraid I didn't know the truth until recently."

I should have felt relief, but disappointment lingered. "Oh."

"I'm sorry that we failed you."

The words hit me straight in the heart. I'd never really known my parents. But if my mom had been from here, and her family had taken me in... *This could have been my home.* "All these years..." I shook my head. Home had never been something I'd considered.

"And now?"

What now? That was the question—a big one. "I don't know," I admitted. "It doesn't feel like I understand much of anything anymore."

"But, with time, you will learn many things, my dear Ivy," he said, his voice full of hope. Those sparkling eyes that danced with something akin to amusement captured mine. Teddy's father seemed delighted that I was here. He looked at his son. "Things we have all forgotten around here."

A thousand emotions warred within me.

What was it I really wanted?

WE LEFT THE CABIN, though we didn't walk back to Teddy's house. Instead, there was a sleigh out front, with Buddy hooked up to the reins.

When had he had time to do this? We'd left his reindeer in the stable, and he hadn't left the room once.

I shook my head, hiding my small smile. *Magic*? Had he gone through the effort for me? Between all the events of the day, I was exhausted and glad not to walk back to his place on foot. Teddy helped me onto the bench before getting us on our way.

"Does your dad always speak in riddles like that?" I asked, biting my lower lip as I inhaled the clean, crisp air, watching the scenery pass us.

He chuckled. "I think he thinks he's wise."

I wrinkled my nose. "And what do you think?"

A laugh left Teddy's lips. "That I'm glad I have *many* years before he expects me to take over for him."

I peeked up at him, keeping the lower half of my face nestled into my coat for warmth. "And you want that? To… take up the mantle?" I assumed that meant that one day, he would be Santa Claus.

"Of course. It's all I've ever wanted." He looked at me

with a strange expression. "I've been learning all I can about my family's company so I can run it all one day."

Teddy would stay here. Of course he would. This place, the North Pole... it was his home. But no matter what his father thought, it wasn't mine.

Did I belong here? I didn't have an answer. What had started as an excuse to experience a white Christmas for the first time was quickly becoming something very different.

The sleigh continued through the snowy terrain, neither one of us seeming to have the right words.

"It's already dark out," I observed, wanting to break the awkward silence. The sun had set while we were inside, yet the way was lit thanks to the lights that adorned practically every structure around.

"Yeah." Teddy nodded. "It gets dark pretty quickly here in the winter."

"And where exactly *is* here? Because the actual North Pole is in the middle of the Arctic Ocean, and you can't honestly tell me this entire place is floating on a polar ice cap?"

He laughed. "*No.* But where, exactly, I can't tell you."

"Why not?" I crossed my arms over my chest.

"It's a secret. And you haven't proven yourself trust-worthy yet."

I clicked my tongue on the roof of my mouth. "Need I remind you that you basically kidnapped me?"

"Semantics, really."

"*Teddy.*"

"Ivy." He stared at me, his face practically inches away from mine, and I had to remind myself why I shouldn't lean in. Why kissing him was a bad idea.

Even though at this moment, there was nothing I wanted more. Just a breath closer, and...

"We're here." Teddy jolted away from me, hopping out of the sleigh faster than a bolt of lightning.

"Oh." I followed him out of the sleigh, stumbling slightly and catching my foot on the lip of the frame, sending me tumbling out into the snow.

Strong arms caught me, heaving me upright. "Are you okay?"

"Fine." Just my injured pride, but I could deal with that. I turned away, heat rising to my face and ears.

What was wrong with me?

"ARE YOU HUNGRY?" Teddy asked as he closed the door behind us in his cozy cabin.

Earlier, I hadn't appreciated just how small it was. It was set out, further away from town, like he didn't want anyone to bother him here. But it was obvious it was lived in, too. Photos hung on the walls: him growing up with his parents, wearing a cap and gown at his graduation. Memories of a life lived. If you looked in my apartment, you'd see none of that —just a blank slate waiting to be written on.

I frowned at the wall.

"Ivy?"

"Huh?"

"I asked if you wanted dinner."

"Oh." I nodded. Despite just having eaten at the diner a few hours ago, I was already hungry again. "That sounds great, actually."

"Alright. I'll whip something up."

"You can cook?"

"Why do you sound so surprised?"

I shrugged. "I don't know. You just don't..." I raised an eyebrow at his form instead of finishing my thought.

"Don't look like I can cook?" He placed his hand over his heart. "You wound me, Poison Ivy."

Sliding on to a barstool at the counter, I let my head rest in my hands. "I guess I just didn't expect all this."

Everything felt so... domestic. I'd never been treated like this by a man in my life. Maybe it was the bare minimum, or I'd just been with a lot of red flags, but I wasn't used to it.

As he rummaged through the kitchen cabinets, pulling out pans and various cooking utensils, I couldn't help but think about his plea earlier. Maybe he was just as lonely as I was.

Maybe this could be something good for both of us. Because as much as he drove me crazy—and he did—I had to admit he wasn't all bad. Even from behind, his well-defined muscles bulged through his shirt. His forearms, now properly on display after he pushed his sleeves up, made my mouth water.

Especially as the scent in the room turned into the most mouthwatering smell of my life. Clearly, he wasn't lying about saying he could cook.

"Okay," I said to his back, trying to ignore the ache between my thighs. How long had it been? Too long, really. Especially with this magnificent specimen of a man standing in front of me. Not that I was going to suggest anything of the sort.

No, I had other ulterior motives for what I was about to say. What I was going to suggest.

"Okay, what?" He turned around, facing me fully.

I took a deep breath, wondering why the hell I was saying this. "This is all crazy. And I can't believe I'm saying this, but I believe you."

His face lit up, those forest green eyes twinkling with satisfaction. "I told you, sweetheart." And, okay, I wouldn't look into that too closely; why he wanted me to trust him so badly or why he seemed so excited that I'd admitted he was right.

"When you asked me to come home with you, I didn't expect all of this. The North Pole, the magic... finding out I'm not who I thought I was."

Teddy nodded, pausing only to flip the meat in the pan. "I know. I'm sorry for not telling you the truth sooner."

"But I still want to have the perfect Christmas."

He blinked at me a few times like he didn't understand my meaning. Or maybe he'd never considered that he'd give me anything but.

My cheeks warmed, and I could feel the heat all the way to the tips of my ears. "I've never gotten to experience what it was like. A white Christmas. With snow and presents and cookies and..." I trailed off. *A family.* I'd never had a Christmas where I was surrounded by people who loved me.

"Okay." He pasted on a big, dopey smile. "A perfect Christmas. We can do that."

Leaving the food simmering and effectively ignoring his current mission in favor of our new one, he moved over to his desk. Rustling through the drawers, Teddy pulled out a leather-bound journal and flipped it open to an empty page, tearing it from the book.

"What are we talking?" His gaze bore into mine as if he was searching my face for some deeper meaning. "We'll make a list."

"Oh. Um." I hadn't really thought this far ahead. "I guess we should do the normal things, right? Bake Christmas cookies. Decorate a tree. Take a sleigh ride at night." I closed my eyes, picturing it. Taking a romantic sleigh ride was something they did in all the Christmas movies, right?

He hummed in response, his hand moving across the paper. "What else?"

"I don't know. I'm not exactly the expert on Christmas here."

"Ivy. You've literally worked at Christmasland for what, seven years?"

"Well, sure… But I'd also drink hot chocolate and turn my apartment thermostat down to the sixties to trick my body into thinking it was actually cold outside. I don't have experience with these sorts of things." The joys of being an orphan.

"But there has to be other things you've always wanted to do. Come on. Hit me."

I bit my lip. "I mean… I guess I've always wanted to do all that traditional family stuff." The words were barely more than a whisper. "You know, matching pajamas and stockings and all that." Shrugging, I tried to appear more casual than I felt. I'd always loved Christmas. And this was shaping up to be my best idea yet.

He took my ideas and added to them, too. Once we were done, our list was complete.

Teddy and Ivy's Christmas Checklist
1. *Bake Christmas Cookies*
2. *Decorate A Christmas Tree*
3. *Take a Sleigh Ride*
4. *Drink Hot Chocolate While Watching a Christmas Movie*
5. *Build a Snowman*
6. *Make a Gingerbread House*
7. *Go Ice Skating*
8. *Visit The Christmas Market*
9. *Ugly Christmas Sweater Party*
10. *Hang Stockings*

11. Matching Christmas PJs
12. Buy and Wrap Presents
13. See the Lights

The list stared back at me in Teddy's handsome script. Damn him—why did even his writing have to look nice? He was all man, and I definitely should not have been drooling over him. Not when he'd been so sincere all day. So patient and kind and—

Letting me sleep in his bed with no expectations.

"Perfect," I whispered, not wanting to break this moment. It felt like we weren't fighting for the first time, and I didn't know what to do with that. Since we'd met, our relationship hadn't been exactly steady. It felt like we were always either flirting or fighting.

When he walked away to finish the food that was cooking, I added one more to the list.

14. Kiss Under the Mistletoe.

Maybe it was wishful thinking. Maybe I'd just imagined the heat between us.

But maybe, just maybe… He felt it, too.

12
teddy

13 days until christmas

*W*hen was the last time my bed had an actual woman in it? Never. The worst part was I wasn't even in it. I groaned, massaging the back of my neck. My couch was comfortable, but nothing beat my bed. It was like sleeping in a pile of clouds.

"Ivy." I shook her ankle lightly. "Rise and shine, sweetheart."

She groaned, sitting up in bed and rubbing at her eyes. "What time is it?"

"Seven."

"In the *morning*?" Ivy flopped back down, covering her eyes with her pillow.

I walked over, taking it from her, looking down at her with amusement. "Yes. Now get up."

"Why are you up so early? It's barely even light outside." She grumbled something into her pillow.

The corners of my lips tugged up in amusement. "We're going to cut down a tree."

There was a magic to cutting down your own tree. To finding the perfect one, carting it home, and then decorating it together. Some of my fondest memories with my parents had been from those days when I was younger. I wanted to share that with her.

Give her memories she would never forget, just like I'd promised her last night.

"What?" Ivy sat up quickly, the comforter falling down onto her lap. "Like, we're cutting it down ourselves?"

"Well, I don't exactly have a tree here to decorate, and you said you wanted to decorate one, so…"

I still couldn't believe she'd agreed to stay. Whatever had gone through her mind, I'd half expected to end up taking her back to Florida after she found out the truth. But she'd stayed.

Whether it was for me or to find out more about herself, I didn't care.

"Oh. Wow. Okay. Um. What do I need to wear?"

"Clothes, preferably." I tried not to let my eyes trail down her body in a blatant perusal. It was hard, considering she was wearing a T-shirt she must have found in my closet. Did she have anything on underneath it?

She packed clothes, so why was she stealing mine? And *why did I like it so much?*

"Teddy." Was she blushing?

"Ivy," I retorted back. Her ears flashed the most adorable shade of pink when she blushed. I cleared my throat, looking away. "Warm clothes. It might be light outside, but it's still freezing."

She looked at the suitcase at the side of the bed, exactly where she'd left it yesterday, since she still hadn't unpacked.

"I know you said to pack warm, but I didn't exactly pack for *this*."

"You can borrow one of my sweaters again and wear my mom's coat." I eyed her feet. She needed some warm boots. "This afternoon, we can go back into town and get you some warmer things." I let my eyes trail down her body. "Because as much as I enjoy seeing you in my clothes, Ivy..." I swallowed roughly. It was driving me crazy.

Our faces were only a few inches apart. What would it be like if I brushed my lips against hers? If I took her mouth with mine, and...

"I'll be fine," she said, shaking her head and putting distance between us. "I don't exactly have disposable income where I can purchase a whole new wardrobe. And I can't expect you to buy me clothes..." Ivy trailed off.

"Let me take care of you," I practically begged. "It's the least I can do."

"Okay." Ivy let out a sigh. "I'm just... not used to all of this."

"What?"

"Someone who cares enough to take care of me." The words were a whispered admission. Fuck, no one had taken the time to cherish her. But I wouldn't make that mistake.

"Well, you better get used to it, sweetheart. I promised to win you over, and I'm going to." I winked. "Now, get dressed, and let's go cut down a tree."

PART of me still couldn't believe she'd agreed to come with me today. That she'd followed behind me, freshly showered —I tried not to notice that she'd used my shower gel and smelled like me—wearing one of my old, too-small selburose sweaters and a pair of boots I'd borrowed for her. A strange sense of satisfaction had run through me as I looked back at Ivy, watching her trudge through the snow.

One that I was trying hard not to think too deeply about.

The distance between us wasn't helping me get my head on straight. I'd been denying myself for weeks, and I knew one thing.

I wanted Ivy Winters more than I'd ever wanted anyone before.

Turning my head back, I focused straight ahead. It wasn't actively snowing right now, but I couldn't help but notice the way her eyes lit up as she took in the view. Even as we walked out of town, there were dozens of little cottages that dotted the landscape. My house was on the far outskirts of the North Pole, away from everyone else—the way I liked it.

I led her back into the woods where she'd gotten lost yesterday. I was pulling a sled behind us—so we could bring the tree back with us on it. It also held the other necessary supplies for cutting down a tree.

"What are we looking for, exactly?"

"The perfect tree. Come on, you'll know when you see it."

We trudged through the woods, and every so often, I had to slow down my pace so she could keep up with me. I kept forgetting how much shorter her legs were.

I wasn't in a hurry, though. It was a beautiful day, and I had a beautiful girl at my side. We were going to work through each item on our Christmas list. Getting a tree was obviously the most important. Since I hadn't been home lately, my house didn't have one either. I'd expected her to tease me about that, but she hadn't.

I liked it much better when we were bickering because then, at least, I knew that Ivy was okay. When she was quiet, I had no idea what was going on in her head.

"What about this one?" she asked, sounding quiet. I

turned, finding her standing in front of a perfectly acceptable tree.

"Hm." I rubbed at my chin. "Not quite."

She groaned. "How long is this going to take?"

"Patience, sweetheart. Finding the right one is the most important part of the whole process."

Ivy grumbled under her breath, and I couldn't hide my amusement.

"Are we still doing this?" She glared at me.

I frowned. "What?"

"Fighting."

"Is that what we're doing?" I hummed.

Maybe not. Maybe it had never been fighting at all. It felt like there was a different word for it entirely. While she was poking around the trees, I grabbed something out of the sled —a peace offering.

"Here," I said, offering no further explanation.

"What's this for?" she asked, looking down into the cup. Her ears were pink again, though at least now I knew it wasn't from the cold.

She was affected by me as much as I was affected by her. I liked that.

"You looked cold," I answered, not skipping a beat.

I should have given her gloves. My sweater and my mom's coat might have been warm, but sometimes I forgot how chilly it was up here in the woods this time of the year. I was used to it, even with my travels.

"Oh." Ivy took a sip, a small moan slipping free. I took a drink of my own, watching her intently.

Damn, it was delicious. I needed to remember to thank my mom. She'd packed us more cookies, too, which I fully intended on winning the girl at my side over with.

"You're welcome, Poison Ivy." A smirk curled over my

lips. I found myself unable to look away from her cheeks and slightly pink nose.

She was feisty, but I liked fighting with her.

A month ago, I never would have imagined that I'd be here. Maybe part of me had grown used to the human realm, but it still wasn't the home I loved. At least, that was how I felt until I saw Ivy Winters smile. Now, I couldn't imagine being anywhere she wasn't.

Maybe it was her little moan that had rewired my brain. I couldn't think straight. Fuck, that sound. Or her tiny pink tongue, swiping a clump of whipped cream from her upper lip. Still, the hot cocoa had been a good choice.

"Teddy." Ivy came to a stop. "That one. I found it."

"Yes." I had to agree. "It's perfect."

Her blinding smile was all the convincing I needed.

After we cut the tree down—though I'd mostly done all the work while Ivy supervised—and I'd loaded it onto the sled, we headed back to my house to get it set up.

By the time it was sitting in the base, ready to be decorated later today, the sun was high in the sky. We both collapsed on the couch, sweaty and starving.

"Should we go into town for breakfast, or do you want to eat something here?"

Ivy turned to face me. "You'd really cook for me again?"

"Of course." I reached out and brushed a piece of hair off her forehead, tucking it behind her ear. "But I want to take you into town, too. And then I can get you the clothes I promised."

"Mmm." Ivy hummed. "Maybe I *like* wearing yours."

I held back a groan. "You're going to kill me, little Poison Ivy."

She stood off the couch, swaying her hips as she walked towards my bedroom. When she reached the door frame, she turned back to look at me. Her eyes were full of heat. *Fuck.*

"Food first," I announced. "Then we'll go into town."

She just nodded, and I left her to change as I made us a quick breakfast.

IVY GRABBED another ornament from the box and hung it on the tree. We'd spent the day exploring the village and all the shops. Her eyes had lit up like a kid in a candy store, which was hilarious considering how she'd been inside the *actual* candy store.

"This is really nice."

"Yeah?" I turned to her, stepping back to inspect our tree. We'd wrapped it with lights together, and now that most of the ornaments were hung, it looked pretty great.

I'd made a lot of ornaments in the workshop as a kid, and I didn't miss how she looked at each one, running her fingers over the smaller details. Some of them had been carved, while others had been sculpted or decoupaged. Not that I was as talented as my father.

"I wish I had some of mine," Ivy said, her voice subdued.

"You can make more here."

"I can?" She raised an eyebrow. "But all of my stuff is back at my apartment..."

"You know my dad has a giant workshop, right? Anything you could ever imagine, every supply you could ever need... you'll find it all in there."

"Oh."

I stepped closer to her, enough that I could hear her breath catch as I towered over her tiny frame. My mouth dipped down towards her ear as I murmured out, "Anything you want, Ivy. It's yours."

She rose on her tiptoes, wrapping her arms around my neck. "Teddy."

"Yeah?"

Her lips curled up in a relaxed smile. "Thank you for today."

"Ivy." My eyes dipped to her lips. Soft. Begging to be kissed.

"Mhm?"

"Look up," I said, tilting her chin up with my finger so she could see what was above us.

Mistletoe. Just like the last item she'd snuck onto the list.

"How..." Her jaw had dropped, like she couldn't believe the sight.

"Christmas magic, I guess," I said, shrugging my shoulders and hiding a little smile. "You know what that means."

Our lips were only inches apart. All either of us had to do to close the distance was to move just a little closer, and we'd be kissing.

"Kiss me, Teddy," she whispered.

I obliged. Pressing my lips against hers, I started softly. The gentle meeting of our mouths quickly turned into more as I poured all of my want from the last week into it. Every time I'd wanted to kiss her and hadn't. Every time I'd thought about how beautiful she was.

She curled her fingers into the hair at the nape of my neck, tugging on it to deepen the angle, and I wrapped my arms around her hips, lifting her up against my body. Her little gasp at the sudden change gained me entrance into her mouth, and I used that opportunity to taste her. Fucking finally.

Ivy tasted like hot chocolate and the peppermint candies she'd been sucking on all night, sneaking them when she thought I wasn't looking. So sweet.

Bringing us to the wall, I pinned her between it, keeping us at the perfect level to explore her mouth with my tongue.

When we broke apart, Ivy wriggled out of my arms and dropped to the floor before touching her fingers to her lips. They were swollen and puffy, and when she spoke, Ivy was practically breathless. "Good night, Teddy."

"Night."

There was one thing I knew for sure—Ivy was going to ruin me.

Maybe she already had.

13
ivy

12 days until christmas

*T*he sunlight streaming through the window woke me, as did the smell of coffee and cinnamon rolls baking. I practically moaned at the sweet scent in the air.

Who was this man, and what had he done with Theodore Claus?

He was spoiling me.

All I could think about was how he'd kissed me last night, practically devouring me. I knew if I had let it, we would have gone farther. Why was I still holding back? I had felt the press of his length against me, and knew from his sheer size he was big, but it was something different *feeling* it.

And damn, I wanted it.

But I'd never been good at asking for things I wanted. Just the idea made my cheeks heat. I wasn't a virgin, but I'd never particularly enjoyed sex before, either. But somehow, I knew that things with Teddy would be different. That when I gave into this heat between us, he would focus his sole attention on me and my pleasure.

No one else would ever compare, and I knew it. Damn him.

"Morning." I leaned my hip against the counter, watching him cook. He was wearing a pair of plaid pajama bottoms but no shirt. I bit my lip. How was he so effortlessly sexy? And he'd been sleeping on his couch the last few nights. I'd run back to his bedroom like a coward after he'd kissed me, falling asleep with the smell of him around me.

That dimple popped in his cheek as he turned to face me. "Hey."

"What's on the agenda for the day?" I asked, trying to sound casual.

"Thought we'd mark off another item off the list."

My cheeks must have been bright red because all I could think about was that last addition to the list. Was that why he'd kissed me last night? "Oh?" I finally choked out.

"Mhm. What do you think about making cookies?" He slid a plate of cinnamon rolls in front of me, and my mouth watered.

"You don't want to go outside?"

Teddy shrugged. "It's snowing like crazy out there. Seems like a good day to stay in. We can even put on a Christmas movie, and I'll make more hot chocolate."

"Okay. Sounds fun."

"You're surprisingly agreeable this morning."

I blushed. "You're doing so many nice things for me. I can't really complain." All the clothes and things I'd purchased yesterday had filled up his extra closet and the house, but Teddy didn't seem to mind. "Are you sure you don't have any work or anything to do?" I frowned.

He'd been working on some proposals back at Christmasland. I hated to think I was keeping him from that.

"Nah. I'll finish them after Christmas. Besides, Dad's always telling me I work too much, anyway."

"Oh. I mean, if you're sure..." I trailed off.

"I'm sure, Poison Ivy. Now eat up before they get cold."

I complied, devouring the plate in record time.

What had I done to end up here? It felt a little like fate that Teddy had walked into my life, swept me off my feet, and then brought me home for Christmas.

"ALRIGHT," I said, standing in the kitchen. Since we didn't have to go outside, I was wearing a simple green dress that I'd packed, while Teddy was wearing a plain blue T-shirt. There was a fire burning in the fireplace, and the entire place felt so cozy. "Let's do this."

Teddy pulled ingredients out of the cupboards.

"I'm surprised your kitchen is fully stocked," I admitted as I watched him. "Aren't you always on the road?"

He sighed. "Lately, I have been. But I try to come home between jobs. Perks of working for your family's company is you have a bit more flexibility with your schedule."

"That makes sense."

"Yeah." He turned, looking directly at me. "It gets lonely though."

"All the traveling?"

Teddy nodded, pulling out mixing bowls and measuring cups. "Constantly staying in hotels. Never being settled. I don't think I even realized how lonely I was until..."

"Until what?" I whispered.

"Until I met you."

"Oh."

I'd never felt as seen as I did right at that moment.

Because here was this man—this very attractive, handsome man, who was telling me things I'd been feeling for years. But I hadn't realized just how empty my life was until Teddy had swept in. Maybe barreled in was a better word for it.

"So, what's first?" I asked him, pushing my hair back behind my ears.

He brandished a recipe card, handing it to me. "Want to measure out all of the dry ingredients?"

"Sure." I grabbed the sugar cookie recipe card and started dumping flour into the mixing bowl. He was using the mixer to cream the shortening, slowly adding in sugar as he worked on the mixture.

I didn't know why I found it so hot watching him, but my eyes were glued to his forearms, and there was more than one time that I almost lost count of what I'd been measuring.

Doing great, Ivy, I scolded myself. I needed a distraction from how delicious this man was. I'd just focus all of my energy on the cookies.

We worked in tandem until the time came to mix all of the ingredients together when I took over, continuing mixing everything in the bowl while Teddy continued to give me instructions.

"Uh-huh. And then you mix it in like that." He stood behind me, wrapping his arms around my body to help me mix the dough. It seemed highly unnecessary, but I wasn't complaining. Not when he was pressed up against me, and his warmth was seeping into my skin. "Afterwards, we'll put it in the fridge and—"

"Teddy." A laugh slipped free from my lips. "I have made cookies before, you know." I poked at his forehead. "It's not hard to follow a recipe."

He groaned. "Why did you act like you didn't?"

I shrugged. "This was more fun." Rising to my tiptoes, I

wiped the hair off his forehead. "And I wanted to do this with you."

Dough forgotten in the bowl, I dipped my hands into the flour, flicking a small handful at his face.

"Oh, I'm *so* gonna get you for that," he said, a roguish smile transforming his face. "My wicked little Poison Ivy."

He grabbed a handful of flour, and I shrieked, running away from him. But it was no use—he was much taller and faster than me—and he caught me, swinging me around in the air, getting the flour all over me.

We were both a mess, flour everywhere yet I couldn't stop smiling. I was still in his arms, and I wiggled from his hold so that I could turn around and look at him.

"Teddy," I whispered, tracing my fingers through the flour on his jaw.

He grabbed my hand off his face and wrapped his fingers around mine before bringing it up to his lips.

"Ivy." His voice was hoarse. Maybe it was his touch that did me in. Or the pleading tone to his voice. Or the fact that standing this close to him, his scent wafted into my nose. He smelled like pine trees, clean air, and... *man*. It made my toes curl in my socks. I leaned up, my lips only inches from his. I wanted a repeat of last night. To know that I hadn't been dreaming when he'd kissed me.

Instead, he shook his head. "I'm trying really hard to control myself right now."

I frowned, not understanding. "Why? When you kissed me..." Maybe I wanted him to lose control. It would be so easy in this position to bring our lips together. But if there was something else holding him back... "Did you regret it?" I whispered. I didn't want him to regret it. *Regret me.*

"*No.*" He looked horrified that I even thought that. "God no, Ivy. But everything in your life changed in the blink of an eye. I just wanted to give you time to process without..." He looked away. "All of this."

"All of what?" I whispered. "All of you? Have you considered that maybe that's what I want, Teddy?" I rubbed my nose along his throat, drawing in his scent. "That I want *you*?"

He groaned, curling his finger around the point to my ear. "Do you not feel overwhelmed?"

"I'm still me," I said, shrugging my shoulders. "Elf or not, I never knew my parents, and I'm not going to now. Unless you're telling me I have a whole family here I don't know about..." I bit my lip. I was still alone. Nothing had changed.

I looked at the ball of dough in the bowl. The recipe said to let it chill for two hours before rolling it out. "Should we watch that movie now?" I asked, changing the subject.

"Lady's choice." Teddy bumped my shoulder playfully, and I turned to give him a small smile, only to find him looking at me with an emotion that I couldn't quite decipher.

Maybe he knew I needed the distraction. But maybe there was something else, too.

I PICKED *RUDOLPH*, of course. It was my favorite growing up, and I didn't care if it wasn't one hundred percent accurate to reality. Though I had to admit, I felt even more fond of the creatures ever since meeting Teddy's reindeer.

After the movie, we finished our cookies, rolling them out and cutting them into various Christmas shapes. There were trees, snowmen, and reindeer, not to mention Santa hats and snowflakes. We whipped up a giant batch of frosting to decorate them, and by the time we were done, it was already dark outside.

The cookies were delicious, though, and well worth the wait. Never mind that I was pretty sure most of the icing had ended up in our mouths instead of on the cookies. They'd still turned out looking—and more importantly, tasting —amazing.

"This is my mom's recipe," Teddy admitted. "She's made them for as long as I could remember."

"I think I could eat these every day for the rest of my life," I said, moaning around another bite. The frosting added the perfect sweetness. "She's a genius."

He laughed. "Sometimes I wonder what her life would have been like if she hadn't married my dad."

That surprised me. "She's not from here?"

He shook his head. "No. My dad... he met her down in the States when he was younger and had one hell of a time convincing her this place was real and to come back with him."

"But she did. And then they had you."

Teddy nodded. "And now she's Mrs. Claus."

"Is it always like that?" I asked, curious. "How does one become Santa Claus, anyway?"

He chuckled. "The Claus family is a long line. As far as I know, it has been. But the last few generations of Claus's have come from the same family. Mine. And they've always found their wives outside of the North Pole."

"Huh." I wasn't sure why I found that surprising—after all, Teddy bore no pointy ears. There clearly wasn't any elf blood in him. "What about you?"

Teddy, who had been taking a drink of milk to go with his cookies, spluttered out, "W-what?"

I didn't know why I was jealous, but I was. For the face-less girl who would become his wife. His *Mrs. Claus*. Because he wanted to take over for his dad one day.

And that woman wouldn't be me.

"Never mind," I said, my cheeks feeling hot. I didn't want to ask him how he was going to find a wife. "Thank you for today. I had a lot of fun."

Teddy leaned against the back of the couch. "We could watch another movie, you know. Split a bottle of wine?"

As nice as that sounded, it was dangerous, too. Because Teddy wasn't mine, and I was already feeling too greedy. The reminder that he would marry someone else was all I needed.

A yawn burst free from me. "I think I'm going to call it a night."

He nodded, looking away. "Good plan. We have more list activities to check off tomorrow, after all."

"Good night," I murmured, trudging over to the door to his room. My hand wrapped around the doorknob, and I looked back at Teddy, feeling guilty. He was six feet tall, and he'd been sleeping on that couch. Meanwhile, I'd been in his bed, cozy and more comfortable than I'd ever been before.

"Teddy?" My voice was quiet, hardly above a whisper.

"Hmm?"

I fidgeted with the hem of my dress. "I think the bed's big enough for both of us, don't you?"

He raised an eyebrow. "Are you sure?"

A blush crept over my cheeks. "It's your bed. I feel guilty."

"Sweetheart." His voice was low. "I can sleep on the couch."

"Come on, Theodore. Before I change my mind."

I heard his footsteps as I turned and walked into his room, not bothering to turn on the lights as I slipped under the covers.

"No funny business," I murmured, turning over to face him, though I could hardly see him with only the moon illuminating our faces.

"Of course not," he agreed, a dopey grin splitting his face. "Whatever you say, Poison Ivy."

14.
teddy

11 days until christmas

"*W*ow, it's really coming down out there, isn't it?" Ivy asked, staring out the window as we sat on opposite ends of the couch.

We'd spent the morning lazing around in our pajamas after breakfast, neither of us bringing up the fact that when we'd woken up this morning, we'd been wrapped up in each other's arms. Her scent was everywhere—on my pillow, clinging to my sheets, and damn if I didn't love it.

I sighed. "I'm sorry. Snowstorms at the Pole are almost unavoidable this time of year."

"Don't be." She smiled. "It's beautiful. Besides, when it stops, that's the perfect excuse for a snowman, right?"

"I just really wanted to take you skating today," I mumbled. "And my parents had invited us over to dinner."

"They did?" Her eyes widened. "I mean... I know I met your dad, but... Wow."

"It's alright, sweetheart." I brushed a piece of hair back

behind her ear. Why was I still resisting this? It was clear we both wanted it. After that kiss the other night, all I could think about was doing it again.

The way she'd tasted. How soft her lips were. My eyes drifted down to hers, watching as her tongue darted out to moisten them.

"Does this feel too fast?" She whispered.

"No," I murmured, answering honestly. "It feels right."

"It feels right to me, too." Ivy's response was breathless. "But we barely know each other."

"We know the important things. I know how you like your coffee—sickeningly sweet and full of sugar. Your day is ruined without your favorite gingerbread muffin. The way your cheeks turn bright red when you're embarrassed. That you love Christmas."

"Well, that one's a given," she muttered.

"I know that I want to kiss you again," I admitted.

"Theodore..." The beautiful strawberry blonde sitting on my couch, wearing a slouchy white sweater and leggings and not a lick of makeup, was the most beautiful sight I'd ever seen in the world. Nothing would compare to her.

No one could. Even if I searched the entire planet, I knew that she was the one I'd been meant to find.

"Ivy." Her head perked up, and those blue eyes met mine. They darted down to my lips, and it took everything in me not to let out a groan.

I was dying to kiss her again.

"Come here," I rasped, beckoning her over.

Ivy climbed onto my lap, her thighs parting as she strad-dled me, positioning herself on top of my straining erection. But she didn't give me her mouth. No. Instead, she asked, "What else do you know about me?"

My voice was rough when I answered. "That you taste like chocolate and peppermint. I know that those jingle bell earrings you wear drive me crazy and that I love how you light up whenever you hear them move. I know that when I first saw you, standing in the middle of my family's theme park, dressed in green velvet, I wanted you even then."

She hummed. "But you didn't make a move."

"How could I? You didn't even like me." Maybe not then. But I'd worn her down. "And yet, I still couldn't stay away." I visited her almost every single day, bringing her muffins and coffee just to get a glimpse of her.

I brushed one shoulder of Ivy's loose sweater off, exposing her bare skin. Placing a kiss there, I marveled at her. "You're the most beautiful thing I've ever seen, Ivy Winters. You make me want to do bad things. To break every rule I have. To want things I shouldn't."

I'd been half-hard all day just from watching her in my space. The way she seemed so at home here. The way she just fit into my life.

Ivy wiggled her hips, pressing my length against her entrance. I held back my groan at the sensation. "Were you ever on the *naughty* list, Theodore?" She traced a finger down my chest, her expression coy as she drew her eyes down to the bulge in my pants. Torturing me.

One corner of my lips turned up. "Wouldn't you like to know, sweetheart?"Her breath hitched as I brushed my thumb across her lips. "You weren't, were you? Because you're a good girl."

"Y-yes," she whispered, worrying her lower lip into her mouth. "*Please.*"

I tilted her chin up, brushing my lips across hers. Not kissing her. Not yet. "What do you want, my Poison Ivy? Use your words."

"Teddy," she moaned. "I want you."

"You can have anything you want, sweetheart." I'd give it all to her. Anything she asked for was hers.

Ivy rocked her lips, pressing her core against my cock.

"Fuck," I groaned. "You're going to ruin me, sweetheart."

She leaned down, her lips only a breath away from mine. "We could have done this before, you know. If you'd come into my apartment after our first date."

"But you didn't like me yet."

She laughed. "Of course I did. I just hated how much I liked you."

"Ivy Winters, do you have a crush on me?"

"Shut up," Ivy grumbled. "You're ruining it."

I rocked against her, causing Ivy to let out a sharp gasp. "Am I?"

She groaned. "Stop talking and kiss me."

"Gladly." I wrapped my hand around the back of her neck, bringing our mouths together. I kissed her like I'd wanted to since that night under the mistletoe when I hadn't been able to hold back anymore. Why had we denied ourselves for so long when it was this good?

The chemistry between us was different than anything I'd experienced before.

Swiping my tongue against her lips, she opened up for me, and I groaned at her taste. Sweet, like the hot chocolate we'd drank.

Ivy tugged my shirt out of my pants, running her fingernails over my abs. "Need this off," she panted as we broke apart long enough for her to pull it off over my head.

"Yes," I agreed, dropping it on the floor and pushing the hem of her sweater up off her hips, and sliding my hands over her leggings to cup her ass. "You're wearing too many clothes."

Her fingernails traced my abs as I palmed her backside. For being so small, she definitely wasn't devoid of curves. Still, I wanted to see all of her. Her sweater joined my shirt on the floor, giving me a full view of the cute red bra she was wearing—complete with a little tiny bow between her breasts. I pressed a soft kiss to the swell of each one as Ivy reached around, unclasping the back of her bra.

Her breasts sprung free, and I lost all coherent thought.

"*Fuck.*" Her tits were full, pink nipples that begged for my tongue. "So pretty."

She whimpered as I bent my head down to capture one with my mouth, sucking on her nipple and running my teeth along the sensitive bud.

Ivy gasped. "More."

"Patience." I switched to her other breast, giving it the same attention. "I'm gonna give you everything you want, sweet girl."

She whined, rocking against my thigh.

I pushed her waistband down, lifting her up so she could wriggle out of her leggings.

Her little red lace panties matched her discarded bra. Fuck me. I didn't even bother removing them before sliding two fingers inside her entrance, groaning as I felt how wet she was.

"I want to fuck you so bad," I muttered, dropping my head against her neck to inhale her scent. "Bury myself in this sweet pussy."

"Do it," she begged, rocking her hips to ride my fingers. She threw her head back, letting out a series of breathy moans.

Unzipping my jeans with my free hand, I freed my cock from my boxers. Ivy reached out, her small hand sliding around my length as she pumped me a few times.

"You're so big," she murmured, her eyes glued on my shaft.

"You can take it."

"Fuuuck. I need to be inside of you." There was no damn way I was spilling in her hand the first time we did this.

Pulling my fingers out, I adjusted our position, dragging her panties down her legs before pushing my pants and boxers down my hips in one motion.

Seated back on the couch, Ivy straddled my lap once again, rubbing her bare cunt over my length. Letting out a groan, I pulled her up, ready to bury myself inside of her, only—"Shit. I don't have a condom." I hadn't needed them before. And now...

Now, the most beautiful woman I'd ever seen was in my lap, her tits glistening and nipples hardened from my mouth, and I couldn't do anything about it.

She groaned. "Do you have any in your bedroom?"

I shook my head. "There hasn't been anyone. Not here."

"Ever?" Ivy blinked.

"I... I've never brought a girl home before. And it's been a while." I squeezed her ass. "But we can stop." As much as I wanted her, I wouldn't do anything to put her at risk. I'd never gone without condoms before.

"Or..." Ivy bit her lip. "I'm on birth control. And I haven't been with anyone in over a year. I'm good if you are?"

"Same." Was I good? Yes. Did I want this? *Yes.*

"Are you sure?" Ivy asked, her breathing rough.

"Am *I* sure?" I repeated. I should be the one asking her that. She nodded, the tips of her ears turning the slightest shade of pink. "I—yes. *Fuck.*" I crashed our lips back together, showing her how much I wanted her with my mouth. Words might have failed me, but my tongue wouldn't.

"Bed?" I asked, my meaning clear.

She shook her head. "Need you now."

"Ivy," I groaned. "Do you even know what you do to me?"

She flashed her teeth, and damn. She knew exactly what she was doing. I was harder than I'd ever been in my entire life, with the girl on my lap, begging for me.

"I just don't want you to regret this," she whispered.

How could I? How could I ever regret her? When I'd wanted her since the moment I'd laid eyes on her? Ever since our date, when I'd seen her in that tight red dress, this was all I could think about.

"I won't." Holding her gaze, I stared into her bright blue eyes so she could see the sincerity in mine. "Later, I'm going to make you come on my tongue so I can prove to you just how much I want this."

"Oh." She let out a sharp exhale of breath.

"You'd like that, wouldn't you, sweetheart? My mouth on you, tasting you?"

Ivy nodded her head, eagerly agreeing as she rested her hands on my shoulders, positioning herself over my cock.

She rubbed the head against her entrance, back and forth until I was coated in her wetness.

"Baby," I groaned as she put me inside of her, sinking down onto my cock. "You're so fucking tight, Ivy. Feels so damn good."

Inch by inch, Ivy accepted me into her body, her wet heat surrounding me. She was so warm, squeezing around me, and I wondered if it had ever felt like this before. So good. So right.

It had never been like this for me. I'd never felt this deep connection, this depraved need to be inside of her, to bury myself so deep that I couldn't find my way out. Like I wanted to live in her body and make it my home. A shimmering cord stretched between us.

"It's too much," she cried out. "I can't…"

"You can," I murmured, coaxing her. "You're doing so good, sweetheart. Look how well you're taking me."

She took the last inch, sliding down until I was fully inside her, buried to the hilt.

Ivy let out a low moan, digging her fingernails into my back. "*Teddy.*"

I gripped her hips, helping her rock back and forth in my lap as I thrusted up into her.

"*Yes.* That's it. Fuck yourself on my cock, sweetheart. Get all messy for me." I brought my thumb to her clit, massaging it in circles.

"You're *so* big."

"You're so good for my ego, sweetheart." I smirked, but then she contracted her inner muscles around me, and I let out a groan.

Ivy tangled her fingers in my hair, guiding my mouth to hers. We were as connected as we could be—in every conceivable way—and all I could think was I never wanted this to end.

Whatever this was between us, I was all in.

Ivy was mine.

And I intended to prove that to her.

15
ivy

$\mathcal{T}$eddy's fingers gripped my thighs as I rode him on his couch, rocking my hips to meet each upward thrust of his. Why hadn't we been doing this from the beginning?

With my hands still buried in Teddy's hair, I brought our lips back together, kissing him deeply. He took the time to explore my mouth thoroughly with his tongue, and it was *everything.*

Sex had never been this good for me—like it was life changing. The way he took such care, lavishing me with attention like his sole focus was on me and my pleasure... I was right. Everything was different now. It was like before, I'd been looking at the world through a pair of rose-colored lenses, and suddenly, I could see clearly.

"Teddy," I said, letting out a moan. "I'm so close."

Each stroke of his cock inside of me and each rock of my hips against him were bringing me higher and higher. It was only a matter of time before I shattered.

I used my knees to slide off him a few inches before dropping back down, repeating the motion until I was panting with need.

He brought his thumb back to my clit, giving me exactly what I needed, and it only took a few more thrusts and his expert fingers at work before I let go. On a scream of his name, I came, the entire world fading out into white, just like the snow that was still falling outside.

Slumping against Teddy's body, I let all the sensations flow through me. He was still buried deep inside me, and I could feel my body fluttering and clenching around him.

"Wow," I murmured in a daze.

"Good?" He kissed my jaw when I raised my head up to look at him. My hardened nipples were pressed against his bare chest, and I loved the way it felt to be pressed up against him, bodies slick with sweat.

I thought about what he'd said earlier and decided to tease him instead of giving my truth. "I'm just going to feed your ego, aren't I, Theodore?"

He grumbled, and I returned the favor by kissing him lightly on the corner of his mouth.

"Better than good," I whispered. "That was…"

"Yeah." He slid his hands down my sides to cup my ass, squeezing lightly again. "But we're not done yet."

Oh. Right. Because I'd come, but he hadn't.

Teddy lifted me up off the couch, wrapping his arms around me as he carried me into the bedroom, wordlessly depositing me on his bed before driving inside of me.

"*Oh.*" I cried out. Every sensation was heightened, every movement inside of me somehow more. Would it be like this every time?

The strands of his dark brown hair fell onto his forehead as he thrust into me, those green eyes dark. I tightened my core, causing Teddy to grunt.

"You're evil," he said before latching his mouth onto my nipple, sucking as he pistoned into me.

With my fingers digging into the comforter, I wrapped my legs around his waist, forcing him deeper into me. He brought my nipple between his teeth, nipping at it, and—

"Oh, *God.*"

If he kept this up, I was going to come again, and that had never happened before. I'd been lucky to even orgasm once during sex and never from penetration. Though I'd never done it without a condom, either, and the feeling of him bare inside of me was *incredible.*

Freeing my nipple with a wet pop, he brought his head up, looking at me from between my breasts. "Come on, baby. Gimme one more."

I shook my head. It was too much.

"Please," I said, not sure what I was begging for.

He grunted as I tightened my legs around him. Teddy was so deep, buried all the way to the hilt, and every time he pulled out and then plunged back in, it sent shudders down my whole body. Another orgasm burst through me, and I could feel Teddy hardening inside of me, my climax setting off his own.

"*Yes,*" I cried as he came with a groan, spilling inside of me. Warmth filled my insides, and I tried to ignore how good it felt.

How right.

Because I was going to get addicted to this, *fast.*

Teddy rolled us, pulling me into his arms so we could collapse on the bed.

He kissed my forehead. "Damn, Poison Ivy. That was…"

"Yeah," I murmured, still feeling breathless. "You're not so bad yourself, Theodore."

He smirked, brushing my damp hair off my shoulder and pressing a kiss to my bare skin.

I wiggled, feeling him softening inside of me, and he pulled out, liquid trickling from my entrance, both of our combined releases.

My cheeks heated, and I hid my face with my hands.

"Hold on," he said, his eyes focused on the pot where he'd just been buried deep. "I'll clean us up."

"Okay," I choked out. Where did he think I'd be going? I certainly wasn't going anywhere with his cum dripping out of me.

He gave me a dopey grin before disappearing into the bathroom, leaving me to spiral into my thoughts.

I'd slept with Teddy. At first, I hadn't been able to stand him, but now... Now, everything felt different. Like it or not, he was starting to burrow his way into my heart.

But I couldn't give it to him. Not when I knew how this would end.

He came back out, holding a washcloth, and settled back onto the bed carefully. After he'd tenderly wiped his seed from my body, I went to the bathroom myself.

After I'd taken care of myself, I looked in the mirror. My face was flushed, my hair a tangled mess, and my eyes were dilated. I looked like I'd just been fucked.

Which, as soft and caring as it had been, was what we'd done. It was pure, carnal need for each other. We hadn't even been able to wait long enough to make it to the bed.

But the way I'd felt when I first slid down on his length, that magnificent way he'd filled me... I bit my lip, holding back a groan.

Fuck, I was in over my head. Because I didn't want this to end.

But how could it not?

YAWNING, I looked over at Teddy. He was awake, playing with the ends of my hair.

We'd fallen asleep, neither of us having bothered to dress after cleaning up. I was perfectly happy cuddling like this, skin to skin. Even if we didn't leave his house today, I didn't find myself complaining.

"How are you feeling?"

I moved my legs, wincing. "A little sore, but good."

He frowned. "I'm sorry."

It was dark outside, though I'd quickly gotten used to how early the sun set here. We were farther north than I could have ever imagined, though I truly had no idea where we actually were. I suspected this whole place was cloaked with some sort of magic, so any random person who happened upon it wouldn't discover the actual North Pole, though I had no proof of that yet.

I wanted to know everything about this place—the way it worked, the magic of Christmas—all of it, but how could I expect Teddy to trust me with that information when I hadn't fully let him in?

Though last night was definitely a start. Part of me wondered what would have happened if he'd come inside after our date instead of going home. Would we have done this sooner? Or would we have ended up here either way?

Maybe there was something to fate after all. Like I was meant to be in this place, right now, with him.

I tucked a piece of hair behind my ear—my long, pointy elf ear—and a thought occurred to me. "Do I have any family here?"

How had I not thought about that before now? I'd been alone all my life. But maybe...

Teddy froze. "I—"

My chest was full of hope. "Grandparents? Or maybe a cousin?" I might not have had parents, but that didn't mean there weren't other people out there who shared the same genetic material as me. Who could be my family.

"I don't know," he admitted.

All I could feel was disappointment. "Oh."

"But we'll find out," he promised, bumping my shoulder. "Even if my dad doesn't know, there are other ways."

That was all I could ask for, wasn't it?

"Okay." I nuzzled against him, using his body for warmth.

"I was just being selfish," he finally said, sliding his arms around my back to tug me closer to him. "Keeping you all to myself."

"Maybe," I murmured. "But I wasn't complaining either." I rubbed my nose against his neck. "I like having you all to myself, too."

I was definitely avoiding all reminders of my real life, sequestering myself up in the North Pole with Teddy. I hadn't even called Sarah and updated her. I'd sent her a few texts here and there after figuring out that my phone *did* actually work—reassuring her I hadn't been kidnapped or murdered —but how would I ever explain this to her?

It made more and more sense why he had kept it from me. This place was unreal. Beautiful, but unbelievable.

Everyone I'd met so far had been an elf, sharing the same pointy ears as mine, though no one commented on my presence here. Did they all just accept it as normal? Or did they know what was going on, even when I didn't?

Teddy had introduced me to all of them in the same way. *This is Ivy.* He never added anything else. What was I to him?

And why did I want to be something *more*?

16
teddy

10 days until christmas

A blanket of strawberry blonde hair was sprawled across my bed, but I couldn't even complain because Ivy was currently using my chest as her pillow. I was doing my best to ignore the press of her body against mine and the way it was affecting me in *other* places. At some point during the middle of the night, she'd cuddled up against me like she was seeking my body warmth.

I was content to stay just like this for a little longer.

"Mmm." Ivy rolled over, throwing her leg over mine.

"Morning."

Her eyes flew open, suddenly realizing where she was.

"Comfortable?" I asked, smirking at the elf draped over my body.

"Oh, I—" The tips of her ears were pink. I ran my finger over them, a shudder running through her body.

"You're so cute. I think I want to keep you in my bed forever." Pressing a kiss to her forehead, I pulled away. If we didn't leave the bed soon, we wouldn't make it out all day.

And as much as I wanted a repeat of last night, I *had* promised her the perfect Christmas.

"Looks like the snowstorm has settled down," I said, looking out the window.

"Oh." Was it just me, or did Ivy look a little sad about that?

"We can go into town, though. The Christmas Market is happening this afternoon."

"Christmas Market?" She perked up. "That sounds amazing."

I traced circles over her bare shoulder. "It is. And we can mark a few more things off our list."

"Mmm." She closed her eyes, and I placed a few open-mouthed kisses on her bare skin. I hadn't left any marks on her last night, but fuck, I wanted to. Wanted everyone to know who's she was.

My girl. *My* Poison Ivy.

Getting out of bed, I headed to the bathroom to turn the water on in the shower. I knew we'd never leave this house if I stayed in bed with her.

Stepping in, I let the water run over my body, grabbing my body wash to pour some into my hand.

Ivy opened the shower door and snuck in with me, a little mischievous smile spread over her face. She wrapped her arms around me, running her fingers over my abs.

"Good morning," I chuckled, ignoring the press of her nipples against my back.

"Hi," she said, pressing her lips against my back.

"What are you doing, sweetheart?"

"No point in wasting water, right?"

"Who are you, and what have you done with my Ivy?" I asked, turning around to face my little elf. *Mine.* I shouldn't use words like that, but it was so hard not to when she was naked and wet in front of me.

In my house.

My bed.

My woman.

She blushed. "I'm just being practical."

"Practical. *Hm.*" I pressed my rapidly hardening cock against her stomach.

"Yup. Saving water." Ivy ran her tongue over her lips. "No other reason."

She took the body wash out of my hands, squirting some into her palm, soaping them up.

"Ivy," I warned.

"Mhm?" She ran her soapy hands over my chest, fingers trailing across my abs.

I groaned. "You're going to be the death of me."

"That's the idea, Theodore."

"*Evil,*" I groaned, though if I was being honest with myself, I'd let this woman do whatever she wanted to me. She was an addiction, and I was quickly growing more attached to her than I should be.

But how could I not when she looked at me like that, with those big blue eyes and that silky hair that I wanted to wrap around my fist? I was fucked. Truly.

"GOD, LOOK AT ALL THIS SNOW." Ivy's eyes were wide. The storm had dumped a bunch of fresh, powdery snow outside, which was glittering from the morning sun. It was an absolutely gorgeous day out—perfect for a trip into town.

"Do you want to walk?" I asked, not looking over my

shoulder as I went to check on Buddy in the barn. "Or we can take the snowmobile—" I had my truck, too, though I doubted the roads would be clear yet. And I didn't want to risk getting stuck somewhere. The walk wasn't bad, especially on a day like today.

Plus, maybe the cold, crisp air would help me clear my head.

Ivy didn't respond, and when I looked behind me, frowning at the lack of my strawberry blonde girl in her fluffy white coat, I was suddenly assaulted by a ball of cold snow.

Right at my face.

She shrieked with laughter.

"Oh, you're going *down*," I said, scooping up a large handful of snow and molding it into a ball before throwing it at her and hitting her shoulder.

This was *war*.

"Guess you'll have to catch me first!"

Ivy threw another snowball at me, missing me this time, at least. She laughed the whole time as I launched more snowballs at her before running after her. We kept it up for a few minutes, pelting each other with snowballs, till we were both covered in snow, and even the tip of Ivy's nose was red from the cold. It was refreshing to see her like this—a genuine smile on her face, happiness radiating from her.

Even as she ran away from me, she was fast, but thanks to my longer legs, I was faster. Catching up with her, I scooped her up into my arms, throwing her over my shoulder.

"Caught you."

"Put me down!" Each word was punctuated by more giggles. "Teddy!"

I smacked her ass. "Who's the naughty one now?"

She pinched mine in return. "Still you, Theodore."

Her eyes sparkled when I put her down, wrapping my arms around her waist and picking her up into my arms. Ivy wrapped her legs around me, and I clicked my tongue against the roof of my mouth. "What am I going to do with you?"

"Kiss me," she answered, breathless.

She didn't even need to ask—I always wanted to kiss her.

IT HAD TAKEN us almost twice as long to get there after we'd both had to change, soaking wet from playing in the snow, but we'd made it.

Booths surrounded us on all sides. The North Pole was notorious for celebrating the season, even during the busiest time of the year. Even though the toys were all done, and most of the work was already completed for my dad's runs, everyone pitched in here.

Ivy's eyes were wide when I turned to her.

"This is... Wow. And I thought Christmasland was magical."

"I told you there's nothing like Christmas at the North Pole."

She snorted. "Yeah, you weren't kidding."

Taking her hand, I guided her down the first row. Every booth was full of handmade items, like scarves and, blankets, and even jewelry.

Reaching out, I grabbed her hand, interlacing our fingers together. "Most of the elves here have some sort of hobby. They make stuff all year, and each Christmas, everyone buys goods from each other."

"That's incredible. I wish I had the time for this."

"You will." I squeezed her hand.

She bit her lip. "How do you know?"

"Just do. I have this feeling, sweetheart. That everything you've ever dreamed of is going to come true."

"Oh." Ivy turned, the tips of her ears and cheeks turning the same color as her jacket. "I don't know about that…"

But I could feel it. As much as I knew what a child wanted for Christmas. "You'll see," I said instead.

Ivy's phone rang, and she looked down at it in surprise, like she'd forgotten it could make a noise. "Oh. This is Sarah. I should really answer her. I don't want her to think I was kidnapped or anything."

"No," I agreed. "Definitely wouldn't want that."

She nodded.

"I can't tell her, can I?" Ivy whispered.

"That you're here?" I frowned. "She might not believe you."

"I know." Her shoulders drooped. "But it's weird not to tell my best friend about this. I've never kept a secret like this from her before."

"It's okay." I squeezed her shoulder. "Do what you feel is right."

"Hello?" she said, picking up.

I could hear her friend on the other line. "Hey, girl! I hadn't heard from you in a few days, so I thought I'd call to check in."

"Oh." She looked over at me, biting her lip. "Everything's great, actually."

Ivy motioned she was going over to a bench to sit down, and I nodded.

Wandering through the market by myself, I smiled as a pair of little snowflake earrings caught my eye. They reminded me of the necklace Ivy wore around her neck—the one she never took off. She'd said it was her mother's, and the only thing she really had from her.

But maybe I could give her something back.

"Teddy!"

"Oh, hi, Mom." I looked up, finding my mother bundled

up in a red coat, her silvery-blonde hair pulled back into a ponytail. I'd gotten most of my features from my dad, except for my mom's eyes.

The fact that my father had fallen for her never surprised me. Sometimes I wondered how he'd convinced her to stay. Was loving someone enough to ask them to make that big of a sacrifice?

Could *I* make it? I wondered what it would it be like to never call this place home again. The thought hurt, but not as much as it did thinking of never seeing Ivy again. Never holding her.

One night, Teddy, I scolded myself. We'd only been together *one* night. I couldn't be thinking about things like forever already.

Mom looked around. "Where's your girl? I thought maybe I'd get to meet her."

I didn't even bother to correct her when she called her *my girl.* Because it felt right. She was my girl.

And I was going to make her see that.

"Ivy's over there," I said, pointing towards the bench, where she sat chattering into her phone excitedly. "Her friend called." No doubt to make sure she was okay because I'd been monopolizing all of her time.

Not that I was going to complain. It had been an eventful few days.

My mom raised an eyebrow. "And how's everything been?"

"Good." I cleared my throat. "We've been working through a list of Christmas activities together."

"Oh, that's so romantic." She pressed her hand over her heart.

"*Mom,*" I protested, feeling embarrassed.

"What?" She shrugged. "I think it's very sweet of you, Teddy. Making sure her Christmas is a good one."

But was that all it was? *No.* It never had been about that at all. It had always been me being greedy and wanting to spend more time with her in whatever way I could.

And now she was here. Last night she'd been in my arms. I'd held her tight and nothing, *nothing* had been the same as being with her. But did it matter if she didn't want to stay? What were we even doing?

"When are you coming over for dinner? Your dad and I would still love to have you both."

"Tomorrow night?" I asked. Tonight, I planned on making dinner and cozying up by the fire next to Ivy. I wasn't quite ready to give that up yet. Plus, if a repeat of last night happened, I wouldn't complain. Just looking at her took my breath away.

Ever since the shower this morning, I'd been desperate to have her again.

"Tomorrow's perfect. I'll make a roast."

"Thanks, mom." I leaned forward, kissing her cheek. "But don't scare her away, all right? I want her to actually like me." I wanted her to more than like me, but I couldn't admit that to my mother.

She gave me a little pout. "So you're saying I can't show her your baby photos?"

"No. Definitely not that."

"But you looked so cute when you were small enough to fit into your dad's hat—" I narrowed my eyes at her. "*Fine,*" she huffed. "No baby photos. But I can't wait to meet her."

"I know, mom."

Hopefully Ivy would enjoy it as much as my mom would. She'd never had a family of her own, after all. Would it be weird for her to be a part of mine?

Would she even want that?

17
ivy

The Christmas market was *magical*. I had an entire bag full of things I'd purchased, too excited to be surrounded by everything to hold back. We'd had apple cider while exploring all the stalls and bought matching pajamas—which felt like a very *couples* thing to do, though, after last night...

Maybe we were.

Neither of us had bothered to put a label on it; maybe that was fine for now. Talking with Sarah had reminded me of that. That this wasn't my home. I might have come from here, but Florida was where my life was.

What did he want, though? He hadn't brought up what happened after. When I went home, back to my life, everything would change.

I didn't want to think about that. Not now. Not when I had this time with Teddy.

"What do you think, sweetheart? Did you find everything you want?" He leaned over, pressing his lips against my forehead.

I looked down at the bags we were both carrying. "Oh. Yeah, I guess. Do you want to head back to your house?"

He ran his hand through his hair, messing up the brown strands. "I was actually thinking we could go talk to my dad."

"Oh?" Was he thinking about our earlier conversation?

"About your family. He knows everything."

I blinked. "Are you sure?" I'd mentioned it yesterday, but hadn't expected him to act on that request so suddenly.

"Yes. Of course."

"But don't you have things you need to do?"

Teddy laughed. "Sure. There's always stuff to do around here. Same with the company. But some things are more important." He looked directly at me when he said that, like he was saying the words, *you're more important.*

My stomach filled with butterflies, and I couldn't explain why I was having this reaction to something so simple— something that should have been a given—but it warmed my heart to know he cared about me finding my family.

"Why?" I whispered.

He shook his head. "I can't explain it. It just feels like something I need to do." He wound our hands together. "Something *we* need to do."

Why? I wanted to ask again, but part of me could feel it too. Like there was something more tying us together than just chance. That all of this felt a little like fate.

"Thank you," I whispered, holding back all my other thoughts.

Maybe one day I would share them.

THERE WAS a piece of paper in my pocket with my grandmother's name and a hole in my heart that felt suspiciously smaller today.

I didn't know how I could possibly thank Teddy for this. For bringing me here, for giving me this. Giving me the chance to have a family.

After we'd gotten back to his house in the early evening, I'd stripped off my outer layers, leaving on my sweater and a pair of leggings, but I discarded the rest by the door.

Teddy made us dinner, and it wasn't lost on me how domestic all of this felt. I was pretty sure I was eating way better than I ever had while working at Christmasland, and I'd never felt so cared for in my life.

After eating, we'd both sat on the couch, cuddled together under a warm blanket as another Christmas movie played in the background. This time, though, I wasn't paying attention to it, too focused on the man next to me. My entire body was on fire, and each of his little touches against me, the way his fingers kept skimming up my thighs, all of it was driving me crazy.

"Any ideas on what you want to do tomorrow?" Teddy asked, running his fingers through my wavy hair. I'd braided it this morning, but he'd taken them out as soon as we'd gotten back from the market.

"What's still on our list?" I asked, trying to distract myself from my needy thoughts and the heat pooling lower in my body.

He pulled a piece of paper out of his pocket and handed it to me. Had it been there all along?

Sometimes I didn't know what he had up his sleeve.

I unfolded the paper. Teddy had added little check marks next to what we'd completed so far, including our mistletoe kiss. Though I hadn't envisioned it happening when it did, I couldn't say I wasn't grateful for it. Especially when it had led to last night.

Moving closer to him on the couch, I rested my head on his shoulder.

Teddy and Ivy's Christmas Checklist
1. *Bake Christmas Cookies* ✔
2. *Decorate A Christmas Tree* ✔
3. *Take a Sleigh Ride*
4. *Drink Hot Chocolate While Watching a Christmas Movie* ✔
5. *Build a Snowman*
6. *Make a Gingerbread House*
7. *Go Ice Skating*
8. *Visit The Christmas Market* ✔
9. *Ugly Christmas Sweater Party*
10. *Hang Stockings*
11. *Matching Christmas PJs*
12. *Buy and Wrap Presents*
13. *See the Lights*
14. *Kiss Under the Mistletoe* ✔

"Technically, we've taken a sleigh ride," Teddy said, pointing at that line. "But that was before we made the list, so I think we need to take another one."

"So we still need to…" I ran my eyes over the list. So far, we'd marked off baking cookies, decorating the tree, drinking hot cocoa, and watching a Christmas movie, and today, we'd marked off visiting the Christmas market. I'd bought some presents today, but we hadn't technically *wrapped* them yet, which seemed like a package deal. "How are we going to get all of this done before Christmas?"

Teddy winked. "One at a time, Poison Ivy."

Rolling my eyes at him, I looked down at the paper. "I don't even have a stocking so we can hang them." I looked at his fireplace mantle. The fire was cozy and warm, but it definitely needed stockings before Christmas. "I should have gotten one today."

"I'll take care of that," he promised. "Also, the town has its annual ugly Christmas sweater party on the twenty first. So, we can mark that off then."

"What you're saying is we need to obtain actual ugly Christmas sweaters?"

Teddy grinned. "Who said anything about *obtaining* them?"

I raised an eyebrow. "Do you have a whole closet full of them hidden somewhere in this house or something?"

"And what if I do?"

"You're crazy."

He flashed his teeth at me, leaning in close to nip at my nose. "If you hadn't figured that out by now, sweetheart, I'd be a little worried."

I laughed. "Theodore Claus, you really are something."

Teddy's hand slid between my hair and my face, cupping my cheek as he ran his thumb over my cheekbone. "And you, Ivy Winters, never cease to be the most beautiful woman in any room. Even in an ugly Christmas sweater."

He leaned in, placing his lips against mine, and I melted. Stroke after stroke, he coaxed me open with his tongue until I was a panting, writhing mess beneath him. I moaned into his mouth, and it was like it unlocked something inside of him.

I panted when we pulled apart, and Teddy slid off the couch, moving in front of me. He pulled my knees apart, positioning himself between them.

"What are you doing?" I asked, looking down at him.

Teddy guided my leggings down over my legs, pulling them off my body. "Having my dessert." He licked his lips, his gaze focused on my panties.

"Teddy—" I squeaked, cheeks heating.

"Told you I was going to make you come on my tongue, sweetheart. I need to taste you." He rubbed his nose over my entrance, inhaling deeply.

My whole body was on fire. And yet, I wanted it. All of it. Whatever he was willing to give me.

He pressed a kiss to the inside of my thigh before hooking his fingers into the sides of my underwear, slowly dragging them down my legs. It was torture.

"Please," I whimpered. Teddy knew what he was doing to me, driving me wild. Not giving me what I wanted.

"What do you want, baby?" He murmured, his hands wrapped around my ankles after he divested me of my panties.

"Your tongue," I moaned. "All of it."

He gave a satisfied hum. "Good girl."

I preened from his praise, which was only made better when he swiped his tongue over my slit, and *oh.* "Do that again," I begged.

He looked at me from between my legs with a wicked grin. "My pleasure, sweetheart." His fingers pried me further apart, bearing everything to him, but he didn't move. "Such a pretty pussy, and it's all mine." Then he brought his mouth to my needy cunt, burying his tongue inside me.

"Yesss," I moaned as he licked me thoroughly, drinking me up like he was dying of thirst and I was the only thing that could sate him.

He was magical, that much I knew to be true. There was definitely something magical about the way he was using his tongue, driving me higher and higher.

And when he refocused his efforts, sucking my clit into his mouth, giving me stimulation that I didn't even know was possible? I came faster than I ever had before, crying out his name.

He didn't stop working me through it, lapping up my release as if he'd die without it.

Teddy licked his lips, standing up to bring our mouths together, letting me taste myself on his tongue. It was dizzying, how fast he could work me up.

"You're way too good at that," I said as my breathing finally evened out.

"Oh, baby." He smirked. "I'm just getting started."

Hefting me into his arms, he carried me into the bedroom, doing just as he promised.

9 days until christmas

"We're so happy to have you, Ivy," Teddy's mom said, smiling at me as soon as we entered his parent's house.

Their house was nothing like I'd imagined. Unlike Teddy's quaint and cozy cottage, their large house was on the top of a hill with large windows on almost all sides, giving you a three-hundred-and-sixty-degree view of the North Pole down below.

"Thank you for inviting me to dinner, Mrs. Claus."

"Oh, please. Call me Carol."

"Right." I nodded, looking around for Teddy.

He'd taken my coat to hang it up, leaving me and his mother in the entryway. I'd worn a white sweater with a plaid skirt and heeled boots, grateful for the opportunity to wear something that wasn't snow boots or leggings for once. He'd cleaned up, too, wearing a pair of slacks and a forest green button up shirt.

We drove over in Teddy's truck—the same one he'd picked me up in for our first date, though I hadn't asked how he had it here—which I was very grateful for since it meant we'd had heat for our drive over.

I followed his mom into the kitchen. "Do you know where Teddy went?"

She waived me off. "Oh, he and his father are always up to something." She flashed a smile. "How's your first Christmas in the North Pole going?"

I ignored the way she said *first,* like there would be more. "Amazing, honestly. Teddy's made it really special for me. Definitely makes up for all the ones I missed as a kid."

His mom turned to the oven, checking on whatever was cooking inside. The place smelled heavenly—like warm baking bread and delicious meat cooked tenderly with spices. I wondered if this was what it felt like to have a family. To eat dinner with them, surrounded by the people you loved, eating a meal cooked for you not because they had to, but because they wanted to... My heart ached.

"Did you... know my mom?" I asked, biting my lip. I didn't know how long she'd been at the North Pole.

She frowned, moving around the kitchen. "I wish I did. By the time Nick and I were together, she'd already left the North Pole."

"Oh."

Carol gave me a sad look. "I'm sorry I couldn't tell you more."

"No." I shook my head. "It's okay. Your husband told me where I could find my grandma. I guess I'm just working up the courage to go over there."

She came over and squeezed my shoulder. "She's going to love you."

Nodding, I sipped on the glass of wine she slid in front of me.

"You two seem like you're getting pretty cozy."

I blushed, thinking about last night. How he'd gone down on me like it was his favorite taste in the world. "Oh, well…"

"He really likes you, you know? I've never seen him like this with anyone he's dated. He's never even brought a woman home with him before."

He *had* mentioned no one had ever been in his house. But was I truly that special? And did it matter if I was going to leave?

Smiling at his mom, I slid onto a barstool. I didn't have an answer for that. "He's a great guy. You raised him well."

She gave me a beaming smile. "I know."

Teddy came into the kitchen, dropping a kiss to my cheek before going over to help his mom get dinner ready.

And *oh*, my heart. I wasn't sure what he was doing to it, but I knew I wasn't going to survive if he kept this up.

18
teddy

*I*vy looked so right sitting at the island in my
parent's kitchen, sipping a glass of wine as my
mom finished dinner. Dad was up in his study, glasses on,
and sketching some new toy idea. After a short conversation,
I'd left him to it, figuring I would check on the girls instead.

It was strange how she fit into my life so well in such a
short time. How much I wanted her here.

I almost could see it, year after year: Ivy wearing my ring.
Children's laughter filling the air. Happiness and love. But it
was too soon for that. I couldn't be thinking about her
that way.

Not when she might not even want to stay.

"What do you think, Teddy?" My mother interrupted my
train of thought.

"Huh?" I forced my gaze away from Ivy.

She had a knowing smile on her face. "About the theme
park. Your proposal?"

"Oh." I nodded. "Yeah. It's going well." Even though I'd
barely thought about it in days.

149

She turned to my girl. "Teddy told me that you've worked at Christmasland for seven years?"

Ivy's face lit up at the mention of her park. "It's an amazing place. Have you been before, Carol?"

I didn't care that it wasn't actually *hers* because it was her spirit that filled the place.

"I have. Nick and I used to go every summer to check on the park. Teddy came along, too, ever since he was old enough to toddle around. It's been a few years now, though. We're getting older, so we don't get down there quite as much."

"Ah." Her gaze swung to me, and she looked confused. "But… I thought you said you'd never been there before?"

"I never said that, sweetheart."

"But, the tour… you experiencing everything the park had to offer, that was just… a lie?" Her voice was soft when she whispered, "Was it all a lie?"

"No." My voice was full of conviction. She had to know I hadn't misled her. That our meeting might have been by chance, but I'd never let her think that it was anything but.

My mom shot me a look. "I'm going to go check on your father."

I nodded, watching her go, before turning back to the girl I couldn't imagine my life without. Did she even know? How much she was in my thoughts, my mind, my heart? She was a deep itch I couldn't possibly scratch, like poison ivy that had seeped under my skin.

She drummed her fingernails on the countertop as I took a deep breath.

"It had been a long time since I'd visited Christmasland, Ivy. Before I'd started college." Before she'd worked there. I tilted up her chin so her eyes would meet mine. "I never lied to you. Not by choice. Maybe I couldn't tell you who I was, but everything else was true. Working my way up through the company meant I made some sacrifices." Twirling a piece of her hair around one of my fingers, I gave her another truth. "I never imagined that I'd find you there. If I had, maybe I wouldn't have spent so long away."

"Okay." She nodded.

"Okay?"

"Yeah." Ivy rested her forehead against my shoulder. "I don't want to fight with you anymore."

I chuckled. "I like it when you fight with me, Poison Ivy. Your claws are cute."

She grumbled against my shirt before pulling her head back. "Teddy?"

"Mhm?"

"Thank you." She leaned up, pressing her lips against my cheek. "I don't feel like I say it enough."

She didn't need to thank me. I was just giving her everything she deserved. But maybe she didn't see that. Maybe she didn't see herself the way I saw her. I gave her a hesitant smile, shaking my head, but before I could clarify that, my mom came back into the kitchen, my dad in tow.

We all worked in tandem setting the table after dinner was done—even Ivy, despite my mom's insistence that guests didn't have to help—before finally sitting down to eat.

"This smells amazing. Thanks, Mom."

"Of course. We're happy to have you both." She smiled at Ivy. "It's nice to see Teddy so happy."

"Mom…" I wasn't usually prone to blushing, but I could feel the warmth in my cheeks.

Ivy reached over, squeezing my hand under the table. I looked over at her, and she raised an eyebrow in a silent question. Like she was asking, *you good?*

I nodded. Did she know how much she calmed me? How much her presence soothed mine? How much I wanted her here?

"Let's dig in."

Squeezing Ivy's hand back, I wove my fingers through hers, letting our combined hands rest on my thigh even as we ate.

I didn't let her hand go all night.

8 days until christmas

I was quickly getting used to waking up with Ivy by my side, and I wasn't sure I'd ever slept as well as I did knowing she was in my arms.

And it wasn't just because we were trading orgasms or she fit perfectly nestled in front of me. It was dangerous how easily she fit into my life. Seeing her in my parent's house last night had been too good.

Leaving Ivy sleeping, I pressed a kiss to the top of her head before I snuck out to check on Buddy and run some errands. Last night, I'd asked my mom for another favor, and she promised to have everything ready for me today. Luckily, she delivered.

I arrived back at my house with a to-go order from the cafe, two peppermint mochas, and all of the necessary ingredients to check another item off our list.

Ivy was awake but still snuggled under the covers as I came back into my bedroom. It had been snowing on my way back, so even though I'd taken my truck, I was still dusted with a light coating of snow.

"Morning," my girl said, yawning as she stretched her arms. She'd pulled on another one of my t-shirts, and I wasn't sure I was going to get any of them back at this point. I also wasn't sure I cared. Ivy looked better in them, anyway.

"I brought breakfast," I said, holding up the bag as I set the coffee carrier on my nightstand.

She inhaled deeply. "Oooh. Smells delicious."

I bent down to put the bag in front of her, and she reached up, running her fingers through my hair. A satisfied hum went through my body from her touching me, and she blushed.

"Sorry, you just had some snow…"

Grabbing her hand, I kissed her knuckles. "I like it when you touch me, Ivy."

She blushed harder, the tips of her ears turning pink, and I traced them with my finger. She shuddered, and I had to pull myself away. Feeding her was my first priority. I pulled out two croissant sandwiches and then handed her the hot cup.

Ivy groaned as she inhaled the scent. "You're not real. I swear. I'm going to wake up one day, and this will all be a dream. It's much too good to be true."

"Better get used to it, baby."

She looked down at her lap, taking a bite of her sandwich before looking at me again. "What are we doing today?"

"Gingerbread houses. Thought we'd mark it off the list."

"Oh, do we have to bake all the pieces of the house, too?"

"Why, because you liked baking cookies so much?" I waggled my eyebrows, thinking about what had happened the last time we were in the kitchen, covered in flour.

Ivy gave me a coy expression. "Well…"

I laughed. "Unfortunately, not today. Mom did that for us."

"Really? Oh. That was nice of her."

Bumping my shoulder into Ivy's, I gave her a smile. "She liked you." They'd talked all through dinner, and it had been like prying them apart at the end of the night.

"I liked her too." She looked at me, so much vulnerability showing through her eyes. "I always imagined what it would be like to have a mom, but I... never imagined someone like her."

"She's the best," I said, meaning every word. "Sure, she's a little overbearing sometimes, but I know how much she loves me."

Ivy sighed, and I wrapped my arms around her, kissing the top of her head. I could almost feel her retreating, withdrawing in on herself.

"It's okay, you know," I whispered.

She twisted her head, looking up at me. "What's okay?"

"To grieve what you never had. To be sad that you missed out on all of this."

"I am," she admitted. "I hate that I didn't get to experience all of this growing up. But you know something?"

"What?"

"I'm glad I get to do all of this with you." A warm smile filled her face. "I think that maybe Christmas means something more with the right person by your side."

"And I'm the right person?"

She blushed again. "I don't know." She paused. "Maybe. Is that crazy?"

I slid my hand around to the back of her neck, kissing her deeply without warning. "I don't know, sweetheart. Does that feel crazy to you?"

"N-no."

Running my tongue over my bottom lip, I went back to eating my food, willing my body not to react. "Exactly."

Hours later, after we had finished breakfast and showered, the sun was high in the sky, making the world a glittering white. It had stopped snowing, leaving an undisturbed layer of powder on top of the several feet of snow that was already there.

Ivy came up behind me, wrapping her arms around my chest and resting her chin against my shoulder. "Whatcha looking at, Theodore?"

"Perfect snowman weather," I said, enjoying the feel of her body pressed against my back.

She hummed, nuzzling into the back of my red flannel. "But it's so warm and cozy inside."

"Well, we'll have to save it for another day then, won't we? We have to check it off the list, sweetheart."

"Teddy."

"Mhm?"

Ivy's voice was soft. "What happens when we check everything off the list?"

I blinked in surprise, turning around to pull her into my arms. "Then I've given you the perfect Christmas, right?"

"Well..." She looked hesitant. "I suppose."

"Okay." I tilted her chin up with my thumb. "Then let's go make that gingerbread house so you can have the best Christmas, hm?"

"Okay," Ivy nodded, and I slipped my hand into hers as I guided her into the kitchen.

I'd already set up all of our supplies—freshly made gingerbread shaped into walls, roofs, and all manner of things we needed for our house, icing made to the perfect consistency to stick it all together, and varying candies to decorate with. There were peppermints, tiny candy canes, gumdrops, red and green M&Ms, and gummy bears.

"What are the bears for?" Ivy asked, raising an eyebrow.

I picked one up, popping it into my mouth. "To eat. Mom always said it was better not to eat the decorations, and she was right. But maybe it's just because I had a bottomless stomach when I was younger. Still, it's always good to have snacks."

"Should we open a bottle of wine, too?"

"Good idea." I kissed her cheek, heading into the fridge to grab one. Thankfully, I'd spent enough time with her now to know what she liked and grabbed one out and poured us both a glass before returning to the table.

Ivy was sitting on one of the chairs, with her legs crossed as she studied the gingerbread pieces in front of her.

"Need help?"

"Nope." She popped the p, taking the wineglass from my hand and taking a sip. "I think I can assemble a gingerbread house, babe."

Chuckling, I sat down next to her, drinking my own wine as I watched her start to assemble the walls. I helped here and there—mostly to hold things up with her instruction—but let her run the show. This was for her, after all. How many gingerbread houses had I built in my life? Dozens. It had been one of my favorite memories when I was younger.

Ivy shrieked as the roof slid down. "Noooo!"

I couldn't stop laughing. "You gotta use more icing, sweetheart."

She furrowed her brows, huffing. "This isn't supposed to be *that* hard."

"Come on, let me show you how the master does it." I took the icing from her hands, spreading it over the sides of the roof panel before holding it to the top.

"Oh, a *master*, huh?" There was a hint of a smile on her face.

Smirking, I crossed my arms over my chest. "I'll have you know I got first place in the annual North Pole Gingerbread House contest for five years in a row."

"Only five?" She poked me in the arm. "You're slacking, Theodore Claus."

"That was before I was put in the adult age category," I said with a shrug. "After that, the stakes were even higher.

And after I got to college, I didn't enter as much anyway. I had a lot more going on."

The roof was now fully attached, and I handed her back the bag so she could start to decorate it.

Ivy bit her lip in concentration as she drew details onto the gingerbread, stopping every few seconds to add an M&M in a pattern on the roof.

"Looks good."

"Yeah? Because I was kinda winging it." She wrinkled her nose.

I pulled her into my lap, pressing a kiss to her cheek. "I couldn't even tell."

She laughed harder, the sound filling my heart, and there was no way I'd trade this moment. Not for the world.

TWO HOURS LATER, our gingerbread house sat on the counter, dusted in a coat of powdered sugar to make it look like it had just snowed. I'd added shredded coconut to the bottom, and thought it looked pretty amazing.

"Look at that. Another item to check off the list."

"Mhm." She leaned back against my chest. We'd finished off the entire bottle of wine between the two of us, and Ivy hadn't moved from my lap.

She wiggled her hips backward, rubbing over my already half-hard cock, and then giggled.

"Ivy," I warned. I'd been doing my best the entire time she'd been sitting on my lap to control myself, but that resistance was slowly slipping away.

She hummed, rolling the icing bag between her hands, her tongue swiping over her lips. "What?"

"Give that to me."

"What, this?" She fluttered her eyelashes, squeezing a dollop of icing onto her finger and then licking it off. "It's sweet."

A groan slipped from my lips. Her lips were pink, begging for mine, but I had plans for her. "Take off your top. Show me those pretty tits, baby."

"Naughty." Ivy wiggled her eyebrows, her tongue running over her lower lip as she toyed with the bottom of her sweater. "You're a little naughty, aren't you, Theodore?"

"Only for you," I grumbled. "Now, off."

Ivy complied, pulling it off and dropping the garment onto the kitchen floor. Flicking open her bra, I let her breasts spring free, baring those pink nipples to me.

"Beautiful." My mouth watered, but I wanted to punish her for torturing me.

She whimpered when I didn't touch her, rocking against me.

"Patience." I flicked my tongue over her ear, standing up and holding her against me, grabbing the icing bag from the table before carrying her into my room.

The place that was starting to feel like *our* room. If she left, if this was all the time we had together, could I be in here without thinking of her? Sleep in my bed without wishing she was next to me? Her sweet, cookie scent was everywhere like it somehow permeated every wall of my house without me even realizing it.

"What are you doing?" Ivy asked as I set her on the bed before picking up the icing.

Smirking, I squeezed a drop of icing out of the bag. "Tasting you."

Her strawberry blonde hair was spread out around her, and she was looking up at me with those beautiful blue eyes as I covered her nipples in icing, coating her skin with the sweet, sticky substance.

Dipping my head down, I captured one of them with my mouth, dragging my tongue over her nipple.

"*Teddy.*" Ivy moaned as I swirled my tongue around, licking the icing off her skin.

I groaned at the taste. "You're a dream, sweetheart."

A dream I never could have imagined. Dragging my teeth across her skin, I sucked her other nipple into my mouth, lavishing her with attention as I licked the icing off of her body.

Her little sounds only succeeded in spurring me on, and she writhed against the sheets, my body on top of hers as I licked each drop of sweetness off her body, swirling my tongue over each hardened bud.

When they were finally clean, I could tell Ivy was close, and I placed kisses up her chest and on her collarbone. Finding her lips, I kissed her deeply, letting her taste the icing on my tongue.

"I need you," she pleaded when we broke apart. "Please."

"Baby," I responded, tugging her leggings down her legs. "I'm all yours." I'd give her anything she wanted. Whatever she needed.

Freeing myself, I positioned myself over her entrance. With one last swipe of my tongue against her nipple, I pushed in, burying myself in her body in one thrust.

A surge of rightness spread through my body.

Mine. She was mine. Ivy was mine.

And there was no way I was letting her go. Not a chance. I'd do whatever it took to convince her to stay.

Whatever it took to keep her.

19
ivy

7 days until christmas

*T*eddy was working with his dad today—something about the factory that I'd tuned out—so I'd decided to go into town by myself to explore. Teddy had given me a house number where my grandma lived, though I hadn't decided what to do with it yet. It was one thing to know that you had family and another to actually show up and introduce yourself.

Would she not want to see me because of my mom? It seemed like they'd been estranged after she left. Did my family know I existed? Would they want a relationship with me?

Throwing my hair up into a high ponytail, I pulled on a cozy sweater dress and a pair of tights I'd brought with me, as well as my new pair of fuzzy boots with little pompoms. I'd spent the morning lazing around Teddy's house, trying to work up my courage to do the thing.

Finally, I gave in and wandered into town, which was luckily only a few minutes walk from Teddy's house. The Christmas Market was still set up, so I wandered through it, enjoying a nice mocha while browsing the different stalls. I'd already had a warm, fresh waffle drizzled with chocolate and caramel, which I was pretty sure was one of the best things I'd ever eaten.

It felt like everyone who lived here must have had some sort of skill or craft, making the selection of handmade items absolutely incredible. Not to mention all the food stalls. I imagined myself set up, selling things I'd made with my own little booth next Christmas. It was a nice dream, warm and fuzzy, with Teddy by my side. If only it was real.

Because it was just a dream.

"Ivy!" Someone shouted my name, and I turned. I was surprised to see Scarlett, our waitress from the diner when I'd first arrived. I'd seen her around, but hadn't had too many chances to talk to her.

"Oh! Scarlett. Hi," I said to her, stopping on the sidewalk as she hurried to catch up with me. "I didn't realize anyone would recognize me."

She looked shocked. "Of course! How could we not? How have you been settling in?" she asked, giving me a warm smile.

"Oh, I'm not... I'm just visiting for Christmas."

"Really?" Scarlett frowned. "I thought... Well, it doesn't matter." She looped her arm through mine. "What brings you into town?"

"Teddy went to help his dad with something at the factory, so I thought I'd take the time to explore."

Her arm was looped through mine like we were best friends and not practical strangers. But maybe that was the way it was up here. We walked through the market, her pointing out different stalls and telling me about the people who worked there, and me asking her questions about the North Pole.

"Can I ask you a question?" I asked, fiddling with the piece of paper in my pocket.

Scarlet nodded.

I pulled it out, showing her the piece of paper with my grandma's name on it. The backside had her address. "Do you know her?"

She made a weird face, raising an eyebrow. "Ivy, that's my grandma."

I froze. "No way." Of all the people in the North Pole, that meant... "Did Teddy tell you?"

"Tell me what?"

"My mom passed away when I was younger, and I never knew my dad. Until this week, I didn't even know I was from here. But I... Teddy's dad gave me the address to my grandmother's house. Which means we're..."

Cousins. She was my cousin?

"Oh." Scarlett's eyes widened, and then she squealed. "No, I had no idea. Oh my gosh! This is so exciting." Her arms wrapped around me, and then I was being hugged. By my cousin.

It was a little crazy how the world worked.

"I can't believe this," I said, laughing. "All this time, and I had a cousin." My eyes filled with tears as she held me tighter.

When we pulled away, she was also a little teary-eyed. "Wow. Do you want to go meet her?"

"Oh, I..." Was I ready for that? This was already a little overwhelming.

"We can go another day. I'll go with you." Scarlett squeezed my hand.

I nodded. "Yeah, I think I'd like that. Thank you."

She winked. "No problem, *cousin.*"

"That's going to take some getting used to," I said with a laugh. "I've never had a cousin before."

We continued walked through the stalls together. Since I'd already done a decent amount of shopping, I was just taking this time to appreciate all the work that went into the market.

"Is that your husband?" I asked, watching as the red-haired elf beside me's eyes lit up as they landed on a dark-haired man. He was working at one of the booths, selling hand-carved items.

She smiled. "Yeah. That's my Jack." Scarlett blew him a kiss. "He's my mate."

"Huh?" I asked, not sure I'd heard her right.

"Elves don't just marry," she informed me. "We mate for life."

"They—what?" My eyes felt like they were bulging. "*Mate?*"

Scarlett nodded. "I'm sure you know by now that magic runs through these lands. It's how, well… this place came to be. Our magic strengthens the barrier surrounding the North Pole, keeping out those who do not understand." She blew out a breath. "The same magic ties us together. Those bonds of fate provide us with our mates. Like a shimmering, golden thread, tying us together."

"Soulmates," I breathed out.

"In a way, yes." She cocked her head to the side. "You didn't know? Teddy didn't…"

"No." I was sure my cheeks were pink, but I hoped I could blame that on the cold nipping at my face instead of the embarrassment I felt at not knowing my own background. "It's not like that between us."

It wasn't, though. Teddy and I weren't soulmates, and we definitely weren't fated to be together. After all, he'd told me about his family, how every Santa had found his Mrs. Claus outside the North Pole... it couldn't be me. Just another reminder that he wasn't for me. I sighed.

She gave me a reassuring pat. "I see."

As if summoned by my thoughts, I spotted Teddy walking towards us. I was surprised to see how close he was standing to a dark-haired woman, having a deep conversation. Looking at them, it was obvious how much they fit like there was a closeness there that couldn't be forced.

Why was it so unsettling? He wasn't *mine*. Sure, we were sleeping together, but what was this discomfort bubbling up in my chest?

"I should go," Scarlett said, giving me another squeeze. "Tell Teddy I say hello." I gave her a nod, and my new cousin left, heading towards the booth where her husband—her *mate* —stood.

When she approached him, he wrapped his arms around her, swaying them softly back and forth. He looked at her with so much love, and I... I wanted that.

Wanted to know what it was like to be loved so deeply.

My cheeks flushed as I watched Teddy approach.

We couldn't be, and yet...

The girl he was with peeled off, waving goodbye, and then it was just Teddy and I standing in the middle of the street. I wrapped my arms around my middle, watching him. Was it stupid to feel insecure? Yes.

But I did.

"Who is she?" I asked, biting my lip.

"Why? Are you jealous?" Teddy asked, a big stupid grin curling over his handsome face.

Damn him. Why did he have to be so hot?

"What?" I said, feeling my cheeks warm. "No, I'm not jealous. Why would I be jealous? I don't care who you talk to or where you've—"

His warm hand slid into my hair, his thumb resting against my jaw.

"She's my cousin, Ivy."

I blinked at him. "Your…"

"Yes." He nodded.

"But…" I scrambled, my brain running at a hundred miles per hour. "How?"

"What do you mean, how? Do you need me to explain how genealogy works?" He tilted his head to the side like there wasn't a smirk glued to his lips.

"No, I just… She's an *elf.* You're… human."

"I am. But her mother and my father are siblings. She's half, just like you."

"Oh." I bit my lip. "So you're not…"

"The only woman I'm interested in spending time with is *you,* my Poison Ivy." He pressed a kiss to my forehead. "Now, what were you up to in town?"

"I thought I'd explore while you were busy with your dad. I ran into Scarlett from the diner."

"Oh?" He cocked his head to one side.

I frowned. "You knew."

"Knew what?"

"That she was my cousin."

"Oh." Teddy brushed a piece of hair off my cheek, tucking it behind my ear. He ran a finger down the point, making a shudder run through my body. It was incredible how sensitive they were, and his touch just reminded me of last night. "I didn't want to ruin the surprise."

I looked away, trying to hide my blush.

"Ivy." He interlocked our fingers, tugging me towards him and distracting me from my thoughts. "Come with me. I want to show you something."

"Okay," I agreed.

Maybe it was time to admit to myself that I'd follow him anywhere he asked. Even if that scared the hell out of me.

MY EYES WIDENED as I took in the sight in front of me. From the top floor of the factory, as far as the eye could see, there were toys and little workstations.

"No *way*."

He hummed. "I thought you'd appreciate it."

Wandering around, I picked up a little soft baby doll from the station next to me. "Yeah. This is wonderful."

He smiled, and I moved towards him, wrapping my arms around his neck. "You're wonderful," I admitted.

"Oh? I thought you didn't like me, my sweet Poison Ivy?"

I punched him in the shoulder, though my fist didn't even seem to phase him because he just kept grinning at me.

"Why are you still smiling?" I frowned.

He leaned down, his lips close to my ear as he said, "Haven't you learned by now that I like when you're feisty, sweetheart? When you have those little claws out?"

I rolled my eyes. "You're insufferable."

"Nah. You like it."

I did.

Shrugging my shoulders, I turned to the toys, running my fingers over the little details the elves had created.

Teddy seemed to read my mind, watching me inspect the space. "The elves who work here are all paid well."

"I always just imagined elves were all children." But that was the farthest from the truth.

He laughed. "The kids up here are more focused on playing with toys than making them."

"As they should be," I muttered. "Kids back home are so focused on growing up I think they miss out on being a kid."

"Was that how it was for you?" Teddy asked. When I turned to look at him, I found him leaning against a table, watching me.

I bit my lip. "I don't know. Maybe it was. My childhood definitely wasn't typical." A sigh slipped from my lips. "Sometimes I just can't help but wonder what it would have been like if I hadn't lost my mom. If she would have brought me back here and raised me with my cousin and my family. Or would we have stayed in Florida? I don't know what brought her there or how she even met my father. But I can't imagine how she loved him enough to leave this place. It's *magical*." Wonderful. I never wanted to leave.

Teddy stood, wrapping his arms around me. "It really is." There was a twinkle in his eye, and I leaned up, pressing my lips to his.

"Come on."

"Where are we going now?" I whispered, even though we were alone inside the factory.

He turned, a little smirk on his face. "You'll see."

20
teddy

*W*hat is this?" Ivy asked, looking around the room.

I scratched my chin. "You know about the naughty and nice list, right?"

She nodded. "Sure. Who doesn't?"

"This is it."

It was a reminder that one day, all of this would be mine to take over. Somehow, the idea of the impossibly big shoes I would one day have to fill didn't fill me with as much apprehension as usual. Maybe it was because I had Ivy by my side now. Everything felt different.

Her mouth formed a little 'o' as she surveyed the walls. "But this place is…"

"Records of all the children of the world."

"This is insane."

She was right. There were more records in here than any one person in their life could ever read. Not to mention, no one could explain how they came here. It wasn't like there were thousands of elves scattered across the world, entering data into tablets as they watched children. No, the answer was plain and simple: *magic*.

In the middle of the room sat the console that collected and analyzed all the data, though it still had to be checked twice each year for errors. Guiding her to it, I explained its history and how it worked.

"So you really want to take over all of this someday? You never considered anything else?"

Running my fingers through my hair, I looked away. "Of course I did." I'd gone to college like a normal kid, and I'd thought about it. What it would be like to walk away. To leave this life behind. "But I can't imagine not being here. Not raising my kids here. Even if I never became Santa Claus, I love the North Pole."

"Right." She turned away, gnawing on her lower lip. Was that too much to process?

"Teddy." Ivy's voice was barely a whisper. "What are we doing?"

"Having fun. What else would we be doing?"

"I just… What happens when I go home?"

I frowned. "What do you mean?"

"It's not like we're going to be in a long-distance relationship. And I know you're only at Christmasland temporarily. So whatever this is between us…" She shook her head. "It doesn't have to mean anything."

My heart sank. It was a reminder that this wasn't permanent. That she still didn't feel like this place could be her home.

A low growl slipped free from my throat. "What do you mean, it doesn't have to mean anything, Ivy? This doesn't mean anything to you?"

"No, I just want to make sure we're on the same page."

"*No?*" She didn't say anything, and what else was there? She was right. We weren't in a relationship. "Right." I stood up, running my hands through my hair. "So I can fuck you, but nothing more?"

"Teddy, I—"

"It's fine. I get it. This doesn't mean anything to you." Not like it did to me.

"That's not what I'm saying at all—"

I let out a deep sigh, smoothing my hand over my face in frustration. "Why do you even want to go back there? What's so great about your life?"

"Hey! I like my life."

"Do you?" I raised an eyebrow.

Ivy closed her arms over her chest, glaring at me. "Yes."

"Because it seems like you're alone. No family, no friends. Living by yourself…" I scrunched my nose, realizing I'd just described my life, too.

Why would I ever want to go back to that after finding her?

"I have friends," she said, offended. "Besides, what else would I do? Stay *here*?"

"Why not?" I asked, my voice quiet. Why couldn't she imagine it?

"Teddy." She looked shocked. "You can't be serious. What would I even do here?"

"You belong here." With her family. With me.

Ivy shook her head. "Do I? Because it all feels too good to be true. I'm just waiting for the other shoe to drop. Honestly… I'm scared. *Terrified.*"

"You never have to be scared of me, sweetheart. I'm not going to hurt you."

Her eyes were glassy. "How do you know that? You can't. Just like my parents…" She shook her head. "I can't lose anyone else. Not again."

I ran my hand down her hair. "You can't live your life like

that, Ivy. Protecting your heart from hurt… It also keeps you from experiencing love, too."

And I knew I was falling in love with her. That I had been. But the clock was ticking. I only had one week left with her.

But if she didn't love me back, if she left… That would be it. It would be over.

And I'd have to live the rest of my life knowing that this wasn't enough for her. That *I* wasn't enough for her. Because it wasn't just sex for me or about her list. It never had been.

"Poison Ivy," I murmured, twirling a piece of her hair around my finger. "Just give me a chance, okay? Give *us* a chance."

She nodded.

"Come on," I said, tugging her hand.

"Where are we going?" She raised an eyebrow.

Looking out the window, I pointed at the snow. "Outside. We're long overdue for building that snowman."

HOURS LATER, I sat at my desk in the workshop, staring at the corkboard in my office. All of my plans, everything I'd been working so hard to achieve all of these years… and suddenly, it didn't feel like any of them mattered.

All I could think about was her.

Ivy, sleeping in my bed. Ivy, the way she looked each morning when she opened her eyes, a sleepy smile curled over her face when she saw me. Ivy, who I'd left to wrap Christmas presents because she'd shooed me out to wrap in secret.

Ivy, who I couldn't imagine my life without.

There was a black velvet box in my top desk drawer, something I'd picked up on the way here, but was it crazy?

Maybe what was crazier was the idea that I would give all of this up in a heartbeat if she didn't want to stay. That I'd follow her anywhere she wanted to go. I didn't need to follow in dad's footsteps someday. What I needed was Ivy. Her laugh. Her smile. Those beautiful blue eyes locked on mine. Losing myself in her, in her body, every night. The future I couldn't stop dreaming of.

It was too soon, and yet, how could I think of anything else?

"Son." He rapped his knuckles against the doorframe. My dad's warm, booming voice filtered into the room, and I looked up in surprise from my desk.

"Hey, Dad."

"What are you still doing here? Everyone else went home hours ago." He was wearing a red snowflake patterned sweater with a pair of black pants, and despite his hair being completely white, he was still in pretty good shape for his age. Of course, he had to be.

I shrugged, tugging at the dark green sweater around my neck. "It's busy season." There were a million things to get done, and he knew it. "Trying to finish up these reports." Plus, I'd been finishing my proposals for the park. Christmasland was important to Ivy, which made it even more important to me.

My dad frowned. "Teddy…"

"I know, I know." I let out a sigh. "It's just…" Things were moving so fast. Too fast for Ivy? Because I knew in my heart it wasn't too fast for me. Not when she'd be gone in a week if I didn't do something different.

I ran my thumb over the snowflake earrings I'd gotten her at the market. The ones that matched that pendant she wore around her neck.

The perfect gift to show her how she belonged here. Her

dream all along had been a family, and she had that here, right?

He cleared his throat, distracting me from my train of thought. "You're different," my father mused.

"Huh?"

"With her. You're different with her. Happier."

I couldn't deny that. "I care about her. A lot." It was too soon to say the l-word, even if I was feeling it. I didn't trust my emotions yet. I let out a groan as I let my head fall back against the chair. "But... What if she doesn't want to stay? What if she doesn't want *me*, Dad?"

"Your mother was like that too," he chuckled. "Even though we'd been dating for some time, when I told her the truth of who I was... she broke up with me. Told me I was *crazy*. That I'd manipulated her feelings. All the things I'd done for her, well... it was a long road to where we are now, but it was worth it. She was worth it." He gave a contented sigh, running his fingers over his white beard, and then his gaze sharpened to me. "So don't mess this up. Don't let her go, Teddy."

"I don't want to. But it's different with us. She belongs here."

"That she does." He nodded. "I'm glad I pushed you two kids together. Without that, you might never have met."

"Wait." I froze. "Dad." Letting out a slow groan, I stared over at him. "You've known all along who she was. Did you have me bring her here so that I could *date her?*"

That was fucked up. I never would have agreed if I'd realized he was just trying to marry me off. Had he realized it that very first phone call?

"Oh." He did his best to look innocent. "Not *exactly*."

"*Dad.*" Narrowing my eyes at him, I crossed my arms over my chest. "What are you up to?"

"Nothing." He whistled, running his hands over his white beard. My father had a sly expression on his face.

I glared at him. Leaning my head back against the chair, I looked up at the ceiling. Should I have just let her be?

No. I couldn't stand seeing the Christmas Spirit ruined, and the North Pole was her home. I'd make her see it.

That was what my plan had been all along. To make her fall in love with it, and then maybe she'd be convinced to stay. And if not, I'd take her back to her empty, crappy apartment in Florida. What was left for her there?

I just had to make her believe in us.

I closed the book in front of me, feeling a new resolve. "Alright, well, I'm going to go home." Standing up, I moved to grab my coat.

"If you give her your heart, Teddy, I promise you won't regret it."

I shook my head. "How can you be so sure? What if I give it to her, and she gives it right back?"

I didn't know how I'd survive.

It was funny because I told her the same thing earlier. That she couldn't hold herself back from experiencing love because she was scared. Was I doing that?

"Love is always a risk, Theodore. But it's worth it." A smile curled over my dad's face. "You'll see."

I groaned, but maybe he was right.

Because Ivy… Ivy was definitely worth it.

21
ivy

6 days until christmas

S tanding in front of the red door of a cozy-looking house with a tin of cookies in hand, I gnawed on my lower lip. *I could do this.* My grandmother—Ginger—lived right outside of town. Though my grandfather had long since passed away, she still lived in the same house where they'd raised my mom.

Scarlett had insisted she could come with me, but some part of me felt like I needed to do this alone. Though it was thanks to Teddy that I was here. Like he was lending me his strength. His belief in me spoke magnitudes.

Yesterday had been hard. But when I'd tried to push him away, he'd held me tighter. And then we'd built a snowman, and everything else had melted away.

But I wasn't here for Teddy. I was here for myself—to gain a piece of *me* back that I'd been missing my whole life.

Finally, I knocked, and a few moments later the door opened.

"Hello, dear," she said, adjusting the glasses sitting on her face. "How can I help you?" Her grayed hair was pulled back, showing her age.

"Hi," I squeaked, suddenly forgetting everything I wanted to say. "I'm Ivy. Ivy Winters." I extended out the cookie tin. "I brought these for you." I squeezed my eyes shut. "I'm your granddaughter. Can I come in?"

If she was surprised by that, she didn't so much as balk. Instead, she opened up the door wider, taking the cookies from me. "Come on in, sweetheart. I've been expecting you."

"You have?" I blinked, trying not to let tears fill my eyes.

She gave me a warm smile, leading me into a cozy living room. It smelled homey and welcoming, like something was baking in the oven. "Oh, yes. Nick told me all about you." Setting the cookies down, she turned towards me.

"I'm sorry I didn't come sooner," I said, the words spilling out of me.

My grandma shook her head. "You never have to apologize to me, my sweet girl. I'm just glad you're here now." She wrapped me up in a hug, her warmth surrounding me. I'd never known this kind of love before. Unconditional. Like she accepted me completely without a single explanation.

"I've always thought I was alone in the world," I whispered into her hug. "That I didn't have anyone. A family." Tears streamed down my face, and I was glad she was holding onto me so tightly so I could cry freely.

Her hand smoothed down my hair. "I wish we had known about you, dear. I'm so sorry you had to grow up all alone."

She held me like that for a few minutes until my tears turned into sniffles. "I wish I'd known about *you*."

"Do you want to sit? I can make you a cup of hot apple cider." She nodded to the couch before heading into the kitchen.

Settling onto the plush couch, I ran my fingers over a plaid sherpa throw as I took in my surroundings. Her house was eclectic, filled to the brim with decor—plates that featured puppies in Santa hats, and a collection of snowmen on her mantle—and yet it was perfect. If I'd have ever imagined my grandmother's house before, I would have hoped it was like this.

"Here you are," she said a few moments later as she handed me a mug.

"Thank you."

She settled on the couch next to me, smoothing her skirt over her lap. "I had twin daughters, you know. Juniper and Rose. They were inseparable growing up. Did everything together. It shouldn't surprise me they both gave me such beautiful granddaughters."

I blushed, not sure how to respond to that. "Do you... know what happened? How she met my dad?" I'd lost them both so young that I'd never gotten to hear their story. How they'd fallen in love.

"Your mother..." she sighed. "Well, Juniper wanted a different life." I nodded at her. I'd gathered that much, at least. "A lot of the elves here never leave the North Pole. We have little reason to. But your mom, she dreamed of seeing the world. Of experiencing what was outside of our little bubble. So she left. Stowed away in the middle of the night, determined to find something for herself.

"She sent me letters, at first. Meeting Joseph. How happy he made her. He was in the military, and they fell in love quickly. She wrote to me, told me how she planned to marry him. He might not have been an elf, but she felt that connection with him."

"They were mates?" I guessed.

My grandma nodded. "At least, she suspected so. But

elves who spend too much time outside the North Pole lose their magic."

"What?" My jaw dropped open. "But what about me?" I looked down at my hands. "I lived outside the North Pole my whole life, and I'm fine, aren't I?"

"I can only assume that she gave up whatever was left when she had you." She gave me a sad smile. "When your dad passed away... it would have broken her. Living without your mate... That's not a fate I'd wish on anyone." Her hand pressed over her heart. "Even now, I miss my Rudy. But I had so many years with him." She gave me a sad smile. "How did she pass?"

"Cancer," I said, my eyes filling with tears. "I was five. My dad passed away a two years before that in an accident."

Her hand slid onto my knee, squeezing softly. "She loved him so much, you know. And I'm sure she loved you even more."

"The only thing I have left of her is this necklace." I pulled it out from underneath my sweater. I'd stolen one of Teddy's again, because it brought me comfort. If I took a deep breath, his scent still clung to it, like pine trees and spice.

Her eyes sparkled. "Oh. We got her that for her eighteenth birthday."

Somehow, it was even more special now knowing its origin. That it came from my family. One I still had.

"Can you tell me more about her?"

Her eyes sparkled with understanding. "What do you want to know?"

I took a deep breath. "Everything."

178

5 days until christmas

Two days had passed since Teddy had asked me to give him a chance. *It also keeps you from experiencing love, too.* My heart had swelled with the possibility.

But it was too soon. And then I'd be leaving, anyway.

So I'd avoided bringing up the future again. Instead, we'd focused on the list. Presents were wrapped under the tree. A snowman sat in front of the house, wearing one of Teddy's scarves. And every night, without fail, we lost ourselves in each other's bodies.

The sex was amazing. I'd never been able to deny that. But I couldn't deny that I was using it to avoid the more serious conversations we needed to have.

Where was this going? Where did I want it to go? The ball was in my court.

And Teddy was... everything. Everything I'd never let myself want. Because having something meant you could lose it, right? Like I'd lost my parents.

I twiddled the snowflake necklace on its chain as I sat at Teddy's living room table, working on a handmade gift for Scarlett. It was still so surreal to me that she was my cousin. Yesterday, while I'd been talking to my grandma, Scarlett had come over, and she'd told us both countless stories about our moms. We were fast friends.

It was filling a hole in my heart. A hole that had been there for a long, long time.

"Ivy?" Teddy called, traipsing through the house.

"In here!" I called back, adjusting my position on the chair.

There was snow in his hair, and his cheeks were red from the cold, but I still thought he was the most handsome man I'd ever seen. Even if he lived in the North Pole and had a reindeer named Buddy.

God, I adored him. What was wrong with me? How come I couldn't just admit it?

He bent his head down, dropping a kiss on my lips. "Hello."

"Mmm. What was that for?" Though I was all too happy to be kissing him any time, without complaint.

"I have a surprise for you," Teddy said with a grin.

Raising an eyebrow, I tried not to show my excitement. "You know how many times you've said that to me?"

"Yeah, well, this time I mean it."

Not saying anything else, Teddy grabbed my coat off the hook, opening it for me. I raised an eyebrow, but he just held it up, and I faced the wall, hoping he didn't notice the way my cheeks warmed from the action as I pushed my arms into the fabric. He slid it onto my shoulders before kissing my neck, inhaling deeply.

"Come on. She's outside."

"*She?*" I asked, wrapping my new scarf around my neck. "What do you mean, she—"

Buddy was standing out front, nuzzling another reindeer.

"Who's this?" I asked, walking over to the second one and rubbing my hand up her nose. She was just as soft as Buddy, though her coloring was slightly lighter and her frame a little smaller.

"She's yours."

I turned to him with my jaw open. "Sorry. Hold on. You got me my own reindeer?"

Yes, because this was the craziest thing to happen to me while staying in the North Pole, I thought to myself.

"You can't just... *give* me a reindeer, Teddy." Not when I wasn't even sure I was going to stay. What if I went home and had to say goodbye?

Teddy walked over to us, and smoothed his hands over

the reindeer's back. "I thought it would be easier. Then you can come and go without having to walk into town. I know you've been visiting with Scarlett and your grandmother."

I rested my hand over his heart. "Teddy, this is too much."

"No, it's not." He cupped my cheek. "Not for you."

Standing on my tiptoes, I threw my arms around him and kissed him. Deeply. It was the best way I could think of to show him how much I loved this gift. Even if I thought it was insane.

"They're a bonded pair, you know," Teddy said after we pulled apart, looking between the two animals. "Her and Buddy."

"What's her name?"

He smirked. "Clarice."

"No way." There must have been something in my eye. It was perfect. Absurd but perfect. "You're insane, do you know that?"

"I might have been told that once or twice." He wrapped his arms around my waist. "Come on, Poison Ivy, say thank you."

I rolled my eyes. "Thank you, Teddy. She's perfect."

"Want to go for a ride?"

4 days until christmas

Ugly Christmas Sweater Party was an understatement. Whatever I'd expected, it hadn't been this. And I loved every bit of it.

The entire town was gathered in the school's gym, though

the place had been turned into a winter wonderland and was barely recognizable. Apparently, they did this every year as a fundraiser for the school. People crammed together, bringing baked goods and dishes, and threw the best holiday party I'd ever seen.

"I love your sweater," Scarlett said, her husband Jack at her side. I'd gotten to know him fairly well, too. They'd both grown up here, going to high school together. The two had eloped after college, and Scarlett had just told me tonight that they were expecting their first baby. I wasn't sure I'd ever seen a couple so happy. That looked so right together.

"Thank you." I looked over at Teddy, who was wearing the same one as mine—just in green. They were ridiculous, but I loved it. We matched, just like a couple.

Maybe there was something to this whole mate business that she'd told me about. But if soulmates were real…

Was it even possible?

My heart yearned for him. If we were mates, what would that change? In my heart, I knew the truth. Everything. It would change everything.

"This party is incredible," I said, gushing for the fifth time. Teddy had left to get us drink refills. "I still can't believe this is all real."

"I'm so glad you're here," Scarlett admitted.

"It has been an amazing trip," I said to Scarlett. "I can't believe Christmas is almost here already."

"And once it's over?" She asked me. "Are you going to go back?"

I worried my lower lip into my mouth. "I don't have any reason to stay." Not yet, anyway.

My cousin furrowed her brows. "Teddy hasn't…"

I shook my head. "No." He hadn't asked me to stay. Not really. He'd asked me to give him a chance, but that wasn't the same thing. I needed the words.

Needed to know what this was for him. Because I knew what it was for me.

That I was falling in love with him. Maybe I'd already fallen, if I was being honest. Somewhere in between cutting down a tree and him giving me a freaking reindeer, I'd been free-falling.

It was just so hard to trust these emotions. To know that he'd catch me. That I could count on this—on us.

"Is that how you really feel?" Teddy asked, a look of utter devastation on his face, two mugs in his hands.

"I don't—" I shook my head. I didn't want to do this here. Not with everyone watching, and listening. "Can we go outside?"

He put the coffee cups down on the table, and I apologized to my cousin and her husband—though the two seemed too happy in their newfound bliss for my disappearance to really affect it—before he took my hand, leading us outside into the Christmas Tree lot.

I could feel the tension radiating off his body, but he didn't say anything even as he kept my hand in his.

"Teddy," I whispered. "Talk to me. Please."

He dropped my hand, pinching his brow before turning away like he couldn't face me. "I thought that maybe..." He gave an exasperated sigh. "Never mind. It's dumb, anyway." Teddy huffed out a breath as he turned back to me, the action pushing the brown strands of hair off his forehead.

Ask me, I wanted to beg. Because as much as I knew I needed to return to my life, something was different here. Something just felt right. And I wanted to understand what that was.

Maybe it was a fluke. But maybe, just maybe...

"You haven't asked," I whispered. "And I... I can't make a decision unless I know what you want. I have a life there." A life I wasn't in any rush to get back to. A life that, without

Sarah, I wouldn't have thought twice about. I was replaceable at Santa's Christmasland, and I knew it. But here…

"You can have a life here, too. With me. Please stay," Teddy begged, stepping up close to me. His hand raised, brushing a strand of hair back behind my ear. "Stay with me."

Shutting my eyes, I let his words rush through me. Did I want that? To stay? *Yes.*

But why couldn't I give him the words?

He seemed to notice my hesitation. I'd tell him soon how I felt. What I wanted. The decision I'd made. But tonight… Tonight, I wanted things to be about him. For him to know how special *he* was. He did his best every day to show me how cherished I was. And he deserved that, too.

"Come on," he said, holding out a hand. "Let's go inside and get out of the cold."

I took it.

"SWEETHEART?" Teddy called from the other room. I'd snuck in here to surprise him after we'd gotten back from the party, wanting to find some way to thank him for everything he'd been doing for me.

The last few hours had been torture. Not being able to leave the party, to reassure Teddy that I didn't want to leave him, to show him how much he meant to me… It was harder than I'd ever imagined.

Luckily, Scarlett had the perfect idea when I'd talked to her earlier, and between all the extra supplies lingering around the house, I'd been able to create the perfect surprise.

Sprawling out across the bed, I propped myself up with an arm, letting my loose hair tumble around my shoulders. A scrap of red fabric covered my bottom half, and I'd found my favorite red fuck-me heels in my suitcase. Where I'd thought I would wear these, I had no idea, but I was glad I had them. I looked *hot*, my lips covered in a deep red, my hair just begging to have his hands buried in it.

"Ivy." Teddy's jaw dropped as he walked in, seeing me ready for him.

I fiddled with the large, red bow I'd tied over my breasts. "Aren't you going to unwrap your present, Theodore?"

"But it's not Christmas yet, sweetheart. And it would be wrong of me to open my gift early, wouldn't it?" He smirked.

"I think Santa could make an exception for you." I traced a finger over my cleavage. "Since you've been such a good boy, haven't you, Teddy?"

"No Santa talk in the bedroom," he muttered, coming to stand in front of me. "I do *not* want to think about my dad when I'm also thinking about the dirty, dirty things I want to do to you."

"Maybe you'll make the naughty list after all." I winked.

"But then I wouldn't get my present, would I, baby?" He leaned close enough that he could whisper the words into my ear before nibbling on the pointed tip with his teeth.

A shudder ran through my body. It was crazy how sensitive my ears were. How just the brush of his finger over them felt like fireworks sparking over my skin.

God, I was wet. The second he touched me he'd realize how much. How much I wanted him. Needed him—this.

"Unwrap me," I whispered. "Touch me. I'm all yours to open."

"You are," he agreed, his voice hardly a murmur. "All mine."

Yes. I was.

Stripping his clothes, he crawled onto the bed in only his boxer briefs—a pair of green and red plaid striped ones with little trees—and then pulled me onto his lap, fiddling with the bow I'd tied over my breasts.

"Fuck, I like this. These pretty little tits, all wrapped up for me."

"Yes," I agreed.

"Makes me wonder what other filthy things I can do to them, Ivy, sweetheart. Maybe one day, you'll let me fuck them."

Nodding instead of answering, I tilted my head back as he pressed a kiss to my neck. "You always smell so damn good, Ivy. Like cookies and all things sweet."

I understood the sentiment perfectly. He smelled like pine trees, and it was almost embarrassing how many times a day I wanted to bury my face in his shirt to breathe in his scent.

"It makes me want to tie you up and never let you go."

"Then do it," I said, moaning as he sucked my sensitive skin into his mouth. "Tie me up. Fuck me hard. Give me *everything*."

He groaned, pulling at the ribbon until my perky tits sprung free. He buried his face in between them, giving them ample attention until I was squirming, painting, and all too aware of the growing wetness between my legs.

Teddy tore the red panties off my body, dropping the scraps onto the ground.

"Fuck," he said, pushing two fingers inside of me. "You're so wet. My naughty girl."

I could barely think as he scissored them inside of me, letting my head fall back as I rode his fingers. Little whimpers slipped free from my throat, and I couldn't control my body's reaction to him. I was so close, so amped up from the way he'd touched me, from everything about him that drove me wild. He was stretching me, filling me with just those magnificent fingers, getting me ready for him.

"Are you going to come all over my fingers, baby?"

Teddy's deep voice said against my ear. He pressed a kiss to my neck, sucking lightly on the spot as his thumb found my clit, and I lost it. I climaxed, my release coating his fingers as he kept working me through it.

He pulled them out, licking them clean as he kept his green eyes pinned to me. Filthy and so goddamn hot. I felt empty immediately, feeling the loss of them inside of me, but I couldn't focus on that for long. Teddy's erection pressed against my still-sensitive clit from my orgasm, and I gasped. He was hard, straining against those boxers, and I wanted— no, needed—him inside of me. Rocking against him again, I let out a low moan.

Slipping my hand inside the material, I palmed his cock, running my hand up and down his length. He was hot and heavy in my hands, hard and yet silky soft as I squeezed his shaft.

"Ivy," he groaned. "If you keep that up, I'm going to come in my pants."

"Then take them off," I said, my voice so husky I barely recognized it.

He complied by shoving them down his hips, repositioning us to get the fabric off his body, and letting his cock spring free. Bending down, I licked the tip, swiping a bead of pre-cum off the top and savoring his salty taste. He was so much bigger than anyone else I'd ever been with, and when I wrapped my hands around his length to fist him again, my fingers could barely wrap all the way around. Teddy grunted, stilling my hands with his. "Sweetheart," he warned. His hands moved down my body like he was exploring every inch with his hands, his fingers curling over my pointy ears before pulling me up so our bodies were lined up.

"Ride me," Teddy said, laying down on his back and pulling me so I sat on his hips. "Let me see those tits bounce for me. I wanna see how your pretty pussy swallows me whole, baby."

"Thought you were gonna tie me up," I teased. But secretly, my pussy clenched at the idea. Why did I like that so much? The idea of him tying me up, made it so I couldn't leave him. Maybe I wanted him to keep me here. The idea of other ways he could keep me here.

"Later." He grinned, his dark brown hair falling onto his forehead as he helped guide me up, lining me up with his cock.

What would it look like for me to stay here? Because I wanted it, *needed* it.

Because I loved him.

I loved him. There was no denying that, even to myself.

Sinking down onto his length, I felt a rush of emotions flow through me, tears pricking at my eyes as he filled me.

"Are you okay, sweetheart?" Teddy asked, tenderly bringing his hand to my eyes and brushing away the tears on my cheeks with his thumb. I nodded. "I didn't hurt you, did I?"

I shook my head. "No." It was the opposite. Everything he'd done for me—he'd been healing my bruised heart. Showing me I could love again. "You didn't hurt me." He couldn't. I knew that now.

Placing my hands on his firm chest, enjoying the feel of his well-defined abs under my fingers, I sank down the rest of the way till I'd taken all of him into my body.

Teddy grunted but held himself still underneath me. Waiting for me to move. Waiting for me to take the lead. He always had, hadn't he? He'd waited for me to to be ready for him. To take those steps toward *us*.

His fingers grasped my hips, digging into my skin as I started to rock my hips against him. I knew it wouldn't take long. Not with this emotion bursting through my chest. Not when he was looking at me with so much care, so much emotion.

"Ivy..." Teddy whispered as I cried out, his hips thrusting up from below to meet me in rhythm. "Let go, baby. It's okay. I'll catch you."

And I knew he would.

I knew he always would.

So I let go.

22
teddy

3 days until christmas

I looked down at Ivy, asleep in my arms, and it felt like all the pieces were falling into place. Like my mind had been this raging, constant blizzard, but now it had calmed. Like, for once, everything felt right in the world. I had the girl in my arms. My girl. And I never wanted to let her go.

In the morning light, the rays streaming in through the open windows, her hair was illuminated like a golden halo with little streaks of red. *Beautiful.* She was beautiful, and she was mine.

Our list was almost done. Christmas was almost over. And what then?

Today, I didn't even want to leave this bed, not after last night. So instead, I held her, my body wrapped tightly around hers. The vulnerability in her eyes as she'd sank down on top of me had almost made me lose it right then and there. To confess how I was feeling, the words I wanted to say.

But it was too early.

Did she suspect what I did? Could she feel that pulsing golden tether between the two of us? How her emotions shone so strongly I could feel them?

Maybe I was imagining it. But all my life, this was how I imagined it would feel when I found my person. *My mate.* Whole and complete. I nuzzled my nose into her neck, inhaling her sugar cookie scent. Ivy didn't even have to try to make me feel like this. She just did.

Ivy's arms tightened around my waist, and I knew she was awake, but neither one of us moved. We both just stayed, wrapped up in each other. Her leg thrown over mine, my morning wood pressed against her stomach, eager to slip back inside of her wet heat.

"Mmm," she hummed as I traced circles on her back, the feel of her bare skin against mine a fucking temptation.

Last night, after she'd come—tits bouncing as she rode me into oblivion, fucking herself on my cock—I hadn't been far behind, and when she'd collapsed onto my chest, pressing kisses to my pecs, it hadn't taken long for me to be ready to go again. I couldn't get enough of her. Would I ever?

I knew the answer without having to ask it. As sure as I knew that what we were to each other was more. No, I'd never get Ivy Winters out of my system. And I didn't care to.

Ivy traced a finger up my cock, the motion making me shudder.

"Good morning," she whispered.

I ran my hands down her back to cup her ass. "It is."

She hummed as I squeezed her cheeks lightly, massaging them with my hands before adjusting the leg she had thrown over mine.

"Are you sore?" I murmured, running a finger up her opening.

"A little." She winced. Maybe the third time last night had

191

been too much, but I hadn't been able to resist taking her from behind, and then I made good on my promise and tied her to the headboard with that fucking red ribbon, leaving her at my mercy.

"I'll go run you a warm bath," I said, kissing her forehead.

"Don't leave," she whispered, tightening her grip around me. "I want to feel you."

I brushed her hair back off her forehead and kissed each cheek. "Are you sure?"

"Uh-huh." She nodded.

Pressing the tip of my cock against her slit, I pushed in just slightly. She was already wet and ready for me, her warmth surrounding the head. But I let her adjust to my size, wanting to go slow.

"Teddy," she gasped, her fingers digging into my shoulders as she held onto me. "How do you always feel so good?"

"Same, sweetheart." She had no fucking idea. I wanted to live inside of her. Bury myself inside of her at all hours of the day. "So fucking tight for me."

She whimpered, rocking her hips like she was trying to force me in deeper. Inch by inch, I slid inside of her, burying myself in her pussy until I was fully seated inside of her, practically kissing her womb.

We stayed like that, front to front, her leg over mine as I stilled myself, trying to let us both get used to the feeling. It was completely different like this. More intimate, with our faces almost touching and her nipples pressed against my chest.

"Fuck," I groaned. It felt too good, her wet heat all around me, and I needed a moment so I didn't spill inside of her like a teenager. I should have been used to this by now, but it felt like something had changed overnight. Everything was different now.

"I can feel you *everywhere*," she gasped, her eyelids fluttering shut. Ivy spread her hand over her stomach like she could feel me inside of her. Thrusting in short, smooth strokes, I pushed in and out of her, careful not to be too rough.

I wondered what it would be like to watch her swell with life. To know that I put it there. To fill her up with my cum, day after day, until she was pregnant and round with our child.

The scene was so erotic, and I could feel myself growing harder as I rocked my hips into her. My balls tightened, and I couldn't keep in my grunt. But I needed her to come first. Always.

"Ivy," I murmured, burying my face in her neck. "Touch yourself. I need—" She wrapped her leg around me, pushing me in deeper, and I groaned. "I need you to get yourself off. Need to feel you clenching around my cock, coming all over me—"

She slipped her hand between us, rubbing circles around her clit, her breaths growing shorter as she got closer. I could feel her squeezing around me, clenching down, and then she spread her fingers into a V, pushing them down so she could feel my cock as I drove in and out of her.

"*Fuck.*"

"Inside me," she said, bringing her lips to my ear. "Come with me, babe." The sensation of her fingers against my cock was too much to handle. She ground her palm against her sensitive bud as she cried out, burying her face in my shoulder and biting down on my skin.

With a roar, I followed behind her, spilling everything I had into her cunt that begged for my seed. Not today, but one day, I'd do just that.

Pulling out, I watched my cum trickle down her thighs, then stand up to go into the bathroom. After cleaning up and starting the bathtub filling it with warm water, and adding a sweet-smelling soothing oil to help relax her sore muscles, I grabbed a warm washcloth and cleaned her up.

"Mmm," she mumbled as I wiped her clean, sounding sleepy and relaxed.

"Come here, sweetheart." I opened my arms. I'd never thought of myself as a cuddler before, but that was before Ivy Winters. Now, all I wanted to do was hold her. To take care of her, whatever way she'd let me. "How about that bath now?"

She nodded, climbing into my open arms and letting me scoop her up to carry her into the bathroom. After letting her slip into the water, a satisfying sigh slipping from her lips, I grabbed us towels before sliding in behind her, wrapping my arms around her wet body.

Ivy leaned her head back against my chest, tilting her head back to look at me. "Thank you," she whispered.

"For what?" I asked, knowing there was a dopey smile on my face.

"You know what."

And I did.

I kissed her forehead. "You're welcome, baby."

Always. I'd always take care of her, just like this.

HOURS LATER, after feeding my starving girl and stopping at the cafe to say hello to her cousin and grab coffees to go, we finally arrived at our destination of the day.

Another surprise on my part, because I hadn't told her where we were going, just to bundle up. She'd worn a pair of denim jeans that hugged her ass and one of the cozy sweaters from my closet, as well as one of the beanies I'd gotten for her when she'd first arrived.

She looked perfect. Like mine.

"What are we doing here?" Ivy asked as I stood in front of the rink, unlocking the fence.

The ice skating rink was quiet—probably because I'd talked my cousin into letting us have it for the night, just the two of us. Ruby had agreed, thankfully, and even the twinkle lights above us were still on.

"I'm taking you skating."

She winced. "In hindsight, I'm not sure this is such a good idea."

"Of course it is, baby. We have to finish the list." I kissed her forehead. "Come on. I'll show you what to do." I'd been skating since I was a toddler. When I was younger, I'd played hockey throughout high school, though I definitely wasn't good enough to play it in college. Still, I loved it. The rush on the ice, feeling the wind whipping through your face as your skates glided along. "You'll see."

Ivy sat on the bench, staring at the ice as she removed her boots. "Are you sure about this? I'm probably going to fall. A lot."

"It's okay." I kneeled in front of her, brushing her hair back behind her pointy ear. "I'll be there to catch you."

"How do you always know just the right thing to say?" Ivy muttered, looking down at her feet.

I grinned. "Just for you, sweetheart."

Unlacing the skates I'd grabbed for her, I helped her into them, tying them tight so they'd be snug on her feet.

Her cheeks flushed pink—and so did her ears—when she looked down at me, kneeling in front of her, and I wondered what naughty thoughts she was thinking about. If she was remembering the time I went down on her on the couch. If I'd told her how many other times I'd thought about it, I'd bet she'd turn even redder.

Sitting next to her and avoiding the temptation, I put my skates on.

"Ready?" I asked, standing up and holding out a hand. She nodded, taking it. I helped her up, wrapping my arms around her as she wobbled a bit, barely avoiding falling onto me. "That's it, sweet Ivy. "

She shook her head. "I'm like a baby deer. I can't even stand up straight."

I brushed a piece of hair behind her ear before adjusting her beanie. "You'll be fine." Leaning in, I kissed her roughly, letting our tongues intertwine and watching the tension pour from her body. She just needed a distraction, that was all. "Come on."

Her dazed eyes snapped to mine, and she nodded, intertwining our fingers as I led her to the side of the rink.

I stepped out onto the ice first, adjusting my stance to turn to face her.

She bit her lip, worrying it into her mouth. "I don't know…"

"Do you need me to kiss you again?" I asked, popping her a flirty smile.

She grunted—though that wasn't a *no,* something I made a mental note of for later—before stepping out onto the ice. I was close enough to grab her hands as she fell, putting her weight onto the second skate. And then, Ivy was on the ice. Well, she was still clutching the wall, but I counted that as a success.

"Now, all you have to do is—" I started, ready to show her how to skate.

"Teddy!" She sounded panicked. She really did look like a baby deer, clinging to the railing on her skates, though she was staying upright just fine.

"That's it, Poison Ivy. You got this." I held my hands open. "Just come toward me and glide on your skates."

Ivy glared at me, her gaze like murder. "If you make me fall, I will kill you."

"No, you won't." I grinned. "You like me too much."

"Do *not*." She huffed out a breath.

Using my magic, I made a blast of air push her off the wall —directly into my waiting arms. I took her hand, skating backward as I showed her how to move her feet.

It only took a few minutes, and we'd already moved halfway around the rink. And I only had to help her stay upright a few times, though our hands had never dropped.

I looked into her eyes, those beautiful ocean blue irises looking back at me. "Look. You're skating."

She laughed. "Huh. I guess I am."

Pulling her into my arms, I twirled her around, and then I kissed her deeply, putting all of my emotions into the kiss.

I hadn't told her how I felt—not yet.

But I would. *Soon.*

I just had to get through Christmas first.

IVY COLLAPSED ONTO THE COUCH, rubbing at her thighs. "I'm sore *everywhere*." She let out a groan. "I didn't realize skating would wear me out like that."

We'd skated for a few more hours, going for a few laps as she got the hang of it. Though she had fallen—a few times— I'd always been there to help her up. And she picked it up faster than I expected for a girl who'd grown up in Florida.

"I know something that can make it better," I offered, wiggling my eyebrows.

Her cheeks turned pink. "*Teddy.*" She scolded.

"What?" I held my hands up in admission. "I meant I could give you a massage."

"Mm. Sure."

Kissing her cheek, I stood up, grabbing something I'd stashed behind the tree. There was still something we hadn't done yet—a very important item on the list. My mantle was bare, needing the perfect item to finish it off.

A fire burned in the background, making the room feel cozy and warm. We hadn't turned on the overhead lights, letting just the lights from the tree and the fire illuminate the room as the snow fell outside.

I handed her the bag, sitting back down next to her on the couch.

"What's this?" She asked, looking at the gift bag. "It's not Christmas yet."

I waggled my eyebrows. "If you're allowed to give an early gift, so am I."

"*Teddy,*" she scolded, looking around like she'd been scandalized.

"I got you something you needed."

She raised her eyebrow, reaching in to pull out the tissue paper that covered the gift I'd had handmade for her. "Oh. Teddy." Her fingers connected with the fabric, and she pulled it out, her eyes filled with tears. "I've never had one before," Ivy murmured, her thumb running over the stitching at the top, spelling out her name in delicate script.

"A stocking?" I asked, frowning at her. Mine was also stuffed behind the tree, waiting with the hooks to put them on the mantle.

Hang stockings—check.

It felt like every second, every item we checked off the list, was taking me farther away from her, and I hated that.

She shook her head, her words quiet when she finally said, "A home."

And it took everything in me not to scoop her up into my

arms. To press her into my chest and beg her to stay. To be mine—for real, for always. Not whatever this was.

Because I craved her. *Needed* her. She was in my system, and I couldn't get her out.

"Baby," I whispered, reaching over and cupping her cheek. "You do have a home."

"No." Her eyes were shut, even as tears dripped out of them. "Not like this."

Fuck it. I pulled her into my arms, plopping her on my lap and cradling her head to my body. And then I whispered sweet nothings into her ear, hoping she knew just how wrong she was.

That she did have a home. And it was here, with me.

Teddy and Ivy's Christmas Checklist
1. *Bake Christmas Cookies* ✔
2. *Decorate A Christmas Tree* ✔
3. *Take a Sleigh Ride*
4. *Drink Hot Chocolate While Watching a Christmas Movie* ✔
5. *Build a Snowman* ✔
6. *Make a Gingerbread House* ✔
7. *Go Ice Skating* ✔
8. *Visit The Christmas Market* ✔
9. *Ugly Christmas Sweater Party* ✔
10. *Hang Stockings* ✔
11. *Matching Christmas PJs*
12. *Buy and Wrap Presents* ✔
13. *See the Lights*

14. Kiss Under the Mistletoe ✓

23
ivy

2 days until christmas

*H*ow could one person be so perfect? It should have gone against all of the laws of the universe. But Teddy Claus—he was that perfect. The way he saw through me, understood me.

Last night, I'd broken down over a stocking. A *stocking*.

The most perfect, handmade, embroidered stocking with my name on it. *Ivy,* stitched in red letters, with a little holly berry and ivy leaves next to it. It was the most precious gift I'd ever gotten, because it was made with love. I knew it was.

And when I'd lost it, he hadn't said anything else, just scooped me up into his arms and let me cry into his shirt. Because I could *feel* it. He was the first person to ever really notice how alone I was. How lost I felt, navigating this world by myself. The first person to really see me.

I hadn't given him an answer yet. He'd asked me to stay, given me all these little signs, and yet, every time I tried to tell him yes, my throat grew tight.

And tonight, *tonight...* The town's annual Christmas Ball was happening. The entire town was decorated head to toe in Christmas lights, and I wondered if you could see this place from space. That was how bright it was.

It was magical. They'd laid a dance floor out to keep us from sinking into the snow. The snow was gently falling, but it somehow didn't touch us, the air warm despite the chill outside. I'd learned a while ago not to question the magic of this place. Because it *was* magic.

And so was he.

Theodore Nicholas Claus was, without a doubt, the most wonderful man I'd ever met.

We danced under the stars, dressed in our finest—me in a long-sleeved, green velvet dress and Teddy in a three piece suit, his tie matching my dress. He held me tight, swaying us to the slow music under a blanket of twinkle lights.

The entire town might have surrounded us, but I didn't even notice.

All I could see was him.

My Teddy.

"Thank you," I murmured against his chest. "For this. For all of this. These last two weeks have been some of the best of my entire life. I never knew..." My throat grew tight. I never knew it could be like this. Life full of so much laughter, and so much happiness.

So much love.

His finger hooked under my chin, tilting my face until our eyes met.

"Teddy," I whispered as his fingers brushed over my jaw, my eyes meeting his dark green ones. I couldn't look away. There wasn't a chance. Not when all of these emotions were flowing through me.

I loved him. I couldn't imagine my life without him.

And maybe it was soon, maybe this was crazy, but I didn't

think so. Not knowing everything I did about this place. About Teddy. He was so *good*, like everything that was right in the world, and he was it for me.

Ever since I'd first run into him in the park, I'd known he would change everything. One flash of those pine tree green eyes and I was gone. Completely under his spell.

And all I wanted was to stay in this moment forever.

If what Scarlett said was true, I might not have to leave. Maybe I *could* say yes. How could this—us—not be meant to be?

He dipped his head down, and I stood on my tiptoes, brushing my lips against his in the softest kiss.

"Take me home," I said, wrapping my arms around his neck. Did he notice that I called it my home too? Because it didn't just feel like *his* anymore. I hoped he felt the same way.

"Gladly," he responded, scooping me up into his arms.

A BEAUTIFUL RED SLEIGH, hooked up to a team of reindeer, awaited us. I wrapped my white fur cloak around my body, the fabric thankfully keeping out the North Poll chill.

Part of me felt like I'd grown used to it, but then again, maybe that was just thanks to Teddy. He always made sure I was warm. That I felt cared for. But still, this was...

"This is too much," I said with a gasp as he set me down. My shoes sank into the snow, but I couldn't focus on that right now. Not with what was sitting in front of us. "Is that your dad's sleigh?"

He smirked. "Yeah. Borrowed it for the night. He doesn't need it till tomorrow."

"Teddy." I gasped. "You didn't."

"Of course I did. Anything for my girl." Bending over, he brushed the hair off my neck to place a kiss to the sensitive skin there. "My sweet little Poison Ivy."

"You're wonderful. Do you know that?"

His lips trailed kisses up my neck. "You deserve it. I hope you know that."

I blushed.

Teddy grabbed my hand, squeezing it before guiding me through the snow to the sleigh. Grabbing my hips, he lifted me inside, following me up before grabbing a blanket to spread over our laps.

We'd ridden in a sleigh before, but somehow this felt different. More *romantic*. And yet I couldn't help but remember it was one of the final things on our list to check off. Saving this for the end felt... *right*.

Though, I supposed that had something to do with the night instead of the sleigh. With who my company was.

"What do you think, Ivy?"

"The perfect Christmas," I said with a dreamy sigh.

"It's not over yet." Teddy winked.

I didn't need anything else. Truly. This trip had been perfect. The North Pole was amazing, but I just needed him.

The sleigh started moving, and Teddy interlaced our fingers, kissing my knuckles. I couldn't look away from him. His beautiful, vivid green eyes focused on mine, and I was lost in them.

"Look," he murmured, moving his thumb over my cheekbone. "It's snowing."

"Oh." My breath caught in my throat, and I forced myself to look away.

Immediately surrounding the sleigh, outside of our little bubble, tiny white flakes fall down around us. The world was blanketed in white, and it was magical. There was nowhere else I'd rather be right now, no one else I'd rather be here with than Teddy.

Of course, it was Teddy.

Who else would it have been other than him? The man who'd brought me here showed me what it was like to have a family, to have a home. To love and to be loved. Because I knew that what I felt for him was bigger than anything I'd ever felt before.

I loved him. I loved Teddy Claus, and for the first time in my life, I wasn't afraid anymore. I wanted to shout it from the rooftops. To proclaim it to the entire North Pole. But first, I needed to tell him.

"Teddy, I—"

"Shhh," he whispered, his finger moving over my lips. He brushed the hair off my neck, placing a kiss on my exposed skin. "Not yet."

Like he knew what I was going to say was going to change us, this, forever.

He dragged his thumb over my cheekbone, caressing my skin. "Sweetheart, you're so damn beautiful."

"You know, when I first saw you, I thought you were the most handsome man I'd ever met."

He chuckled. "Good. Because I'd have to chase off anyone else. You know why?"

I straddled his lap, breaths coming out in puffs from the cold air. But I wasn't cold. I was burning up. For him— only him.

My green dress pooled around my hips as I settled over his groin.

"Why?" I breathed out the word.

"Because you're *mine*, Ivy Winters."

I made a humming sound, running my fingers through his soft hair, messing up the strands. I was, wasn't I? I was his. Ever since he'd claimed me for the first time. The first time I'd slept in his clothes, wanting to be surrounded by his delicious scent. Or maybe I had been ever since that first date.

"This reminds me of something," he said, a little grin as he slid his hands up my thighs. Slowly. Everywhere he touched me, where his fingertips brushed my skin, it felt like sparks were exploding.

"Oh?" But I knew exactly what he was talking about. The first time we'd had sex on his couch. When I'd ridden him on his lap because neither one of us had been able to make it to the bedroom.

We wouldn't be able to make it back to his house now, either. Not when we were this desperate for each other. Not when I needed him this badly.

He hummed in response, ripping a hole and dipping his fingers underneath the waistband of my panties. "So impatient, sweetheart."

"Teddy," I whimpered as he rubbed circles over the thin fabric. My hips rocked against him, desperately seeking friction.

"Do you need me to take care of you, baby?" Teddy asked, his mouth finding my neck.

"Here?" I asked, looking out of the sleigh.

We were surrounded by white and trees on all sides, though thanks to Teddy's magic, I was perfectly warm. A bubble ensconced us, keeping us safe from the snow and the outside weather.

He grinned. "No one's going to find us."

"But—" Silencing me with another kiss, Teddy pulled the top of my dress down, revealing my red lacy bra. My nipples pebbled, quickly hardening from the exposure to the outside air.

"You make me insane. You know that?"

I moaned as he sucked my nipple into his mouth, lace and all. *"Teddy,"* I moaned.

"Yes, sweetheart?" He grinned as he left a wet circle on my bra before moving to the other side.

But I couldn't think. Not with his mouth on me, his cock pressed against my entrance, and his hands keeping me firmly in place. Squirming, I wiggled against him, but that only succeeded in making it worse.

Were we really going to do it here? In the middle of the woods, on the bench of his father's sleigh?

Teddy swapped our positions, spreading a blanket over the bench before laying me down. His suit coat hit the floor, followed by his vest and tie, and I admired his figure as he loomed over me. His hands, so strong and big, the perfect size to cup my breasts. Like they were made to fill his hands. Everything about us so perfectly matched. We just *fit*.

I reached my hand up, combing through his hair. "I want to remember this moment forever," I told him, everything feeling so meaningful. So reverent. It didn't matter where we were. It just mattered that we were together.

Teddy unzipped his pants, pulling out his cock, fisting it a few times before positioning it at my entrance. But he didn't plunge in right away, instead rubbing himself back and forth across my clit, making my hips jolt off the bench each time from the sensation.

"Don't tease me," I whined.

He ran the tip through my wetness, coating his length in it, before finally pushing inside me. I wasn't sure what it was about this position—flat on my back, with him perched above me, the stars above us as the world was enveloped in a blanket of snow—but everything felt different. Like the world was more vivid and crisp. And when he slid his cock inside of me, I cried out, feeling too much. He was so big, and every part of my body felt the stretch of him inside me every time.

"That's it," he encouraged, watching the spot where his length disappeared into my body. "Take every inch like the good fucking girl you are. Fuck. You're always so wet for me. So tight. That pretty pussy so ready to be filled up."

"Yes," I agreed, though I might have been chanting the word, I wasn't sure. "Teddy, *Yes*." My fingers scrambled for something to hold onto as he thrust roughly inside of me, burying himself to the hilt. Every time he bottomed out, it felt like the stars erupted in front of me, little fireworks exploding.

I clenched around his length, causing him to groan. "So fucking good. So right. Like you were made for me."

"I was," I agreed. Teddy grabbed my leg, bending it and changing the angle, forcing himself in deeper. The stretch of my leg only added to the bite of pain, but I liked it. "Only for you."

"Because you're mine."

I nodded, crying out as he dipped his head down, sucking my nipple into his mouth as he ravished me. The stimulation was too much, and I didn't even have the time to warn him before I was coming, my muscles contracting around his length.

Teddy popped off my nipple, circling it with his tongue before kissing me roughly, fucking my mouth like he thrust inside of me, not giving me a moment to breathe. No, he just kept fucking me through it.

Determination showed on his face, his brow dotted with sweat that made his brown hair fall onto his forehead. I liked it when it did that—because it gave me an excuse to touch him, thrusting my hands into his hair. Running my fingers through the soft strands and tugging at them roughly.

He stilled, and I could feel him getting close, grunting as he hardened even more inside of me. It was a good thing I was on birth control, or the sheer amount of times I'd let him fill me up would have definitely gotten me pregnant. Maybe one day. A shudder ran down my spine.

We hadn't even talked about kids yet. But we would. We would have time for all of those things.

Because there was no way I was leaving him.

"Tell me you're mine," he said, breaking the kiss. "I need to hear it, Ivy."

"I'm yours," I promised.

"Tell me you're not going anywhere," he begged. "Tell me you'll stay with me."

I nodded, tracing his jaw with my fingers before cupping his face. "I'm not going anywhere, Teddy. I'm here, with you."

"Thank fuck," he groaned. He nuzzled his head into my shoulder, burying his teeth in mine like I had with him, and it only took a few more thrusts before he was spilling inside of me, messy and wet and *perfect*.

Not yet. I didn't want to tell him I loved him during sex.

Tomorrow.

Tomorrow was Christmas Eve.

That was when I'd confess.

Teddy straightened my dress, pulling me into his arms and cradling me like we hadn't just christened his father's sled. Like he didn't have a care in the world.

And for the moment, I didn't either.

24
teddy

christmas eve

J looked at the list one final time, pinned up on the wall. Almost everything had been checked off. The last thing to finish just required us to change into the absolutely ridiculous matching pajamas we'd gotten together last week while at the market.

Teddy and Ivy's Christmas Checklist
1. *Bake Christmas Cookies* ✔
2. *Decorate A Christmas Tree* ✔
3. *Take a Sleigh Ride* ✔
4. *Drink Hot Chocolate While Watching a Christmas Movie* ✔
5. *Build a Snowman* ✔
6. *Make a Gingerbread House* ✔

7. Go Ice Skating ✓
8. Visit The Christmas Market ✓
9. Ugly Christmas Sweater Party ✓
10. Hang Stockings ✓
11. Matching Christmas PJs
12. Buy and Wrap Presents ✓
13. See the Lights ✓
14. Kiss Under the Mistletoe ✓

It was officially Christmas Eve, which meant that tomorrow was Christmas. And we'd accomplished everything on the list. I had to admit, I'd never had so much fun completing anything before.

Maybe I'd see if she wanted to make a Christmas list with me every year. Of course, we could switch things up. Some things would be tradition—cutting down the tree, kissing her underneath the mistletoe—but we could mix things up, too. I'd be up for the challenge.

"What are you doing?" Ivy asked, walking out of my bedroom in only a towel and wrapping her arms around my waist.

"Looking at the list," I admitted, willing myself to ignore the fact that she was totally naked under that towel and her tits were pressed against my back.

"Ah." She made a sound in her throat. "The list."

"Mhm." I turned my head back to look at her. "We did it."

"We did."

She didn't sound very excited about that. I spun her around, frowning as I looked into her beautiful blue eyes. Her hair was damp, hanging loose around her shoulders, and she didn't have a lick of makeup on, but goddamn, she was gorgeous.

Gorgeous, and all mine.

"Why aren't you excited?"

"We didn't talk about what happened when the list was over," she whispered.

I furrowed my brows. "I didn't think we had to."

Ivy wriggled out of my grasp, heading back to the bedroom. "Of course we do."

"Then let's talk!" I shouted, not sure why she was leaving in the middle of this conversation. *The* conversation. The most important one we'd ever had.

I knew she loved me. She was going to say it last night, wasn't she? She said she'd stay.

And I loved her too. So why were we dancing around this?

"Ivy." I came into my room, finding her pulling one of her new sweaters on over her head. "Talk to me."

"It's your dad's big day," she said, biting her lip. "We should go see him off."

"Is that what you want?"

Ivy grabbed her brush. "I just... everything's about to change, Teddy. Can we just have this? One more day?"

I took the brush out of her hand, my hand grasping her chin roughly to force her eyes to mine. "What's wrong, Ivy? What did I do?"

Tears spilled from her eyes, but she just shook her head. "Nothing's wrong. That's the problem. Everything's *right.*"

"Sweetheart..." My voice was low.

"But if I say it now, if *we* say it now, we're not going to leave this house today, are we?" I shook my head. Probably not. "And I know it's fucking crazy, that all of this is certifiably insane, but I'm just—we're in the *North Pole*, Teddy. Your Dad is *Santa Claus.*"

I nodded. And I knew what she was doing. That she was doing this for me as much as she was for her. For us.

"And I really, really want to see him leave on that fucking sleigh." She laughed, tears spilling from her eyes. "But I don't want to fight with you. I mean, I always want to fight with you because fighting is our flirting, and flirting turns into kissing, and no one's ever kissed me the way you do, Teddy. Because no one's ever cared about me the way you do." She slid her hand over my heart. "So tonight, okay?"

"Tonight," I promised. I took her hand off my chest, kissing her knuckles before sliding my free hand around the back of her neck, bringing her lips to mine. Then I kissed her because dammit, she was mine.

I was hers.

Tonight.

But first, I had one more surprise for her.

THE SLEIGH WAS LOADED, which meant that all that was left for Christmas to truly kick off was my dad in the sleigh, guiding the reindeer to the houses of children all over the world who were dreaming of Santa Claus. They'd have no idea that he was sneaking in, dropping off toys right under their noses.

But that was the magic of Santa, wasn't it? The same magic that flowed through my veins. Through all of us.

I wrapped an arm around Ivy, tugging her closer to me. "What do you think, sweetheart?"

"I think we're missing the big man himself." She raised an eyebrow at the empty sleigh.

A grin filled my face. I couldn't help it. "I was thinking I had a better idea. One last Christmas surprise up my sleeve."

"Teddy..." Ivy warned, looking around us.

I held out my hand for her. "Care for a ride in Santa's sleigh, baby?"

Her jaw dropped. "You're joking."

"Uh-uh." I shook my head. "I'm as serious as they come. We're gonna fly."

"No way!" Ivy shrieked. "I can't believe you."

Dipping my head down, I kissed her until she was breathless, smiling up at me, and then I took her hand, guiding her over to the sleigh.

It hadn't taken much convincing for my dad to let me take her out. We wouldn't do the whole route, after all, just a stop or two. After we were back, my dad would take over, heading out to deliver presents to all of the good children of the world.

Grabbing her waist, I lifted her in, and she giggled as she took the seat next to me, covering herself in a plaid blanket.

"Do you think they know what we were doing in here last night?" Ivy asked, leaning over to whisper in my ear. The tips of hers were pink, and I laughed.

"Let's hope not. Or else my dad will disown me."

She gasped as I flicked the reins, looking at the reindeer. "Let's go boys!"

And we were off, the reindeer picking up the pace with their hooves before we lifted into the air. *Flying.*

Ivy's face was alight with joy and wonder. "God. I can't believe this is happening. That this is real. This is *crazy!*"

We left the North Pole's barrier, flying high in the sky as we took flight around the world.

Some day, I'd show her all of it. Take her to Tokyo, Paris, Moscow, São Paulo, Seoul, and even New York City. Anywhere she wanted to go. But tonight, I wanted to show her *this.*

"It's beautiful," she whispered, the northern lights coming into view. "Wow."

"Do you like it?" The North Pole stretched below us, hidden by the protection barrier that kept the outside world from discovering us. The world was covered in a blanket of snow.

"I love it." Her cheeks were red, frost-bitten from the wind, but the smile on her face was enough to reassure me that this had been worth it. "Thank you for showing me this."

Her arm wrapped around mine, and though I could have stayed up here with her forever, I knew we had to get back.

My dad had his rounds, after all.

We landed back at the Pole, and as soon as we hit solid ground, Ivy was launching herself at me, throwing her arms around my neck. "That was amazing!"

I grinned, holding her up. "You're welcome, sweetheart."

Ivy pressed her lips to mine in a quick kiss before realizing we had an audience, dropping back down to her feet. "Thank you." She looked up at me, her ocean blue eyes meeting mine, that beautiful smile covering her face. "I think I want to spend every Christmas here."

"You do?"

Ivy nodded. "I mean… if you'd want that. I know we haven't really talked about it…" Because we'd been too busy having sex and fucking each other's brains out, but I wasn't about to get technical. "But I do. I want to stay."

"Poison Ivy, I think you've made me the happiest man in the North Pole."

She rolled her eyes, but I wrapped my arms around her waist, tugging her in tight against my body.

"All I've ever wanted was you," I said, whispering the words against her ear as I held her tight. "We're meant to be together, Ivy."

She looked up at me, surprise in her eyes. "But—"

"I know it's crazy. But it's true. You're my mate." I'd always figured I'd never find my person. My perfect match.

But here she was. Standing in front of me, strawberry blonde hair spilling around her shoulders, ocean blue eyes shining, and she was the only woman who I could ever imagine being with. There was no one else for me. There never would be.

"I—" Ivy's mouth formed a little 'o'. "How long have you known?"

"I've suspected for a while, but I didn't know, not for sure, until last night." I rubbed the spot over my heart. Last night… when I'd wanted so badly to tell her I loved her. That I could see the golden threads of fate shimmering between us. Our bond, locking into place. "You can't tell me you don't feel it too."

"How is this even possible? That we could be…" She shook her head, laughing. "Scarlett had told me, but I couldn't bring myself to hope—"

I could see that glittering string between us, what had only gotten stronger since last night. It pulsed, like our hearts beat in tandem—perfectly in sync.

Picking up her hand, I kissed her knuckles. "My whole life, I think I've been looking for you," I admitted. "I could have come home after college. Started learning the ropes up here to take over for my dad."

"But you didn't."

"No." I shook my head. "But I didn't. I decided to take my time. I have years to learn, anyway. But I knew something was waiting for me down there. I just didn't know that something was *you*." I took a deep breath. "My dad thinks that the reason you ended up working at Christmasland was that the magic there called to you. But I think it was more than that. I think that whatever brought us together called both of us there."

"You really believe that?" Her eyes were wet.

"Yeah. I do. You and I have been destined from the beginning, Ivy. You were made to be mine, just as I was made to be yours."

"This is crazy," she whispered.

I wasn't disagreeing. It *was* crazy. But that was fate, wasn't it? "I know. But I can't imagine my life without you in it. I know it's a lot to ask, but I want you to help me make every Christmas this special, Ivy. Because this has been the best one I've ever had. And it's all thanks to you."

"I'm the one who should be thanking *you*."

"No." I shook my head. "This is all for you. It's always been for you. The list, everything we did this Christmas… It was me trying to convince you to stay. To show you how good life could be up there. I know you love the theme park, but I wanted you to love this place too. I wanted you to fall in love with *me*."

Stay. Stay with me.

"Teddy…" Her voice was soft.

Tell me you're mine, I'd begged last night. *Tell me you're not going anywhere. Tell me you'll stay with me.*

I'm yours, she'd whispered back. *I'm not going anywhere, Teddy. I'm here, with you.*

Words that I knew were true. Words that I needed to hear again until I believed them. Because I couldn't believe the woman in my arms was mine. That everything I'd ever hoped for—a mate, a life of my own—was in reach.

"I'm yours. I've always been yours. But tell me you'll be mine too." I needed to hear it more desperately than I'd ever needed anything in my entire life. *Tonight.*

This was tonight, and we were here, surrounded by the lights of the North Pole, confessing our feelings like no one else was around to hear us.

"Of course I'm yours. I choose you, Teddy. I choose this life with you."

Picking her up by the waist, I twirled her around, a giggle slipping from her lips.

"You're stuck with me now, you know," she murmured against my lips. "Because you're mine, Theodore Claus."

I liked the sound of that. "We don't have to live here full time, you know. We can still spend time at the park." Setting Ivy down on the ground, I wrapped an arm around her.

She smiled, shaking her head. "Anywhere you are, that's where I'll be too."

"Good." I pulled her in closer to me. "I can't think of anything better." Dropping a kiss to her lips, I whispered the words I'd known in my soul. Words I'd never given anyone else. "I love you."

"I love you, too, Theodore." They were the best words I'd ever heard.

"Again."

She squealed as I spun her around. "I love you."

I kissed her softly.

"I love you, Teddy," she murmured, sliding her hands to cup my face.

"I don't think I'll ever get tired of hearing that," I whispered. "I love you, Ivy Winters."

She hummed, giving me her lips. I kissed her deeply, swiping my tongue over her lip, seeking entrance. Ivy returned it with as much fervor, our open-mouthed kiss quickly turning passionate.

Someone cleared their throat behind us, and we pulled apart. Ivy blushed like we were teenagers who'd just gotten caught making out instead of two people who'd just confessed their feelings.

I love you. Those words lit my soul up from the inside out.

"Congratulations, you two," my dad said, wearing his full Santa suit. "I knew you crazy kids would figure it out eventually."

Ivy laughed, glancing over at me. I just shrugged, like, who knew, right? My dad had known all along. He'd just let us figure it out ourselves. And fuck, if I wasn't grateful for that.

"Be careful, Dad," I said, releasing Ivy so I could give my old man a hug before he set out.

He grinned, his rosy cheeks warming his face. "Always am, son."

My mom stepped up beside me, and Ivy and I gave them privacy as Dad climbed onto the sleigh, getting ready to deliver presents.

Once he was set, he turned to us, that smile still firmly in place. "Merry Christmas to all, and to all, a good night!" He flicked the reins, and the reindeer were off, flying into the sky just like we had before.

"Worth it?" I asked Ivy, tucking her under my arm.

"Definitely." She turned her head towards mine, her lips begging for another kiss. So I gave her one. "Love you," she murmured. "And that was even more than worth the wait."

I picked her up in my arms, carrying her bridal style all the way back home, her giggles filling my heart.

My girl. She was mine. My mate.

The woman I loved.

"TEDDY," Ivy murmured my name as I peeled her clothes from her body, dropping the sweater on the floor that she'd put on this morning to delay our conversation.

"Ivy," I responded, kissing her neck.

She was right. As soon as we'd confessed, I wanted to claim her immediately. How had I avoided this for so long? I'd felt it—the bond between us—but I'd ignored it, too worried she would never choose this. Choose *us*. But now she was mine. And I was hers, and all I wanted to do was prove that to her, over and over.

Starting with tonight. But I didn't want to rush this, either, so I undressed her slowly, taking my time with each piece of clothing. Shimmying her leggings down her thighs, I pressed a kiss to the inside of each one, running my nose up the seam of her panties.

Fuck, she smelled good. Like *mine*. I wanted to paint her skin with my scent to make sure everyone knew exactly whose she was. The possessive feeling was growing, and I already knew I wouldn't want to leave this bed tomorrow. Or the next day. Maybe I'd keep her here for a whole week.

I rubbed her clit through the fabric, enjoying the little breathy noises she made from the contact. Standing back up to my full height, I plucked each bra strap against her skin, and Ivy let out a small moan.

"Please," she whined.

I shimmied out of my sweater, dropping it to the ground, and Ivy reached for my belt, undoing it and unzipping the fly of my jeans before I could stop her.

She reached into my boxers, wrapping her hand against my half-hard cock. Not that it would take too much for me to be ready—her small hands around me, the feel of her skin against mine, the way she ran her tongue over her bottom lip —was all so erotic. Even when she wasn't trying to be, she was the hottest thing I'd ever seen. The most beautiful woman I'd ever laid eyes on.

My mate. My woman.

I wanted her wearing my ring. With my baby in her belly.

"Bed?" She panted.

I shook my head, walking her backward into the wall. "I want to fuck you right here," I said into her neck, hoisting her up so I could position my tip against her entrance. "Take you against the wall."

There'd be time for slow and soft later. For making love with the woman I loved.

"*Oh,*" she gasped, giving a sharp exhale as I pushed inside of her with no warning. "Teddy," she cried.

Had I ever been so hard? So fucking ready to explode, just from this? Her insides squeezed me tight, and I had to shut my eyes, counting to ten before I could move. I held her up against the wall, keeping her pinned between me as I buried myself deep.

"Going to fill you up," I promised. "Give you so much cum that no one doubts whose you are. So they all know you're *mine.*"

"I am," she agreed, her fingernails digging into my shoulders like little claws as she cried out from my rough thrusts. "I'm all yours."

"*Yes,*" I grunted.

Ivy wrapped her legs around my waist, pushing me in deeper.

My heart thumped in rhythm with hers, and I couldn't hold myself back.

"I love you," I groaned, pressing my face into her neck as I let go, pouring my release inside of her. Rope after rope of cum spilled out of me, filling her up.

When I'd finished, I let Ivy drop down to her feet, pulling out of her as a rush of liquid spilled down her thighs.

"Looks like we made a mess," she murmured.

I ran my finger through it, pushing it back into her. "Worth it."

"I love you, you maniac."

I grinned. "You took the words out of my mouth, sweetheart." Grabbing her hand, I tugged her behind me into the bathroom, setting her on the bathroom counter so I could clean her up. I ran a washcloth over her sticky skin before cleaning myself up, finally shedding the rest of my clothes.

Then I carried her back to bed, content to just snuggle with her until we fell asleep.

Except ten minutes later, our hands were wandering, and I was driving into her again, her legs on my shoulders as we lost ourselves in each other, again and again.

25
ivy

christmas day

*M*erry Christmas, sweetheart." Teddy's smiling face was there when I woke up, holding a mug of delicious, steaming coffee.

"Merry Christmas, Teddy," I responded back, yawning in the process. "What time is it?"

His eyes sparkled with amusement. "Seven."

"Seven?" I groaned. "Why do you hate me?"

Placing the mug on the nightstand next to me, he leaned over me, one of his hands resting on the mattress, caging me in. "I can assure you, Ivy, hate is the last thing I feel for you."

I hummed in response, and he leaned down to kiss me softly. "Good morning."

"It's better now," I agreed.

"Oh?"

"Yeah." Sitting up, I reached over for the mug and took a sip. "Because you brought me coffee."

He chuckled, moving off me so I could drink the mocha he'd made me.

"Spoil a girl this much, and she's never going to want to leave."

"That's the idea," Teddy agreed. "Come on. It's present time."

"Presents?" I perked up.

"Now I've got her attention," he said with a laugh. "Come on, Poison Ivy." He held out his hand, and I took it, interlacing our fingers together as I slid out of bed.

Grabbing my mug, I walked with him towards the living room. We were both wearing the ridiculous matching reindeer pajamas we'd gotten at the market.

Like a couple. Which we were, now, I supposed. *Officially.* He was mine, and I was his.

Teddy was my boyfriend. A smile curved over my face. The words had never filled me with so much rightness before.

A surprisingly large stack of presents was piled under the tree, but my favorite part of the room was the two stockings that hung over the fireplace, our embroidered names looking so right side by side.

Putting my mug on the side table, I turned to him, my heart feeling so full I thought it might burst. "You know, I don't need any of that," I said, gesturing to the presents.

"I know." He grinned. "Most of them aren't even from me."

"Really? Who—"

"My parents. Scarlett and Jack. Ruby and her husband. Your grandmother. They all wanted to make your first Christmas here special."

"Oh." My eyes filled with tears. Dammit, I needed to get it under control so I wasn't crying all day. "I don't know what to say."

"Say 'thank you, Teddy, for bringing me here and giving me the best Christmas ever.'"

"Thank you, Teddy," I said, repeating his words as I rested my hands on his shoulders. "Thank you for asking me to come home with you for Christmas and making this the most memorable Christmas of my life." I meant every word.

"Not quite the wording, but I'll take it."

"Shut up," I said, rolling my eyes.

"Gladly," he responded, dropping a kiss to my lips. "Now, want to open your gifts, sweetheart?"

I did. I really, really did.

Two hours later, we sat curled up on the couch, our bodies completely pressed together. All the boxes were gone, the wrapping paper cleaned up off the floor, and I had a stack of beautiful presents from the people who were quickly becoming my family. It was strange to think about.

"I have something else, too." Teddy stood up, pressing a kiss to my forehead as he got off the couch.

"You do?" I looked up at him in surprise.

He nodded. "Wait here. I'll go get her."

"*Her?*" I repeated, but Teddy didn't answer, already gone.

A few minutes later, he came back with a basket in his arms, holding the world's smallest bundle in them. My eyes widened.

"Teddy?"

"I know how much you've always wanted one," he said, placing the basket onto the floor in front of me and lifting the puppy into my arms. He'd even tied a big red bow around her neck, just like I'd always dreamed of.

The puppy barked happily, jumping on me to lick at my face. He'd listened to every word I'd ever said, hadn't he?

"But..." My eyes filled with tears. Damn him, but this really was the perfect Christmas present. How was I ever going to top this? "How did you even do this?" I looked down at my lap, stroking the dog's soft fur.

She was mostly black, with little brown markings over her eyes that looked like eyebrows and white that went down the middle of her body, accented with more brown spots. Beautiful. The cutest puppy I'd ever seen in my life.

A little smirk made one corner of his lips tilt up. "I had help."

I snorted. "You're ridiculous."

He hummed, leaning down to drop a kiss against my lips. "I know."

The baby girl in my lap gave a little yip as I tilted my head up to kiss Teddy deeper—obviously, I was *not* allowed to ignore her.

"Sorry, sweetheart." I rubbed my nose against her cold, wet one. "I promise mommy won't ignore you again."

Teddy cleared his throat. "At least, not *most* of the time." He winked, and I rolled my eyes.

"You're insatiable."

We both were. We could barely keep our hands off each other since we'd said those three little words. Since we'd confessed our feelings. The bond between us was new, but I could feel it. Like whatever magic I had was growing inside of me, strengthening the pull I felt to him. I hoped it never dulled.

"You like it."

I hummed in response. There was no denying that I did. "I love you," I whispered the words against his mouth.

"I love you too." He kissed me again and then kissed our puppy's forehead. "What are you going to name her?"

I looked down at the darling puppy in my lap. After making fun of him for naming his reindeer Buddy, I knew our puppy needed a good name.

Ours. The word settled into my heart, and it felt right. I'd meant what I told him yesterday—that anywhere with him was home.

This was home. I couldn't imagine saying goodbye. I loved his cozy little house. The tree we'd decorated soon after we'd first arrived still sat in the corner, our stockings hanging from the mantle like they were meant to be there. Like I'd always been meant to be here, with him.

Snuggling my head on his chest, I ran my hands over the puppy's soft ears. She was beautiful. What was a name worthy of that?

I wanted her to have a name that reminded me of this Christmas and all our wonderful memories. There was one thing that kept popping up in all of them. I smiled.

"Coco."

Teddy chuckled. "Coco?"

How many cups of hot chocolate had we shared as I'd fallen in love with him? The puppy in my lap gave a yip of agreement.

"Mhm." I nodded, holding her up so her nose was pressed against his. "She looks like one, doesn't she?"

"Yeah." He smoothed a hand over her head. "She does."

And then, snuggled up with the man I loved with the dog of my dreams, I felt like my heart was so full it was going to burst. Because I knew I'd never been this happy. So deliriously happy.

Merry Christmas, indeed.

PART of me couldn't believe I was doing this. Leaving my entire life behind to be with Teddy. But also, I couldn't imagine anything else.

I stood staring at my empty apartment. All the decorations had come off the walls, and all of my stuff was currently piled in boxes, ready to be shipped to my new home via express delivery.

That delivery was, of course, in Santa's sleigh. Unreal.

How was this my life?

Part of me felt like I should be sad. I was closing a chapter in my life. Saying goodbye to Florida and the first apartment of my own. Except I couldn't bring myself to feel anything other than joy. I was opening a new chapter of my life, one full of love. Of a family who'd accepted me with open arms. I'd found exactly what I was looking for.

Who knew all it would take was going home with Teddy and coming to the North Pole?

I turned around and finding Teddy leaning on the doorframe, watching me. He looked absolutely delectable in his dark green henley. God, he was handsome. And he was all mine.

I snuggled Coco to my chest, burying my face in her scruff. I hadn't been able to leave her at home earlier, not wanting to be parted from the best Christmas present ever.

The only better gift was the man who'd come with me.

"You don't have to move, you know. You can still work at the park, we could live here..." He gave me a hesitant smile.

"No." It was time for a new adventure. An adventure with Teddy. Wherever that took us. "I want to see the world with you." It sounded amazing, and I couldn't wait for everything. "But... I do want to come back and visit." Of course I did.

Maybe one day, we'd be bringing kids of our own here, just like his parents had with him. And until then, whenever I was homesick for candy cane forests or the best gingerbread muffin on the planet, I knew exactly who could bring me back.

"We can come back as much as you want," Teddy promised, as if he could read my thoughts. Maybe he could.

There was so much I still didn't know about the golden string that tied us together. I couldn't wait to explore that. "I still have to finish my development projects, after all."

"Good." I smiled, giving my apartment one last look.

"Well, are you ready to go?" He asked, crossing his arms over his chest. The action made his biceps flex under his shirt, and damn, he knew what he was doing to me.

"Yes," I agreed. I'd never been more ready.

He stalked over to me and pulled me into his arms, our puppy in between us.

Home. Home was being wrapped in Teddy Claus's arms. I knew that like I knew it was the air I was breathing and that Christmas magic was real.

"Take me home, Teddy," I whispered, wrapping my hands around his neck.

"With pleasure, my Poison Ivy."

A FEW HOURS LATER, the sun had set, and the interior of our house was lit up by the glow of the fireplace and the Christmas lights strung around the room. My stuff now joined Teddy's in the house, and my craft stuff now had its own space in the loft. It was perfect. I was home.

"What do you think?"

I hummed, nuzzling my face into his shoulder. "About what?"

Coco was asleep in her bed at our feet, her brand new collar sporting a red bow.

"Look at the time," he whispered, and when I did, I realized that the clock had crept over to midnight. *Christmas was over.* "Did I succeed in giving you the perfect Christmas?"

"More than," I said. "The best one ever. We even managed

to check everything off our list." The list, framed on the kitchen wall, each item brings us closer together.

I'd been falling in love with him the whole time through each of them. Every item, every experience he'd given me... They were all firsts that I couldn't imagine having given anyone else.

He pressed a kiss to my forehead. "That's good."

"Why?" I raised an eyebrow, confused.

"Because I have one last gift for you."

I blinked at him as he got off the couch. "You didn't have to do that. You already gave me everything I could have ever wanted." A home. A family. Love. A puppy. Not to mention the other things I'd already unwrapped. A new coat and boots. A gorgeous red velvet dress I couldn't wait to wear. Little snowflake earrings that matched my necklace.

Kneeling, he brandished a small gift box from behind his back, sliding it into my hand.

"Just open it," he said, grinning at me.

Raising an eyebrow at him, I turned my attention to the box, slowly pulling the red ribbon off the top and sliding the lid off.

It was an absolutely gorgeous ornament, gilded red and gold. And somehow, without even having to ask, I knew that he'd made it in the workshop. Because what couldn't this man do with his hands?

"Oh." My eyes felt wet. "Teddy, it's beautiful."

"The first one for *our* tree. I'm sure there will be many more in the future." He wiped a finger under my eye. "Take it out and look at what it says on it."

"Huh?" I said, doing as he instructed. Pulling it out of the box, I spun it around to read the writing. "What..."

Will you marry me? Was etched above the hinge, and I had a feeling I knew what I would find when I opened it up.

"Teddy, I—" Looking at him, I found him down on one

knee in front of the couch. He gently took the ornament from my hands, opening it up to reveal a beautiful diamond ring nestled among the red velvet.

The smile on his face was dazzling. He was the most handsome man I'd ever seen, and knowing he was mine made him even more so.

"Ivy Winters, you have to know by now that you're the best thing that ever happened to me. Part of me knew when I found you that day, red in the face from arguing with an ungrateful park guest, that I was in love with you. And thank god I found you. Because you are my *everything*, my Poison Ivy. I know it's soon, but I couldn't wait another moment without asking you to be my wife."

Tears were streaming down my face, but I supposed what they said was true: *when you know, you know*. And I definitely knew with him.

I'd known it since the first moment he asked me to come home with him, and I'd said *yes*. Had there ever been another choice for me? He was it. The man I was meant to be with. My fated soulmate. And I wanted this, too. This life with him. Being his wife, starting a family of our own. The future was brighter than ever with him in it.

Looking up, I found a bundle of mistletoe hanging from the ceiling, and his face was transformed in the most dazzling smile I'd ever seen in my life.

"Will you marry me, Ivy? Make me the luckiest man in the North Pole and be my wife?" His deep green eyes held mine, and I could see the love in them. I never wanted to look away.

"Yes," I said, nodding, even as tears filled my eyes. "Yes, Teddy. I'll marry you."

He slid the diamond onto my finger before I was in his arms, kissing him senseless.

It might have been soon, but I'd never felt more sure

about a decision in my life. I admired the ring on my finger, the beautiful princess cut ring with a band that almost looked like ivy decorated with stones. It was perfect. I'd never have picked it for myself, and yet I couldn't imagine anything else.

"Thank fuck," he said against my lips. "Otherwise, buttering you up with Coco so you'd say yes would have been really awkward."

I laughed, smacking his shoulder. He didn't need to butter me up, and he knew it. Teddy slid his fingers into my hair, bringing our lips back together. We kissed for what felt like hours but was probably only minutes, lost in each other. In the world we'd created. His tongue tangled with mine, tasting me, and I straddled his thighs, taking his face in between my hands.

"Are you sure you want to marry me?" I asked when we pulled apart, breathing rough. "I'm not too stubborn, am I?"

"Sweetheart." He grinned. "You're the most stubborn woman in the world. It's one of the things I love most about you." He ran his thumb over my bottom lip, swollen and tender from his kisses.

I rocked my hips against him, brushing my overly sensitive core over his jean-clad erection, aware that there were too many layers between us.

"What else do you love about me?"

He placed a kiss to my neck, sucking lightly, and I let out a small gasp. "How responsive you are for me." Teddy brushed his fingers over my nipples, already hard for him, even through my bra. "How beautiful you are." He kissed my collarbone. "Inside and out, you're the most beautiful thing I've ever seen, Ivy."

I was all too aware that I was dry humping him on the couch, but I couldn't move. Not when he was touching me like this. Dropping my head back against the couch, I let out a low moan as he rocked against my core.

"Take me to bed, Teddy," I breathed, "I need you. Please."

"You never have to ask, my love."

It was a promise I knew he'd never break. That he'd love me with all his heart. That no matter what happened, no matter what trials we faced or fights we fought, we'd always come out of them together.

He swept me into his arms, and I tightened my legs around his waist, my arms around his neck, finding his mouth once again as he carried me into the bedroom—our bedroom—and showed me just how much he loved me all over again, with his fingers, his tongue, and his cock.

Teddy made love to me in the quiet of our house, with only the fireplace and the lights to illuminate our bodies, and nothing had ever been better.

Merry Christmas to me. It was definitely one I'd never forget.

epilogue

Teddy

one year later...

*I*t was the best Christmas Eve I could remember. All because of the woman by my side. The woman who I'd married today. *My wife.* Ivy looked absolutely breathtaking in her white wedding gown, the same color as the snow. My mate.

There was no chance I'd ever forget a night like tonight. We'd talked about having our wedding during the warmer season—when the North Pole wasn't completely frozen over —but Christmas was special to both of us. We'd had a tent put up, string lights above us giving the space a warm, cozy glow. Of course, given the freezing temperatures outside, we'd also had portable heaters throughout the room so all our guests could be comfortable.

It was magical, and I hadn't even used my powers. Well, at least not much. I'd kept Ivy warm all night, though she never knew I used my abilities to keep her wrapped in a cozy bubble.

I'd never let her freeze.

The entire North Pole surrounded us to celebrate our wedding, which was held in the middle of town as the snow fell around us, and the entire world was a blanket of white. But all I could see was her. She radiated with happiness, practically glowing as she chatted with her best friend, Sarah.

She sipped from a glass of sparkling champagne as she chatted, her cheeks pink as she spoke excitedly about something.

In the last year, I'd gotten to know her even better. Her likes and dislikes, the way she loved to dance in the rain, and how every single time—without fail—her eyes lit up when she tried a new sweet treat. Lately, it felt like she couldn't get enough of *all* desserts. I was pretty sure she'd had four pieces of wedding cake.

Who was I to tell her no? This was the North Pole, after all. Dessert was at the top of our food pyramid. And as long as she was getting her nutrition, and eating healthy, what did it really matter?

We'd traveled all over the world, spending the months after Christmas had ended going anywhere Ivy wanted to go. We spent two weeks in the Bahamas, soaking up the sun, and I was pretty sure we'd spent more time naked in bed than we had actually outside with clothes on. Not that I minded one bit. I couldn't wait to get her into bed tonight, to peel that beautiful white dress off of her, and see what she had on underneath.

My mom slid by my side, patting me on the shoulder. "Congratulations again, Teddy."

"Thanks, Mom." I looked at my wife. Our dog was curled up at her feet, perfectly happy outside in the snow. She'd been a part of the wedding, carrying our rings up to the altar, and was now content to sleep next to Ivy. "I'm the luckiest man alive."

She laughed. "That's true. She's special."

"I know. I've known it since the first moment I saw her." Red faced and yelling at a disgruntled guest, and yet she never lost her composure. No, the only person she did that with was me. But we still liked fighting with each other. It was our foreplay, and there was nothing better than the make-up sex after we fought.

It was easy to see how obsessed I was with her. Even a year later, I couldn't believe she was mine. That out of everyone in this world, I'd found her. My mate. My wife.

Putting that ring on her finger had been the best decision I'd ever made.

"I'm proud of you. Your dad and I both are. One day, you're going to do such an amazing job up here."

"Not for a long, long time," I promised. "Because I have a lot of things I want to do first." And my Dad was the best Santa the world could have asked for.

She laughed. "Hopefully, one of those things involves grandkids."

I grinned. "We'll see." That was definitely on the agenda, though I wasn't quite sure *when*.

Ivy had gone off her birth control a few months ago, but these things took time. Still, I couldn't wait till she was pregnant. Picturing her with a baby in her arms just felt *right*. Our baby.

"Don't try too hard," she said with a wink.

My cheeks flushed, and I tried to hide my embarrassment. *"Mom,"* I groaned. "Can we not?"

"What?" She acted all innocent. "I'm just saying."

"Carol!" My dad wrapped his arms around my mom's middle. "I've been looking everywhere for you. Did you get some cake?"

"Hm?" She looked up at my dad's face. He'd cleaned up for tonight, putting on a tux—which felt like one of the first times I'd seen him dressed up in something fancy that *wasn't* his Santa suit. "Oh, yes. I did."

He pressed a kiss to the side of her forehead. "Well, good. Let's leave our son to find his wife and get some more anyway."

She laughed, waving goodbye, and then I turned to find Ivy walking over to me, her hips swaying with each step in her wedding dress.

My mouth was dry as I took all of her in. God, I loved her. I loved her more than I'd ever thought was possible. Her strawberry blonde hair hung in loose curls down her back, and her eyes looked bigger than ever, those brilliant blue irises locked on mine.

"There you are, Mrs. Claus," I said, planting a kiss on Ivy's cheek.

"Well, hello, Mr. Claus." She wrapped her arms around my neck.

Placing mine on her hips, I rocked us in a small circle. "Are you having fun?"

"Mhm." She rested her head on my shoulder. "So much fun. It's nice having Sarah here. And I'm glad Scarlett and Jack could bring the baby." Her cousin and her mate were in the corner, bouncing their baby girl in their laps. Ivy's grandmother sat next to them, her eyes shining with happiness at seeing her great-grandchild. "It's nice having them here. My family." Her eyes locked on mine. "Thank you."

"Of course." I gave her a small peck on the nose. "But you have an even bigger family now, you know?" She had me, and now, she had my family too.

"Our family," she whispered, a small smile spreading over her face. "That's my favorite."

"Mine too," I murmured back. "It'll always be my favorite."

Swaying to the music, Ivy rested her head on my chest,

and I knew there was nowhere I'd rather be than right here, right now, with her.

ivy

Snow flurries fell around us as the reception music continued, and I stopped to look at Teddy. He was as handsome as ever in his tuxedo, a bowtie around his neck, and a wedding ring on his finger.

My husband. My heart clenched as I looked over at him, finding a dopey smile splitting his face. Sometimes, it still didn't feel real. That this was home—that I was *here.* That he'd found me.

But I was grateful for all of it, and I couldn't imagine tying the knot any other time of year. Christmas was always magical—and now it was extra special.

We danced, toasted, and cut the cake while greeting practically everyone in town. It was like no one wanted to be left out of the celebrations today. My family was here: my grandmother, who had made me feel so loved I couldn't believe I hadn't known her my whole life, and my cousin, who was more like a sister at this point, and all of the extended family I'd met in the past year. Everyone had come out to congratulate us.

Even Coco was here, my big puppy who couldn't bear to be parted from my side. Whenever I sat down, there she was, laying next to me or draping her head into my lap. Her nose brushed against my torso, and I ran my hands over her little brown eyebrows.

Finally, though, Teddy collapsed back in the chair next to

me at the head table. I needed a break, my feet aching despite my comfortable shoes. No fancy heels needed for a wedding here.

After he'd proposed last year, I knew there was no other time I wanted to promise my everlasting love to him. Even if it was busy season. Soon, though, we'd be on an extended honeymoon, enjoying some place warm and tropical, drinking beverages out of pineapples and coconuts. I gave a happy sigh of contentment.

Teddy leaned over, a curious expression on his face. "What was that for?"

"Nothing." I shook my head, playing with the tulle veil still pinned into my hair. But I couldn't help but smile as I rested my head against his arm. I'd barely been able to go five minutes all night without touching him in some way, but he was the same way with me. His palm rested on my knee, a possessive hold that made a shiver run down my spine. "Just happy."

"And to think, a year ago, you *hated* me."

I scrunched up my nose. "Hate is a strong word."

"Merry Christmas, my wife," he murmured, placing a kiss to my forehead as we stared towards the giant Christmas tree in the town square, all lit up in dazzling colors. This whole place was a spectacle. Having our wedding out here, in the same place as the Christmas Ball, was the perfect decision.

"Merry Christmas, husband," I said back, interlacing our fingers.

It was a beautiful place for a wedding reception. Even as the snow fell around us, I didn't feel it at all. My beautiful white gown was lined, and though it didn't have sleeves, the velvet cape I wore around my shoulders kept out the chill.

As did Teddy's hand on my lap, even as he pulled me into his arms.

"I love you," he said, kissing my lips this time as the snow fell around us. *Magical*. But that was him. My husband, every bit of Christmas magic I'd ever wanted or needed. "My Poison Ivy."

I wound my arms around his neck, not caring who saw as I kissed my *husband*. "I love you more."

He snorted. "Not possible."

"No?" Curling my fingers in his hair, I tugged his lips down so they were hardly a breath from mine.

"No," he agreed. "Because every time I see you, my chest fills with so much love I think it might burst."

I smacked his chest, laughing, though that smile stayed plastered to my face as he kissed me deeper.

"How are you feeling?"

"What do you mean?" I bit my lip. I'd been hoping he hadn't caught the amount of times I'd run to the bathroom over the course of the evening. "I'm great."

Teddy nodded. "Okay. You want another glass?" He tilted his head at my empty champagne flute.

I shook mine. "No, I'm good." Probably had something to do with the fact that I hadn't even drunk the first one. I'd had Scarlett slip me sparkling cider instead.

"Okay." He kissed my forehead. "I'll be right back."

I smiled up at him. "Don't be too long. I don't like to be kept waiting, husband."

"Oh, I don't plan to make you wait, wife." He winked, and my heart did a little flip in my chest.

Usually, he was the one surprising me, giving me the most perfect gifts of all. But tonight, I had one more surprise for him. I couldn't wait to see his face.

WE CURLED up on the couch in our living room, staring up at the Christmas tree. After we'd gotten home, he'd stripped my wedding dress from my body, taking the time to appreciate the white lacy undergarments I'd gotten just for our wedding night, before making me come three times— once on his tongue, and then twice with his cock. But I wasn't complaining.

And now, we were curled up in our matching pajamas— snowmen, this year—watching the fire crackle and enjoying the warm ambiance of the lights.

"You know, I always wished for this," I murmured, turning my head to give Teddy a small smile.

"What?" He asked, so quietly, tenderly. Teddy brushed a finger over the tip of my ear, like he still couldn't believe I was real. That this was real.

I couldn't stop the tears from trickling down my face. I was just so happy. "Christmas with a someone who loved me. A family surrounding us. A life full of happiness." My hand curled over my stomach, thinking about that word. *Family.*

Our little, growing family. Coco was curled at our feet, fully grown now. She was the perfect dog, keeping me company always, especially when Teddy was working at the workshop.

He placed a gentle kiss against my lips. "I always wished for you. So I guess we're even."

I laughed, though the sound came out garbled through the tears. "Maybe."

Above all, I was glad for moments like this. The Christmas season wouldn't always be like this for us—and I knew it, just as much as he did. One day, he'd take over for his dad, and Christmas Eve would be me sending him off into the world, a sleigh full of gifts for one impossible night each year.

But for now, I had him.

And the little secret I'd been keeping all day.

"So… I have something for you," I murmured, standing up to grab the little box I'd stashed behind the tree this morning, when I'd taken a test to confirm what I already knew. "Merry Christmas, Teddy," I said, placing the box in his hands.

"I thought we said we weren't doing gifts this year?" He asked, looking up at me with a furrowed expression. "With the wedding, and all."

I shrugged, a secret smile on my face. "Just open it."

The box was tied with a pretty red ribbon, and after untying it, he pulled open the lid, grabbing the wrapped item from inside. It was practically a tradition now in and of itself, us making each other ornaments for our special occasions. It had been, ever since he'd proposed with one.

"An ornament?" He asked as he delicately peeled back the tissue paper, a look of interest on his face. Which then morphed into surprise as he read the words on it.

Baby's First Christmas, the ornament read, with next year's date written underneath.

"Ivy?" He looked up at me, eyes wide—brimming with unshed tears—and I just smiled because I was happy. So deliriously happy.

He pulled out the test that I'd stashed underneath. "You're—"

I nodded. "Congratulations, Daddy," I whispered into his ear. "I'm pregnant."

"Holy shit." He pulled me onto his lap, and in the blink of an eye I was straddling him, my hands on his shoulders as his held onto my hips. "We're having a baby?"

I nodded, sliding a hand over my abdomen.

"When did you find out?"

"This morning, but with the wedding, and everything, I didn't want anyone to find out before you. And it's still early, so…" I brought my hands to his face. "Are you happy? I know it's soon, but…"

It had only been recently that I'd gone off birth control. We both wanted kids, but I had no idea how quickly it would take. Trust Teddy's super sperm to knock me up this soon. The man could do anything he set his mind to, I swear.

"I'm so fucking happy. God, Ivy, you don't even know how ecstatic I am. I love you so much."

I thought I could guess. The same feeling ran through my veins. Feeling his emotions wasn't always easy, but the bond that flowed between us had only grown stronger with time. And it made all of this worth it.

"Thank you for finding me," I said, resting my forehead against his. "For giving me all of this."

A house, a home. A life I'd never imagined but always dreamed of. A family. *Our* family.

"I love you," he said, placing a reverent kiss to my lips before sliding a hand on top of mine. "And our little Christmas gift."

"Guess this means all of my drinks on our honeymoon will have to be virgin."

He barked out a laugh. "That's why you didn't want more champagne earlier."

"Guilty. I had Scarlett slip me sparkling cider instead for the toasts. So… she might suspect." My cousin was my best friend now. I'd had a hard time not telling her my news as soon as I'd seen her this morning, getting ready in the bridal suite.

"Everyone's going to be so excited." His green eyes lit up. "My parents—fuck, they'll be so happy." He cups my cheek. "This is the best present. But I, uh, actually got something for you too."

"You did?" We really *had* said no presents because of the

wedding, but here he was, surprising me anyway. He loved to surprise me, that much hadn't changed.

"It's nothing too big." His cheeks turn a little pink. "Nothing like, well…"

"A baby?" I smiled.

He laughed. "Yeah." Teddy held out a hand to me. "Come on. It's upstairs."

I raised my eyebrows. "This house has a second floor?" How had I lived here for a year and not realized that?

He laughed. "Technically, it's an attic, but dad and I worked on finishing it." He squeezed my hand. "That's not the whole surprise, though. Come on."

Taking my coffee out of my hands, he placed the mug on the side table, guiding me over to a door I'd never noticed before. He hefted me into his arms, carrying me up the stairs.

"Teddy." I poked his stomach. "Put me down."

"No. I'm carrying precious cargo."

I laughed. "I'm barely even pregnant. I can walk up the stairs."

He hummed in response, finally setting me down when we reached the top and he clicked on the light.

Tears filled my eyes again. Dammit, I was emotional. I was blaming it on the pregnancy, even though it was just that he was so damn thoughtful.

"What is this?" I surveyed the room. "How did you…"

"I thought that maybe…" He swallowed roughly. "You'd like a studio of your own. You know. For your office." He looked over at me. "For whatever you want it to be. For your crafts, if you'd like. I know you love living here, but I wanted to give you a place to work on your own projects too."

I'd been fine over the last year—partially because we'd spent a lot of time traveling and he'd kept me so busy I hadn't even had time to think about my hobbies. But I loved this. I loved how thoughtful it was. Like he wanted to make sure I always had a way to follow my passions.

"How did you do this?" I finally finished my question.

He clicked his tongue. "A good magician never reveals his secrets."

"I'm never going to be able to figure you out, am I?"

Teddy laughed. "No, I don't think so. That's the whole point, wife. I want to spoil you. To give you everything good in the world. And if I can't use a little bit of Christmas magic to do that, what's the point?"

"I love you," I murmured, wrapping my arms around his neck.

"I love you too, Ivy Claus." He pressed a kiss to my lips. "And don't you ever forget it."

I wouldn't—because he reminded me of that every day. How he was the perfect man for me. That golden thread of fate, tying us together, sparkled more and more every day.

If someone had told me a year ago that this would be my life, living in the North Pole, married to the son of Santa Claus, and that I was the daughter of an elf—I never would have believed them. But that was my reality.

And I was the luckiest woman in the world that he'd found me.

WANT A GLIMPSE INTO IVY & Teddy's future? Click here to sign up for my newsletter and read a bonus scene, or visit https://dl.bookfunnel.com/6s7pzo5v5x.

extended epilogue

Teddy

several years later...

*L*ittle squeaks echoed through the house, followed by giggles.

Ivy and I were curled up on the couch, the only light in the living room coming from the enormous tree.

"Looks like someone's awake," I murmured in her ear.

"Mmm," my wife said, snuggling against my chest. "They're just excited."

Christmas was tomorrow.

The season had been busy, but it was surprising how much better my work/life balance was these days now that I had someone to come home to. Multiple someones, in fact.

While I loved the cabin I'd called home—the small house where Ivy and I had spent our first days as a couple, and then as husband and wife—we'd started building a new house shortly after our wedding. After we'd found out she was expecting our first baby. That one-bedroom cottage might have been cozy, but it wasn't conducive to a family.

"Of course they're excited," I said, keeping my voice low. "They want to see what *Santa* brought them."

"He's made monsters out of them."

I laughed. "I think my mom might have had a hand in that. Who knew how much Santa and Mrs. Claus would spoil their own grandkids?" Though Ivy's grandma had also had a hand in that, wanting to spoil her granddaughter and her great-grandkids alike.

"Oh, I definitely did."

"You did, huh?"

"Mhm. As soon as I met them, I could tell how much they loved you. They're like the biggest set of green flags I know." Ivy grinned, patting my chest.

"Even if my dad was the reason I brought you here?" He'd meddled, even if I hadn't known it at the time. Everything he'd done had been to ensure Ivy and I had met. Though falling in love—that had been all us.

"You mean when you knocked me out, kidnapped me, and effectively trapped me in the North Pole with you and only one bed?"

I hummed in response. "Yeah, that."

"Just a technicality." Ivy leaned over, brushing her lips against mine. "Thanks for finding me."

Palming her neck, I eliminated the space between us, kissing her deeply. Nipping at her bottom lip, she opened up for me, and I swept my tongue inside, groaning at her taste.

Grabbing her hips, I dragged her onto my lap, pressing my erection against her core. No matter how long we'd been together, it only took the smallest thing for me to be hard for her.

Especially when I got to see her like this. The Christmas tree illuminated her face, and I ran one of my hands through her strawberry blonde strands as the other kept hold of her hips.

"Teddy," she whispered, a needy whimper coming out of her throat.

"I know, baby," I groaned, rocking against her again. I was five seconds from ripping off her pajama bottoms—ones that matched mine, even after all these years—and burying myself inside of her when the sound of a creak upstairs made us freeze.

"Daddy?" That was Charlie's voice. We sprung apart, like we were teenagers who'd just gotten caught making out instead of parents who didn't get enough alone time.

Little patters of footsteps came down the stairs, and then our five-year-old son was standing in front of us, rubbing his eyes and wearing a pair of reindeer footie pajamas. Technically, the kids had matching pajamas to ours, too, though Charlie couldn't be separated from his reindeer pajamas. He was obsessed with them, wanting to spend almost every moment out at the stables with Buddy and Clarice.

"Hey, buddy. Aren't you supposed to be in bed?"

"I couldn't sleep." He climbed between Ivy and me on the couch, his little head of strawberry blonde hair—just like his mom—settling on my chest.

Ivy ran her fingers over his hair, brushing the strands over his slightly pointed ears. They weren't quite as elf-like as Ivy's, though he didn't get my human-like ones either. "Are you too excited about tomorrow, bud?"

He nodded, his deep green eyes looking up at her. "Grandpa Santa is gonna come and bring us presents, right, Mommy?"

"Yeah, buddy." She kissed his forehead. "But only if you're a good little boy and go back to sleep."

"Aww." He snuggled deeper into our sides, and I didn't have the heart to make him move.

Another little pitter of footsteps came, and then Holly was

there, dressed in her pink pajamas that were covered in gingerbread men.

"There's my little angel," Ivy said, opening her arms for our little girl. If Charlie was Ivy's mini-me, then Holly was mine, with my dark brown hair and my nose. Though her eyes were all Ivy's.

"Hi, Mommy."

My wife gave a little happy sigh as our three-year-old climbed up onto her lap, like she was the most content just like this, surrounded by our little family. Our daughter laid her head against Ivy's belly. "You couldn't sleep either, sweetie?"

"No. Presents yet?" she asked, her big blue eyes looking up into Holly's.

"Not yet," my wife said, rubbing her back. "You have to wait till the morning."

"Oh." She pouted. "Why not now?"

"Because Santa hasn't come yet, Holly," I said, still cuddled up with Charlie, whose eyelids were already drooping shut.

"Granpa?" She asked, her little face looking up at me in awe. Holly loved her Grandpa. She had him wrapped around her tiny little finger, and had since the day she was born.

"Yes, baby. Grandpa won't be by till later though, so you have to go to sleep."

"Okay, Mommy." Holly nuzzled her face against Ivy's tummy.

"Will Grandpa bring the baby presents too?" Charlie asked, his eyes peeking open as he turned his head towards the girls.

Ivy rubbed her pregnant belly. "Not this year, bud. She's still got a few months left in here before she gets any presents."

"Oh." He made a noise before curling back up on my lap.

Ivy and I made eye contact, and I did my best not to laugh. We'd been cockblocked by our two sleepy kids, who were too excited about presents to sleep, but also couldn't seem to keep their eyes open.

Even though we lived in the North Pole and they got to see Grandpa *Santa* almost every day of the year, they still loved it. Their eyes lit up with happiness when the Christmas decorations went up.

Four stockings hung on the mantle, though I knew Ivy had already started embroidering the fifth one. Another tradition we'd kept up with.

I leaned over, pressing a kiss to my wife's forehead before whispering in her ear, "I love you."

"I love you too," she murmured, pressing a soft kiss against my lips.

"What do you say we get these kiddos to bed so I can unwrap *my* present?"

She looked down at the sleeping form on her lap. "I think that's the best idea you've had all night."

ivy

I kneeled in front of him, unzipping his pants to free his generous length. The kids were finally in bed, asleep this time, which meant we had some alone time. I intended to make good use of every moment.

Wrapping my hand around his length, I pumped him once, twice, and then leaned down to lick him when he stopped me. "What are you doing?" He asked, sliding his fingers into my hair to tilt my chin up towards him.

"Tasting you," I replied. "It's your present."

Teddy groaned. "I'm supposed to be the one taking care of you, Ivy. I was going to do something nice, like rub your feet."

Reaching out, I swiped my tongue over his cock. "You can do that afterwards. It's been too long since I've had you like this."

"You're pregnant," he grunted in opposition, even as I took him into my mouth. "You shouldn't be on the floor."

Humming instead of acknowledging him, I focused on his dick, sucking him like a lollipop, running my tongue over the crown. I knew he wouldn't give me too much, or let me go too far, but I liked it when he let me take charge for once. The man was all alpha male, but he still liked to make me happy.

Fighting or flirting, it was all the same to me.

"Ivy, sweetheart," he groaned as I took him further into my mouth, squeezing his shaft with my hand as I focused on him. "It's too much."

I shook my head, not stopping. Teddy buried his hands into my hair, helping guide me back and forth over him, being careful not to go too deep or to make me choke. With my free hand, I rubbed my clit, already feeling wet and needy.

When he finally pulled me off, I knew he was close. I swiped my tongue over my lips. "I wanted to taste you," I whined.

"Not tonight, baby," he murmured, untying my robe and exposing my naked body to him. "I want to come inside this pretty pink pussy."

"You already got me pregnant again," I mumbled. "Not much more you can do there."

There was a glint of amusement in his eyes, and he gave me a light smack against my ass. "Talk like that, and I'm gonna put another one inside of you as soon as this one is born."

"Okay," I agreed, surprised at how much I wanted that.

He blinked, as if surprised. "You want a fourth baby?"

I nodded. "I've always wanted a big family. I think it makes sense. Besides, Charlie keeps asking for a little brother, and Clara doesn't quite meet that quota…" I trailed a finger up my belly.

"Fuck, I love you," he muttered, pulling me up so our lips would meet. His hands palmed my breasts—bigger and fuller now, during pregnancy—and I let out a low moan as he rubbed his thumbs over my nipples. "I can't wait to fill you up again. Stuff you so full that you'll be leaking my cum for days."

A moan slipped from my lips as he ran his fingers over my entrance. I wasn't wearing any panties, and he could feel how wet I was. "Damn, baby. So ready for me."

"I need you inside," I begged. "Please."

He laid down on the bed, pulling me on top of him so I straddled him. His cock was pressed between us, and I rubbed against it, the sensations as my clit ground down against him sending shockwaves through my body. But as much as I could come just like this, I wanted him inside of me. Wanted to be connected in every possible way.

His hands cupped either side of my belly as I lifted myself up, guiding him to my needy cunt that begged for his length. Putting him in, I sank down, enjoying the feel of him stretching me. The fullness was incredible, and all my sensations were heightened during pregnancy.

"God, you're so big." My eyes fluttered shut as I took him in fully into my body.

"I do love it when you stroke my ego, baby."

"Shut up," I groaned, rocking against him. Each time my clit ground down against the root, I saw stars.

I opened my eyes to glare at him, and he grinned. "You like it. Don't try to deny it."

"You're the most ridiculous man I've ever met."

"Says the woman riding my cock like she can't get enough."

"*Fuck me,*" I groaned, needing him.

"With pleasure," he said, taking over as he thrust up into me.

After that, I was lost to it. To the pleasure, to Teddy, driving me higher and higher, all these years together meaning he knew exactly how to drive me wild and make me come, and to all of the love I felt for my husband. When we'd both come down from our orgasms, I was nestled against his body, falling asleep with his hands cradling my belly, feeling loved—and completely sated.

teddy

"Merry Christmas Daddy!" Holly pounced on me. The other side of the bed was already empty, which I assumed meant Ivy had already trudged downstairs.

Giggles erupted from my daughter's mouth as I picked her up, throwing her up into the air.

"Merry Christmas, baby girl." I pressed a kiss to her forehead. "Should we go see the presents?"

"Yeah!" I settled her at my hip, heading downstairs to the large living room and the tree that was *overflowing* with presents. Courtesy of two parents *and* grandparents who loved to spoil them. They didn't know how lucky they were. I knew for Ivy, she was making up for all the Christmases she never got as a child, being in foster care and never knowing her family.

She had one now though. One big, noisy, happy family, and an entire town that loved her. A dog that still slept at her feet, even all these years later.

Coco was currently licking Charlie's face, like she thought she'd find leftover food there.

As soon as we'd reached the rug, Holly squirmed in my arms. I put her down, and she shot off like a rocket, joining Charlie in inspecting the presents under the tree.

My wife had one hand resting over her large belly, the other holding a brand new stocking for the mantle.

"Finished it this morning," she said, hanging it on the empty hook. *Clara* was embroidered in elegant, cursive letters —the name we'd picked for our new baby girl, even though Ivy wasn't due until early spring. "I couldn't sleep. The baby was kicking like crazy." She rubbed her side.

It was crazy to think that this was our eighth Christmas together, and we'd officially been married for seven years today. Eight months after that, we'd welcomed Charlie into the world.

"You could have woken me up," I murmured, wrapping my arms around her middle. "I'd have kept you company."

She shook her head, even as I buried my nose in her hair. She smelled the way she always did—like cookies, faintly of peppermint, and like *home*.

Like *mine*.

"You looked like you needed the rest," she said, turning her head to whisper directly into my ear. "Especially after last night. Even if you weren't on the clock, you've been busy all season. I know how hard you've been working."

I cleared my throat, feeling tightness in my chest. "Well, Dad's getting older, and it's my legacy too."

She stood up on tiptoes and brushed her lips against my

cheek. "Still, I didn't want to interrupt a few precious hours of sleep."

"Can we open presents now, Mommy?" Charlie's voice called out, interrupting our quiet moment together.

"Of course, baby. Let's see what Santa brought you, huh?" My wife smiled, taking my hand. "Shall we?"

We gathered around the fireplace, all four of us now in our matching Christmas pajamas, watching as our kids opened their presents.

Sighing happily, I kissed the crown of Ivy's head.

"What was that for?"

"Because I love you," I answered honestly. "Because I'm so grateful I found you."

"Me too," she whispered. Ivy snuggled into me, and we both rested our hands over her belly, our baby girl choosing that moment to kick, before both of our kids came over. They joined our snuggle pile, and my heart was so full of love.

Coco came over to my wife, curling up in her lap and pressing her nose against Ivy's belly, just like she had during each of her pregnancies.

I love you, she mouthed.

Life was perfect.

It was better then, somehow. I had a mate I adored—a family I cherished. I was the luckiest man in the world, because I had the best job in the world. A job that gave me time to soak up all of these cherished memories with the people I loved.

That was what made every Christmas together the best Christmas yet.

acknowledgments

Thank you to everyone who picked this book up and gave Ivy & Teddy a chance! I truly wouldn't be here without all of you and I am so grateful for every person who has read my books and supported me in this journey.

To all my author friends: thank you for being the ones I turned to when I was struggling and wanted to throw this book in the trash (like three times). You keep me going and inspire me in so many ways, and I'm so grateful to have you in my life.

To Autumn: I can't say thank you enough for everything! I love how our calls turn in to multiple hour chats, spending time plotting with you, and am so grateful for all you do for me. So excited for this next year working together!

To my family: thank you for all your support and love, and to my mom for always being my assistant at book signings. Couldn't do it without you. (Even if I won't let you read my books.)

also by jennifer chipman

Best Friends Book Club

Academically Yours - Noelle & Matthew

Disrespectfully Yours - Angelina & Benjamin

Fearlessly Yours - Gabrielle & Hunter

Gracefully Yours - Charlotte & Daniel

Witches of Pleasant Grove

Spookily Yours - Willow & Damien

Wickedly Yours - Luna & Zain

Castleton University

A Not-So Prince Charming - Ella & Cameron

Once Upon A Fake Date - Audrey & Parker

S.S. Paradise

A Love Beyond the Stars - Aurelia & Sylas

A North Pole Christmas

Elfemies to Lovers - Ivy & Teddy

about the author

Originally from the Portland area, Jennifer now lives in Orlando with her dog, Walter and cat, Max. In her free time, you can find her with her nose in a book or going to the Disney Parks. She loves writing romance heroes who fall first and hard for their women. Jennifer writes Contemporary Romance, Paranormal Romance, and Sci-Fi Romance.

Website: www.jennchipman.com

- amazon.com/author/jenniferchipman
- goodreads.com/jennchipman
- instagram.com/jennchipmanauthor
- facebook.com/jennchipmanauthor
- x.com/jennchipman
- tiktok.com/@jennchipman
- pinterest.com/jennchipmanauthor

Made in United States
Troutdale, OR
11/13/2024

24737888R00153